Reilly
– Running Full Circle

3rd book in this trilogy of Reilly's exploits

Amber Jo Illsley

BALBOA.
PRESS
A DIVISION OF HAY HOUSE

Balboa Press books may be ordered through booksellers or by contacting:

Balboa Press
A Division of Hay House
1663 Liberty Drive
Bloomington, IN 47403
www.balboapress.com.au
1 (877) 407-4847

Print information available on the last page.

ISBN: 978-1-4525-3087-1 (sc)
ISBN: 978-1-4525-3088-8 (e)

Balboa Press rev. date: 10/08/2015

CONTENTS

CHAPTER ONE

"A New Day Dawning"

It was going to be one of those days - a day when one's normal routine goes awry; as my mother would have said when we were little: 'I was not myself today', and our usual response: 'who were you then?' There would be no further comment from Mum, but just an irritated look.

My cat Reilly's behaviour was worse than usual, if that was possible, and I could easily imagine my mother saying in gruff tones: "that blasted cat!" Reilly's behaviour quite often seemed to be worse than usual. He had scratched me several times, given me cheek, and tormented the neighbour's cat and spied on the neighbours on the other side of the nice townhouse where I lived – staring down at them through their dining room window until they closed it with a very decisive bang. I am sure I wasn't mistaken in hearing some rude words tossed our way.

In fact, Reilly proved it in the next few seconds.

"Well, I like *that!* How dare they slam their window in my face? *And* say naughty words, too! Why, they should be putting money in their 'Naughty Words' tin, to give to charity. Or preferably, to give the money to *me*, so I could go and buy some lovely cat food."

"You mean, *I* would go and buy you some lovely cat food," I corrected him.

"Thank you for offering."

He sat back on his haunches, while perched at the back of my lovely cream velvet sofa. Although I was annoyed with him for bringing added wrath from the neighbours, I admired his beautiful colours afresh. Even now, it seemed hard to relate the magnificent looking cat, perched there on the sofa in apparent innocence with the sheer mischief he got into. But then, I added to myself, he wouldn't have been Reilly, the most dreadful, adorable cat I have ever owned, otherwise. And nor would he have given me material for three books. I say *owned,* but as all cat lovers know, it's really the other way around!

"Actually Reilly, you were very rude in staring down into their dining room window like that," I said easily. "I for one, would not like the idea of a cat staring at me while I was trying to eat. In fact, you two do it to me all the time, and it's most disconcerting."

"Of course! That's why we do it. Dogs do it all the time, don't cha know? And *they* get away with it. Now *dat* is disgusting!"

"I don't know about *dat*...er, that," I said.

"Anyway, I have come to a great decision," Reilly announced, yawning as if great decisions were an everyday thing for him.

"What, yet another one?" I said good-humouredly.

Reilly lowered one eye at me and added in a rather grandiose manner, even for a cat, that is: "well, you know the saying, every dog – oh, must I *puke* - supposedly has its day. I am saying that every *cat* has its day."

I was slightly puzzled with his turn of conversation. "That's not quite how the saying goes," I retorted. "It's every *dog* has its day!"

"Dog! *Dog?* Why should it be a dog's prerogative? *I'm* saying that every cat has its day, and what's more, every cat has its day... *every* day!"

"Have it your way then," I replied, suddenly tiring of the conversation.

He looked smug. "Oh, but I am! After all, haven't you heard the saying every cat has its day, *every* day?"

"You just made that up – you changed the original to suit yourself."

REILLY — THE BLEEPING TOM!

"MEOW CAN BE A FOUR-LETTER WORD."

"Of course! That's a cat's prerogative. I have made several quotable quotes today."

"Any quote is quotable," I said, yawning.

"Some more than others," Reilly responded. "Like mine for instance."

**

I was getting terribly tired; my pay packet was miserable in relation to the amount of hours I worked and yet I had prayed so long for a chance to stay at home to write books. But being a freelance journalist, I could not work on them in between stories for the simple reason that I was just too darned tired when I had caught up with my assignments.

"Woman, you look dreadful, if you don't mind my saying so."

"Well thanks very much, cat!" I retorted. "That sure makes me feel better."

"Oh I am glad about dat! Because I was thinking that if dis was gonna keep up, I should give up all dis running around reporting and taking photos of cows and sheep and whatnot, plus their behind views, if I wuz you. Hey, I'm a poet yet again!"

"Your speech is bad again, cat. So who would provide food for you and a roof over your heads if I stopped going out to report and take photographs?"

"Oh how incredibly droll. Pictures of cows and their behinds, shelter belts, more cows, sheep and their lambs and their lambs' behinds, working dogs...ugh! Droll, droll! Anyway, haven't you often said God will provide?" Reilly said smugly, ignoring my remark about his speech.

"Yes I have," I agreed. "But God doesn't expect us to sit on our rears and expect Him to do all the work, either!"

"Why did you say God will provide, then?"

"Because that's what He does! I think I need a rest, but I also need a decent income." I rubbed at my eyes.

"Ask God then," said Reilly. He was suddenly in such a nice mood it made me very suspicious.

"Oh Mum, *look!* Reilly's sticking his tongue out at you!" piped little Katie, who had been very quiet until now.

I spun around. "I *thought* your nice behaviour for five minutes was too good to be true!"

"Katie, youse is a little *sneak!* I could *hit* youse for dat!"

He smacked her with a Garfield-style uplifted paw and Katie squealed.

"Mum, Mum, Reilly *hit* me!"

"I don't understand why you have to be such a bully. Leave Katie alone!" I took a few menacing steps towards Reilly and he shot away under my bed and snickered. I picked up Katie and cuddled her in close. "Never mind Katie, I still love you no matter what."

"I know, but I've a good mind to leave home. I know a nice lady who would take me in right away!"

"Aw, Katie, I would miss you *so* much if you left home!"

"I know, but as much as I love you and love Reilly, he is such a bad cat, and he doesn't care about anyone's feelings except his own."

"That's not exactly true!" he called from my bedroom.

"Oh yeah?"

"Well actually, I quite like you two, and I quite like the neighbours."

"We're very honoured, I am sure," I said drolly, "and I'm sure the neighbours would be too."

"That's what I thought!" Reilly announced, scampering back out into the living room, pirouetting a couple of times and then racing around in the bathroom. "I'm bored with dis house!" he added, sing-song.

"Buy us a new one, then," I called back, yawning again.

"You wanna live in a cat-house?" Reilly asked smugly.

I screwed up my face and shook my head.

"I thought not! Why can't we go back to Carter's Beach?"

"Oh, not on about that again, are you?" I groaned.

"You heard me woman. We are sick and fed up wid you working all da hours dat God gave you, aren't we Katie?"

She looked and him and blinked; her great green eyes were beautiful in the last rays of the sun slanting through the living room window. "Oh, I don't know about that, Reilly..." she began, and then Reilly pounced.

"Don't *know*? Don't *know*?" he screamed at her, much to my disgust. "Weren't you complaining to me just the other night about the restrictions we have here? Weren't you saying how nice it would be to be back on the West Coast?"

"Okay, so what if I was?" she blinked owlishly and innocently at him. "Anyway Reilly, I didn't originally come from there, so I don't have the same feelings about it as *you* do."

Reilly narrowed his eyes at her. "Hmmm...getting a bit too cheeky for a female."

He hunkered down, wriggling his bottom as he prepared to pounce on her.

"Stop that this instant!" I shouted.

And to my surprise he did.

Then he nonchalantly started washing himself.

"Good heavens, Reilly!" I exclaimed. "You actually did what you were told, for a change."

He stopped washing himself to gaze at me.

"Oh, did you say something?" he smirked.

And he carried on washing.

**

I began to prepare my solitary evening meal...I say solitary, but it was hardly that, since I had the company of two lovely cats, both of whom were extremely good at staring imploringly at me with their beautiful eyes, Reilly's so golden and Katie's so green. They made it so hard for me to eat my meal in peace, without feeling under a heavy obligation to offer them tidbits, even though I had already fed them. Cats are past masters and mistresses at laying guilt trips on us suckers of humans, I decided, and I did my best to ignore their stares.

I had just finished eating my meal when the telephone rang. It rang so often that it was nothing short of a miracle to actually eat a full meal without the telephone ringing. Tonight was a night for a miracle, it appeared. I was, however, glad of the small respite from seeing and hearing about Reilly's bullying ways.

"Hello...hello?" There was a small whining, grizzling sound in response to my greeting. "Is there anybody there, said the listener," I quoted musically, making my words seem a little ridiculous. "Is there anybody there?" I said again.

"*Whuff, sniffle, snort,*" came the answer.

Then my friend Big Mike came on the line, laughing.

"I was coming out of me office when I heard someone's voice far away, and I saw Mickey standing over th' phone," Mike said in his strong English accent. "Mickey must have bumped off the receiver and put his paw on the quick dial button for yer number!"

"You mean - your little dog telephoned me?" I asked, giggling.

"Yeah, it looks like it!" Then I heard him chatting in an aside to his dog. "Mickey, what are you doing, phonin' up Amber and making a nuisance of yerself?"

"I heard that Mike! Actually, I thought I might have been getting a nuisance phone call."

"You did!"

"In a manner of speaking, but I wasn't expecting one from a dog!" I laughed and told Mike I thought that was really cute; that not everyone gets a phone call from a dog.

"It depends on what she looks like!" Mike chortled.

"What do you mean? Oh...I see. Huh, you chauvinistic sod, you."

But this only made Mike laugh even harder. I winced at the sound. Soon after, we rang off and I turned to see Reilly looking at me with an expression that I can only describe as a mixture of smugness and cynicism.

"Hard up, are you?"

"What's that supposed to mean?"

"*That* hard up that even a dog phones you up for a natter. And, might I add, an *excuse* for a dog! Ohhh, puke, *puke!*"

"Reilly, I swear you get nastier as you get older."

He appeared to huff on his claws. "Haven't I always said I will get even with humankind?"

"Yes, often enough, but by heck, I believe you've made up for at least twenty cats' revenge on humankind."

"Only *twenty?* Good heavens, then there's no time to waste, is there? Mike and Mickey, Mike and Mickey; oh the large and the small of it all. Why does such a big man have such a small dog? Oh ha ha, I must correct myself; why does such a big man have such an *excuse* for a small dog?"

"Because he likes him," I said simply.

"Da giant corncob has a toothless lambie-dog for a pet. It doesn't make sense."

"Put Mike in his big yellow raincoat and hand over his little dog to him and it makes sense all right," I said with a smile. Sense to Mike anyway, who loved his little dog fiercely.

"Yeah well, there's no time ter waste, woman!"

"What are you on about *now?*"

"Revenge, woman, revenge!"

With that, he made a leap onto the loose-weave cream and blue drapes and he clung there, smirking at me while I chastised him. He leaped down and sat on the sofa, nonchalantly washing his paws while I viewed with dismay the pulled threads in the drapes.

It appeared to be a re-enactment of that time in Carter's Beach, except that this time the railing didn't fall down.

Suddenly there was a kind of soft 'whump' sound when the drapes, rail included, fell on top of Reilly who let out a screech and clawed his way through to land on the floor. Correction, it *was* fully a re-enactment of that time at Carter's Beach!

Reilly viewed the bundled drapes with deep suspicion.

"It just goes to show, you can't trust *anything*, these days!" he snorted.

"Amen to that, cat," I said with glee, despite the thought that I had some work in drape repair ahead of me.

"It's not that I mind, but that pukey cream colour with blue stripes is just not *me*," he said, and scampered off into my bedroom.

"Me neither," I said with a wry smile. I had never liked those drapes, but they came with the place I was renting, so I'd left them there. The way I felt, why change things around when who knows when I would have to move on again?

I didn't say that to Reilly of course, otherwise he might get the idea that we were moving straight back to the West Coast.

**

One weekend soon after, I was feeling so bogged down with fatigue that I made the decision to telephone the "Star" on the following Monday, to tell the chief reporter that I was no longer going to work for the newspaper and it's subsidiaries on a freelance basis. Or on any other basis, come to that. I fretted all weekend; I knew it was time to do something positive. I had been caught in a vicious circle of having to work even harder to get enough return for my needs, due to the fact that the "Star" paid so little. It had really come to crunch point several weeks earlier when I received my payslip, to discover that for all the many hours of work I had put in that particular week, the return - after tax, did not even cover my rent.

I was in constant pain with RSI and arthritic problems as well. Reilly eyed me sternly that weekend.

"Enough is enough, woman," he said. And then sat moodily on the sofa, observing me moving slowly and painfully around the room, trying to tidy up. I knew he was right.

On the Monday morning I telephoned the chief reporter. "I can no longer afford to work for your newspaper," I said bluntly, trying to soften my words a little, since the man I was speaking to is such a nice person. But alas, he didn't make the rules on how much freelancers were to be paid. And that was a real shame. Or I most likely would have still been working for that newspaper today. The chief reporter, now the managing editor of that newspaper and its subsidiaries, was very upset at the time, and suggested alternatives. But they were most unlikely anyway, given the fact that the "Star" managing director at that time seemed to have no soul, and in addition he was tight-fisted when it came to paying freelancers.

Over twelve years of freelance journalism and photography were almost at an end. I felt more was to come. It did just three days later, in the form of one of the advertising salesmen from a New Zealand-wide publishing company telephoning me to ask if I had been paid for my work on two of the magazines under the three-magazine umbrella of that particular publishing company. I had worked diligently for that company for over five years and had travelled to many remote parts of the country, and also overseas, in the course of my work. I told the advertising salesman that I had been speaking to the editor of one of the magazines just three days before. He had telephoned me from Auckland with new assignments for me.

"Then you won't have heard?"

"Heard what?"

"That the head guys of the two big publishing companies were in the pub a couple of days ago, having a drink and they agreed that one company should be taken over by the other." He paused for a few seconds for the information to sink in. "I hope you got paid," he added.

"I was paid for some of my work, but I'd better get in touch with them quickly."

We agreed that it was amazing how major decisions, involving millions of dollars could quickly be made over a glass or two of beer. And the fact that many livelihoods would be changed in the same instant was almost hard to comprehend.

I never did receive all the money that was due to me, in spite of repeated requests and invoices. But that appeared to be par for the course at the time. So many companies going under, and so many people owed pay and left to wonder what was going to happen to them next.

So in just a few days, my career spanning over 12 years was over. I felt lost, and very, very strange. And yet at the same time, I felt an enormous sense of relief. God had answered my prayers – not in the way I had expected of course (as is God's way so often), but they had been answered all the same.

"Now what are yer gonna do?" Reilly asked, reverting back to his uncouth speech. Katie said nothing, but just gazed at me in sympathy from her perch on the back of an armchair.

"Have a rest and trust in God," I said firmly.

"I hope He's listening," Reilly smirked.

"He is, and He's listening to you being smart, too."

"Good to know I'm being taken notice of!"

"How could anyone *not* take notice of you?" I retorted. "You are such a smart-mouthed cat!"

"Gorgeous too," Reilly replied, and sauntered away to see if there was any food left in his bowl.

***

CHAPTER TWO

"To Err Is Human"

It was Christmas time. Big Mike asked me if I would like to go to his house for dinner on Christmas Eve. His mother would be there, Mike told me, and he was going to cook a big dinner. Every instinct told me to say no. I talked to Reilly and Katie about it. Katie yawned and walked away to my bedroom without a murmur, but Reilly stayed for his several dollars' worth.

"If ya don't wanna go, then don't!"

"It's not that easy, cat."

"What's so hard about saying no, and sticking to it?"

"I hate to hurt people's feelings."

"Yeah, no matter how many times they hurt *yours!* Didn't dat chief reporter in Westport tell you one time dat you were too *nice* to be a reporter? Nice? Hmmm...now, I could have told him a thing or two about how riled up you can get!"

"Huh, when was that? Whenever you goaded me into it?"

"Well, if *goaded* is the word you wanna use...I personally would have said *teased* you a little."

"Actually, it's *you*, cat, who has the swift temper! How many times have you bitten me?"

"Well I don't know woman. I don't count small, insignificant incidents like those."

"You didn't see them as insignificant at the time!" I held out my right arm and showed him the scarring. "Look at these *scars!* See what you have left me with for life!"

Reilly squinted his eyes and pretended to be peering hard at my arm.

"Where? I don't see anything except some freckles...hmmm, and the odd hair or two here and there. Oh yes, I see you have a hint of ginger there. Well, at least we all know you're a genuine blonde. I did wonder..."

"Reilly, you really have been horrible to Mum! I can see the scars from here!" piped little Katie, who was in one of her favourite spots, on the window ledge in the lounge-dining room of the flat.

"Go take a run at yourself while in the air, small cat. I will not, I repeat not, have you interrupting my scintillating conversation with your Mumsy-wumsy! We have just been determining that she's a genuine blonde."

"Have we?" I asked sourly.

Katie gave a sound that was somewhere between a scoff and a sound of long-suffering. Perhaps it was the latter. I looked at the dear little cat afresh. She appeared to have moved away from us in spirit. I so loved her; her dainty ways, loving heart, beautiful oriental black smoke coat and her enormous green eyes. As with Reilly, I never tired of looking at her. I often marvelled at the way the Master Painter had created such depth of colour; such a blend of shades that shifted with the slight easterly breeze.

"Where did ya go?"

"I was thinking about you cats and the Master Painter."

"Not about the scars you reckon you have from me?"

I looked down at my forearm and studied the scars. "Well, they haven't gone away in the meantime."

"Sarcastic woman! Anyway, you could always tell people you got them during the course of your work."

"That wouldn't be so far out, either. Now, what were we talking about before?"

Reilly gave a chirrup of glee. "Woman, you are so easily distracted!"

"Am not."

"Are too! Isn't that right, Katie?"

"Asking *me* for my opinion? Ooh Reilly, you are so gallant!"

"Huh, another sarcastic female. I should leave, that's what I should do."

"But you won't," I said, while pondering on what it was we had originally been discussing.

"Not yet, anyway."

"Please let us know when you are about to leave, Reilly, so we can have a going-away party for you," Katie piped, her big eyes blinking in seeming innocence. "Mummy could bake a cake for you too!"

"Just for that, I think I shall stay here, just to annoy you."

"That's what I figured," I said drolly. "Say, what were we talking about before?"

Reilly blinked too, and appeared to smile. "We were discussing whether or not you should go to dinner at da giant corncob's mother's house. Think of it this way, it would save you cooking a meal, and she's probably a very good cook. Oh, dat's right. It's da giant *corncob's* house you're going to! And he's gonna be da cook! Maybe there would be some nice roast chicken left over that you can bring home to us poor starving cats. Some *corn*, maybe?"

"You're not making it easy for me, cat."

"Who said life was easy? Would you like life to be so easy that all you had to do was crook a finger and servants would come running, to meet your every need? Hmmm...maybe not *every* need..."

"What do you mean?"

"You still need a man in your life, heh, heh."

"I still say you are a very rude and crude cat. Now, back to going to Mike's house..."

"You mean you have finally made up your mind to go? I thought you didn't want to go there?"

"You finally persuaded me! No, I do not want to go, but I think I would feel worse if I didn't!"

"Have it your way den, woman. I suppose you'll spend ages wondering what to wear."

"You know I am not like that." And I wasn't.

**

I duly agreed to go, even though my instincts were loudly telling me that it would not be a successful evening. I called on my inner resolve, telling myself that at least I would have made two other people happy, and if the giant corncob...er, I mean Mike - offered some chicken scraps for my cats, then I would not turn them down.

Mike arrived, in a rush because his mother had telephoned him in the meantime, to ask him to pick up some sherry. She had intended to bring a partially made trifle, and complete it at Mike's house.

"But I couldn't bleedin' well *find* any sherry! The shops must have sold out," he complained.

"I've got some fortified wine," I offered. "She is welcome to have that."

"Nope, if it don't say 'sherry' on the bottle, she don't want it," Mike said in his broad accent.

"There's not a great deal of difference between the two," I pointed out. Although having said that, I have no doubt there are many connoisseurs who would strongly disagree with me.

"It don't matter. If Mum says she wants sherry, that's what she bleedin' well wants!"

I sighed. "Then we'll try another shop on the way over."

Mike was already on his way out the door. He hesitated, looming very large in the doorway. "No time. Mum'll be waitin' for us! She's already complainin' about me being late all the time!"

"Then why don't you leave earlier then, to save the complaints?" I suggested.

Reilly sniggered in the background.

"What's that funny noise?"

"Reilly having a quiet snigger at you."

"Don't be daft! Cats don't snigger!"

"Don't they just? Reilly does it quite often! Don't you Reilly?"

"Only when the occasion sees fit!" he responded.

"Only when the occasion sees fit, he said," I repeated.

"You still think that damned cat can speak to you don't you?"

"Of course I do, and he does! So does Katie, for that matter!"

"I was told writers are a daft lot, and now I know fer sure!"

"We might be a daft lot as you say, but we know how to enjoy life," I retorted.

"You haven't been doing much of that lately!" Reilly called as we began our exit. "For instance, you didn't want to go out tonight!"

"I made up my mind to go out tonight, cat, and that's what I am about to do!"

"Eh?" Mike gave me a puzzled look. "What are you on about?"

"Er, nothing," I hedged. "Reilly's just make a smart remark."

Mike rolled his eyes skyward. I just smiled to myself as I locked the door. Mickey was already barking.

"Why not eat that excuse for a dog, that *lambie*-dog for dinner!" Reilly called. "After he's had a jolly good scrub-up of course, and that could take a while, he's so dirty."

I paused to see what he would say next.

"After all, *you're* all done up like the dog's dinner! Oh, heh, heh, silly me, I just can't seem to help being so witty. Now, dat excuse for a dog ...oh *must* I puke yet again..."

"I sincerely hope not!" I said as we headed towards the very dirty and untidy car we were to go out in, namely, Big Mike's.

"Reilly's talking about being sick," I replied. "But he won't. He's just trying to needle me."

"You're weird! Are yer coming or not? Hurry up, girl! Mum'll be waiting!"

"Da giant corncob's mumsy-wumsy is waiting," Reilly called. "Oh hurry, hurry woman! I wonder if she's a giant corncob too? Perhaps a smaller one, a bit bent over? A corn cob-*ess,* perhaps?"

At that remark I walked down the steps. Mike was already revving his car engine and Mickey the 'lambie-dog' was yapping excitedly. But neither noise was too loud that I couldn't hear the refrain from Reilly singing: "Oh what a night; it really was such a night..."

What a cheeky cat! I was very amused all the same.

Mike drove dementedly through the streets to his mother's house. I asked him to slow down but I was wasting my breath. Mickey yapped all the louder and he had a bad case of halitosis. Already I was feeling sick, and we hadn't even reached his mother's house.

Mike drove into her driveway with great gusto.

"Damn! She ain't out here ready and waiting like she said she would be!"

"Well, she's an old lady, Mike. Perhaps she'd sensibly rather stay inside out of the cold breeze," I reasoned.

"What bleedin' breeze? There ain't any! Look at me, I'm sweating like a pig!"

My nose twitched. I silently agreed with him.

"Damn," Mike said again. Then he tooted the car horn. When his mother didn't arrive in the next few minutes he decided finally to go inside and fetch her.

She came down the ramp slowly with her huge son. His patience at that moment was amazing to see, given his *im*patience just moments before, at my house and on the way to his mother's house. Mike opened his car door and pulled back his car seat to let his mother into the back of his small hatchback car. A short, but solidly-built woman, she leaned on the seat to give herself balance as she clambered in. I wondered why Mike's face was contorted. In fact, his whole mouth appeared to have been sucked in and his eyes went crossed, while swift deep colour flooded his face.

"What's wrong?" I asked.

"Bleedin' hell Mum!" he gasped. "You're squashing me bleedin' *hand!*"

Bleeding it may well be, in a moment, I thought. The day had worn on into evening and my reflection was cast in the passenger window. I pulled faces at it. Sometimes this helped me through situations that did not look as if they would improve as the night wore on. I resolved to tell Reilly all about the dinner the next day.

"Stop complaining, Michael," his mother said in her strong English accent. "You're always complaining!"

Mickey yapped even louder as Mike painfully got back into the car after his mother was safely seated in the back. "Shut up Mickey!"

"Yes Michael, I do wish your dog wouldn't bark so much," came the voice from the back seat. "Oh, and Michael, it's about time you gave this car a good clean. It's filthy!"

I agreed with her on both counts, but said nothing. Mike's face was already contorting again, this time with suppressed annoyance.

"Yeah, when I've got time, Mum! I'm too busy running you around everywhere! If that blasted lazy sister of mine got off her flamin' chuff and took you out sometimes it would help *me!*"

I agreed with Mike too, on *all* counts.

Mickey yapped some more, excited at the fizzing of annoyance in the air.

"Sit down Mickey," said Mike's mother. "Pooh, he's got bad breath, Mike. He badly needs a bath too."

"He'll get one when I have time to give him one!" Mike snapped.

Or when you bring him to my house and I give him a bath for you, I thought. But kept my thoughts to myself. The air was stiff with tension as it was.

"It should be soon. Oh be *quiet*, Mickey! Michael, you really ought to clean out this car. It's very dirty and untidy," his mother commented again.

"I said before that I haven't got *time*, Mum! Now, where are we gonna get this blasted sherry from?"

"How about Liquor King, Michael?"

"Okay, we'll go there then." And Mike zoomed away up the road. I felt he led a very charmed life and so did his Mitsubishi car. I hoped too, that our lives would be as charmed. I quietly prayed that we would get there in one piece, and would not be stopped by a policeman. Luckily we reached Liquor King safely and were not pulled over by a policeman. Mike whipped the car into a small space which was not designated for parking, next to the Liquor King store.

"I don't think you're supposed to park here, Michael," his mother commented.

"Too bleedin' bad. There ain't any parks left anywhere else. Flamin' heck, look at that *queue!*"

He clambered out of his car, walked briskly over to join the queue, while his mother, Mickey and I stayed put. I was concerned that very soon someone would want to move his or her car from the parking area, and Mike's would have been in the way. At the mood that was developing in Mike, I doubted if he would be apologetic to the person or people concerned, and indeed, was likely to have 'given them a mouthful'.

"I do wish Michael would clean out his car," his mother commented yet again. Mickey yapped in my ear. I reeled back from the noise, and the smell of his bad breath. "I wish he would get Mickey's teeth cleaned too," his mother added.

"That would be a good idea," I said quietly. "I'll mention it to him soon." I didn't say to her that I had already asked him several times to get Mickey's teeth checked out.

Mike came storming back.

"That bleedin' queue was even longer than I thought! There are at least thirty more people inside! I ain't waitin' around here any longer!"

He practically flung himself into the car, inasmuch as a very large man can fling himself into a small car, and tried to start the engine.

"Your car isn't going, Michael. It won't start," his mother said.

"Do you think I don't bloody well *know* that?" he shouted, while continuing to try to start the engine.

"Now don't shout at me dear. That's not nice." I couldn't see, but she had obviously turned her head to my direction. "He always bullies me like this, you know Amber. It's not fair on an old lady."

"You'd try the patience of a bleedin' saint!" Mike snapped.

Mine's being tested rather well this evening too, I thought.

"Maybe it's the points," I said mildly. "Maybe they're a bit dirty."

After one or two more tries a very exasperated Mike got out, flung up the hood of the car and fiddled around with the distributor.

"I think the points are a bit dirty!" he shouted. People walking near our car stared in at us. "I'll fix them in a minute!"

"Yer whole bloody car looks a write-off," said a casually-dressed man, walking past in a wobbly manner. It appeared that he had already begun his Christmas celebrating.

"And so will your face if you don't keep your opinions to yerself!" Mike said headedly.

"*Ooh*, who's in a nasty bad mood at Christmas, eh? Now Santa won't bring you any toys!"

When Mike made a move towards him, the man, eyeing up the enormous size of Mike and the menacing look in his eyes, decided to make a swift retreat, albeit a wobbly one.

My stomach knotted with mirth. Mike slammed down the hood and got back in the car.

"I showed him, didn't I?" he said, pleased with the small exchange.

"Oh yes you sure did Mike," I agreed, the mirth threatening to spill over. I was glad Reilly wasn't there to make his usual kind of comments. I imagined he might say something along these lines: "Read all about it in this morning's Press: Literally The Corniest Story of the Week! Giant Corncob beats up drunken man!" I did not want to imagine any more. Mirth was warring with a developing big yawn. We still did not have the sherry and already I was getting very tired.

"You really need to clean this car out, Michael," said his mother from the back seat.

Mike let out a hiss of fury when the car still wouldn't start.

"Perhaps the gaps in the points are too wide, Mike," I said - helpfully, I'd thought.

He flung himself out of the car again, muttering furiously and lifted the hood of the car again. A moment or two of messing about and then there came the announcement: "I just closed up the gaps in me points a bit. She'll be right, now!" He blew a bit of remaining dust out of the distributor cap, fastened it back into place, wriggled a few more things around and slammed the hood down again. "Just as well I know what to do!" he shouted.

Lucky for you that I'm here, I thought wryly, wishing I could voice my thoughts, as mirth rose up again.

Back in the car, he turned the key in the ignition. *Honk! Honk!* came the sound of someone trying to get out of the car park.

"Shift your bloody car!" shouted an irate man.

"Up you too!" shouted Mike, giving a very rude two-fingered sign. Once would have been enough but no, Mike had to continue the gesture for several seconds. I slunk down in embarrassment in the seat. The bird was well and truly being flipped. I sneaked a quick look at the man on the receiving end and he too, was flipping the bird, back at Mike.

One more stroke and you're out, I thought wildly.

"Oh do hurry up, Michael!" his mother said.

The man in the tooting car started to get out. Mike turned the ignition key one more time and the car burst into life, puffing out clouds of smoke. And I mean *real* life! Mike backed his car around in a great sweep and shower of stones and almost hit the car in which the irate man was now staring from, his eyes wide with fright. He had a greyish look to his face which I just *knew* came from the smoke from Mike's car exhaust. Oh, and maybe fright also had something to do with his facial colour. Foolish of him to have his window open so the exhaust smoke could billow in, I thought inanely. But then he didn't know Mike, or know that Mike's car often had smoke billowing from its exhaust.

With another rude gesture and another shower of stones, Mike whirled the little Mitsubishi out the driveway and barrelled onto the main road, almost hitting a car being driven quite legally from the other direction. I had quickly glanced back at the entranceway to the Liquor King store and noted the smoke from Mike's car still hanging in the air. More tooting of horns and shouting, and then finally we were on our way again.

"I think we'll go to New World," Mike said, his humour having been miraculously restored.

It must have been the vigorous two-fingered gestures that did the trick.

Mike parked with a flourish outside the New World supermarket. "We should be able to get some bleedin' sherry here, Mum," he said cheerfully.

"Oh I do hope so Michael. When are you going to clean this car up?"

"Bloody *never*, Mum, if you keep bloody harping on about it!" he snapped. His good mood had disappeared in an instant.

"That's not nice, Michael. It's Christmas, too."

"Oh don't I bleedin' well *know* it!"

He clambered out, and was beginning to walk over to the big supermarket when Mike's mother made the comment: "Oh, I forgot to ask Michael if he would get me some bananas, too."

I called to Mike but he didn't hear. I tried to wind down the window but the lever came off in my hand. I stuck it back on, wound down the window while pressing again the lever so it wouldn't come off again and called: "Mike, your mother would like some bananas, too!" He heard me this time, turned to look at us, rolled his eyes, turned back and carried on.

Fifteen minutes later he emerged. "I got the bally bananas, but there's no bleedin' *sherry* left!"

My heart sank. At least an hour had gone by since we had left my flat. The journey to Mike's flat was normally only a nine or ten minute one. Why didn't I get out and help? For the simple reason that Mike not only wanted me to stay to keep an eye on his mother and his little dog, but also the fact that my back was very sore. And walking only made it worse.

It started to rain and the temperature dropped suddenly. The rain on my face was quite icy. The window on my side of the car was still wound down, so I attempted to wind it up at the same time as Mike made a fast U-turn in the middle of a busy street. The handle fell off again and I tried to fit it back on and re-wind it. A sudden stab of intense pain caught me in my wrist. I yelped with the shock of it.

"Getting' old, are we?" Mike said in a good-humoured voice.

A rush of anger welled up, coupled with the thought that I knew, just *knew* it, that this evening was going to be fraught with problems! I think I was madder with myself than anyone else, that again I had ignored my instincts and gone against them. Oh yes indeed, I would have been *soooo* much happier to stay at home with my cats!

"Speak for yourself," I said, trying not to sound snappy.

"Oh I am, I am. Me back tells me every day that I'm gettin' old!"

It was good to see that Mike's good humour had been restored, but now mine was swiftly ebbing.

I took a deep breath, tried to ignore the stabbing pain in my wrist and counted to ten...hmmm...a hundred would have been better.

"Look out, Mike!" I exclaimed when Mike, turning to make a comment to his mother, almost drove into the rear of another car.

"He should blimmin' well watch what he's doing!" Mike snapped.

"He was about to do a parallel park," I said in what I thought was a reasonable, helpful tone.

"He should bloody well do it somewhere *else* then!"

Oh dear, the good humour that had appeared had been on a very temporary basis. It came and went so quickly it could make a person's head spin. Namely mine. But I tried to look on the bright side. I only had about three more hours before I could go back home. I had Mike's nice dinner to look forward to and I could have a small glass of sherry – not the one for cooking, though – and not worry about whether I was over the limit.

"I think we'll go to Richmond," Mike said. "There's a liquor store there."

Well, at least we're almost at Mike's flat, I thought. *Only another two or three kilometres to go.*

At the Richmond liquor store, Mike scrambled out his car. Mickey started barking again, this time even closer to my ear. I leaped in fright. Halitosis wended its way round the car and I felt sick all over again.

"He does that to me, too," Mike's mother commented about Mickey's barking. "It's just as well I am a bit deaf."

"I thought I was a bit deaf, until Mickey did that to me," I replied, thinking this was one time when I wished I didn't have such a good sense of smell, too.

"What's that you said, dear?"

"I said I thought *I* was a bit deaf too, until Mickey did that to me," I repeated.

"Yes dear, Mickey *does* get what's left over."

"Eh?"

"Mickey *does* get what's left over. Yes, dear, you *are* a bit deaf!"

I sighed. This was a pointless conversation. I wished Mike would hurry up. It took another fifteen minutes before Mike emerged, his good humour restored yet again.

"Met a bloke I know. I haven't seen him in months."

Great, I thought. *We'll get to Mike's flat eventually.*

"I thought of calling around to his place for a few minutes."

"Michael, do hurry up! We don't have time for you to go visiting! I'm tired and hungry and your dog needs a bath."

That's really telling your little boy, I thought wryly.

"Shut up, Mum. What's Mickey needing a bath got to do with the price of fish?"

"Nothing, dear. Are we having fish for our dinner?"

"No!" Mike snarled. His mother fell silent. Which was just as well, I thought. I could easily visualise his mother being put out of the car and yours truly having to help her all the way, step by painful step, to Mike's flat, and Mike saying from his doorway "what kept yer?"

I quietly resolved to stop letting my imagination run away with itself...at least for the time being.

Eventually we reached Mike's flat and amazingly the evening passed by without any major incidents, except when his mother got stuck on the toilet and I had to pull her off. Several hours later, Mike dropped his mother off home and then took me home. I was exhausted.

"Had a super time, Mumsy wumsy?" Reilly sniggered while yawning. I didn't know cats could actually do that, until I met Reilly. Sniggering and yawning at the same time is interesting to see in a cat. "Did you get us any chicken?"

"Yes I did," I replied, and held out a plastic bag full of delicious chicken morsels. I would have liked to eat them myself, except that I was already over-full. "It was lovely food that Mike cooked," I added. "Although it took us a long time to get there." I proceeded to tell Reilly, almost verbatim, what happened over the course of the evening.

"Oh, it really was such a night," Reilly began, sing-song. "Was the moon out in full too? Did the dogs howl?"

"The only one that felt like howling was me," I said, grinning. "But after I had a full tummy it all didn't matter any more."

"To err is human…" Reilly began.

"What are you talking about?"

"Well, you know how you're always saying that you should listen to your instincts and not do what you feel you *should* do?"

"So?"

"You feel duty-bound, woman. A human failing."

"You don't have any of those failings, I suppose?"

"Of course not. Coz I'm a cat! But as it happens, the evening turned out all right in the end. Perhaps it's just as well you erred, in not listening to your instincts, coz we wouldn't have got any chicken!"

"Glad you think so, cat," I said wryly. "Merry Christmas, darlings!" I gave them each a gaily wrapped little gift which Reilly promptly tore open. Katie did the same, only more slowly. I had given them each a catnip mouse and they played with them happily for the next few minutes.

Then I opened the bag of chicken pieces and put equal amounts into the cats' bowls. There was silence for two minutes while they contentedly ate their supper. In unison they turned to look blinkingly at me, their pink tongues licking tiny scraps of chicken from their mouths. It was almost as if they had rehearsed the actions, so in unison they were.

"Merry Christmas, woman!"

"Yes, Merry Christmas, Mum!" piped Katie.

"Thank you my darlings. Now let's all go to bed."

"How sublime," Reilly said in a leering way.

But I didn't make a comment on that. I was bone weary; my back and wrists ached and I had eaten too much.

My bed had never looked so inviting.

***

CHAPTER THREE

"On the Road Yet Again"

Knowing I could not go back to work for a while, I applied for the unemployment benefit. The caseworker supervisor, a former nursing supervisor, took one look at my swollen left hand and told me I obviously had occupational overuse syndrome, which was the new term for RSI (repetitive strain injury) and I should be seeing my GP immediately about it; that under the circumstances I would not be able to apply for the unemployment benefit. Her eyes grew larger when I said I preferred the old name for the syndrome as the new one in its shortened form sounded like a disease. Whose idea was it to call it OOS? I'd asked her, saying it sounded like some disgusting, creeping disease, as in 'OOZE.' She looked at me as if I was a bit of an oddball and that one should not question the authorities' decisions on these health matters and terminology. Oh how often had I seen that look before? She said I was obviously in no fit state to work, should a suitable job became available. She looked at me in amazement when I told her that I had been a freelance journalist for over 12 years and it had been a matter of putting up with the pain.

"Then it's just as well you gave up now, before anything else happened to you," she said briskly.

For the next two years I went on a medical round; there was one specialist after another. Doctors, radiologists, arthritis specialists, occupational therapists, nurses, accident compensation specialists...and so on. I also had to attend a local gymnasium twice a week, which I found a bore and a chore, and very painful. And I discovered how snobbish some people are – acting as if going to a gymnasium was the be-all and end-all of what one should do in life when one is successful.

Reilly was not amused when I came home one day, stiff and sore from the workout to help improve my lower back muscles. He eyed me cynically.

"You look a damned sight worse than before you went to dat place."

"I feel it too," I sighed, after one particularly hard session. The only bright spot was when I met a very gentle young man who was learning to become a Reiki specialist. He was shy and kind – quite different from the many other people whom I met there.

Soon I was seeing so many specialists that there no longer appeared to be any time left for even working on a book. I tried counting my blessings; that at least I was in close proximity to specialist help and that at least I was granted a small income while receiving the help. It made me feel better to think of it as the 'writer's dole' rather than the Accident Compensation Commission payment. The latter however, still had its expectations of recipients – that they must be deemed fit enough to go job searching, which under my circumstances at the time, was ludicrous. Simply because there was no time left to go searching and as one New Zealand Employment person bluntly told me: "No editor would want to give you a job now, with those RSI and arthritis problems you've got."

That comment only served to make me even more determined to prove myself all over again, painful as her words were. But at least she'd used the RSI term, which warmed me a little towards her. And at least I wasn't lumbered with that ghastly 'OOZE' label!

Reilly was more cynical than ever about the whole thing.

"I am utterly fed up with you going to this specialist, and that specialist," Reilly said one day. "Do you realise woman, you are getting worn out all over again with going to all these people?"

"I know," I sighed, preparing for another stint at the sports gymnasium. I went there twice a week for three months...and hated it. But I still had to do it under the terms of ACC (Accident Compensation Corporation), and I also had to accept home help, which was something I had never had in my life. I had always been too fiercely independent. But at least I had been able to make the stipulation, that since I was being forced into receiving home help, then I wanted my sister Sandy, an extremely good, kind and caring person, to be the one to help with some of the housework. Sandy works for a large nursing association that takes over most of the basic work formerly done by district nurses. At first they disagreed, saying that in their experience it was not a good idea for family members to do the work in this situation, otherwise it could cause conflict. I agreed that maybe that was so in some cases, but not with my sister Sandy, whom I love dearly. She and I did not fight.

So after some consideration, they agreed that it would be okay. I think the occupational therapist must have recognised the determined look in my eyes.

"Steely look," Reilly commented blithely. I was amused. I was always amused or *be*mused when Reilly read my thoughts.

"Well in that case, be warned, cat, that you can't always mess with me and get away with it!"

"Think I look silly?" he said as he strolled away again, apparently unconcerned. But his sudden washing of his paws gave him away.

Patience had to be the key, in getting well again. I did not realise how much energy my work had taken out of me, and I felt burned out. I spoke to a doctor about it but he pompously said it was difficult to decide *exactly* what burn-out was. I told him: but that's how I *felt* – completely burned out, sore and very weary in both body and spirit. He looked at me as if I did not know what I was talking about. I could have reminded him that it was *my* body that I lived in, and it was *I* who was experiencing the health problems, not he. Otherwise I would not have been consulting him. However, I knew I would be wasting my breath, so I let it be. I was annoyed all the same, and secretly hoped that one day he might be in a similar position and then he would understand a lot better how his patients had been feeling.

"Doctors often forget to really *listen* to their patients, don't they?" Reilly said to me when I returned home one day, sore and dispirited again. I agreed with him. Really, that darned cat seemed to know everything there was to know about...well...*anything!*

"Of *course* I do!" Reilly responded, reading my thoughts. "I am, of course, the Esteemed One, amongst other lofty titles."

"So I remember," I said, cheering up a little when I thought of Reilly when we were back in Archer Place on the West Coast, racing around with a tea-towel draped elegantly over his back, informing all who would like to hear that he was The Caped One.

It took some getting used to, the almost daily grind of trying to get back into work, which is what ACC people were trying to get me to do. But the pain was too much. Oddly, one morning during the early winter, I suddenly decided to fetch a newly-bought exercise book, and an old telephone book as a support, and I sat in bed all morning, writing my new novel in my own form of shorthand. With the stress of meeting deadlines gone, my hands could function reasonably well again. And the feeling of elation and fulfilment, that finally I was able to do what I had been trying to do for years, was almost overwhelming. I could not remember when I had last been so happy! Sure I was aching and very stiff from being in a cramped position for hours on end, but the feeling of achievement was worth every little ache and pain. It seemed so strange than only a short time before it was a concentrated effort to write just a few words by hand, and yet here I was, able to write up to two or three thousand words in a day, and all by hand.

I completed the novel in less than three months and sent it away. It was accepted, to my delight.

Life was looking up again.

**

My sister Sandy gave me the option of a cheaper place to rent. It was a fairly large house, then belonging to Sandy and her husband, and they preferred a family member who would, for cheaper rent, look after it plus the enormous amount of gear my sister and her husband had inherited along with the house about a year before. In addition, there was gear left by their eldest son, who had rented the house before me and was moving overseas. The object was to gradually sell the gear off for my family members, which I eventually did, bit by bit.

But I felt daunted by the prospect of moving there. The ten or so gardens had twitch and oxalis in them and my back was still causing me a great deal of pain. I knew they were hoping I would say yes to their offer, and of course I was tempted by the cheaper rent. At twenty-five dollars less a week, it made a big difference to how I could manage financially. I weighed up the pros and cons of moving again.

"What? We have to move *again?* But you promised that the next place we moved to would be the West Coast!"

"I know what I promised and believe me, if it was in my power to do so we'd go back there tomorrow. But at least we'll be moving near the beach."

"*You* just pack up your gear, get a truck and a driver and *move*, woman. Like you always do!" Reilly looked furious, his tail swishing alarmingly. Katie, who had emerged from the bedroom after a long sleep, blinked at him, saw the swishing tail and made a hasty retreat.

"And what do you cats do in the meantime?"

"Sit in the corner and watch the workers!"

"Very funny."

"I thought so too."

He yawned as if the whole conversation was beginning to be rather a bore. Many times had I seen that same pose!

Katie spoke up. "If I can't go back to the West Coast, I think I will leave."

I know she had said things along those lines before, but I guess a part of me did not believe her.

"Huh! Who would take you in?" Reilly sneered.

"I know a very nice lady who would, and I am not going to tell you where she is because you might come looking for me, to pick on me all over again."

Oh dear. Katie looked so tragic I began to wonder if it had been a good thing taking her home in the first place. But then I reminded myself that she had been very thin, undernourished and full of worms when she first came to stay. I'd fattened her up until she was strong enough to have her little operation and we had been together since then.

"Please don't go," I begged her. "I would miss you *so* much, Katie."

"I would miss you too, Mum, but I need to be in a home where there are no other cats to pick on me."

"That's coz you are such an icky, softy kind of cat!"

"You see what I mean, Mum?" Katie's beautiful green eyes had never seemed so huge, and nor so sad. My heart ached for her.

"I know what you mean, Katie. But won't you reconsider? I'm sure Reilly will be nicer to you from now on." I gave Reilly a stern look; maybe he would interpret it as one of my steely looks. At least, I hoped he did.

"I'll think about it for a while, Mum, but not for much longer. You know we cats need to be on the move if life isn't working out for us."

"I have never known you to be like this, Katie," I said sadly. "You never really said. Oh, you did say little things from time to time, but I thought you were simply getting some of your feelings out, and that it would all blow over."

"But not for long this time, Mum," Katie said firmly.

My heart ached for my sweet little cat, and I was torn between the two of them. I simply adored them both.

"But what about Reilly? I thought you really liked him?"

"Oh I do, but he's *such* a bully."

"Hey! I don't like dat sort of talk! I am not a bully! I am just an inspired cat of great intelligence, strength and cunning. And forcefulness, too, I might add."

"You have a very big head too, Reilly."

Reilly narrowed his great golden eyes at her. "What's got into you all of a sudden, eh? This isn't like you! Aw c'mon, come and give me a wash!"

To my amusement, that's exactly what she did. Reilly watched me smugly as Katie purred and washed him. I knew that the bad moment had blown over, at least for the time being.

**

After much thought, I agreed to moving out of my rented townhouse, and moving to Parklands, which was not so very far from the beach. In fact, each night when the traffic sounds had stilled somewhat, you could clearly hear the sea and also smell the sweet tang of salt on the air. If we couldn't get back to the West Coast, then this was almost the next best thing. Reilly and Katie reluctantly accepted the move, but only because I had told them it was near the beach. Having a sea-faring family background, I too, never liked to live too far from the coast. Whenever I had no choice in the matter as to where I lived, I always felt deprived.

And so did Reilly. It was never more obvious than when we had finally made the huge move, which happened to be on my birthday.

"Another birthday, woman? How many does that make now? A hundred?"

"Don't be cheeky, cat. I refuse to get any older than thirty-three!" I retorted.

"Hmmm...a wee while back there you did look near a hundred!"

"Thanks, I *think!* But you know I wasn't well."

"Don't I *know* that? I kept trying to tell you, but heck, woman, you're more stubborn than what you first appear to be."

"It's that determinedness that kept me in a career and kept food in our tummies and a roof over our heads, I will remind you, cat."

"Granted. But I hope you don't think you're gonna get back into all that journalism stuff again. Deadlines here and deadlines there. Editors to meet and to telephone. And da phone ringing here all da time! Why, we cats could have had a breakdown with all the stress dat caused us."

I eyed his silky, gleaming fur. "Yeah sure," I said cynically.

**

It was a huge move to Parklands because it meant moving out a great deal of furniture and doing some cleaning before I could even move in. The garage was absolutely stacked at the rear with furniture and other household goods that Sandy and John had inherited. Some of the goods dated back to World War Two days.

The move was also huge in that it was a very painful exercise for me. For several days afterwards I could barely walk. On the first Saturday morning after moving, I tried to put things up in the cupboard, but they fell out due to the amount of gear still packed in the cupboards. When my friend Big Mike arrived, I felt like bursting into tears. But a cup of coffee and a rest did wonders for my morale.

Although it was rather daunting in that there was a lot of ground to keep tidy and goods to sell on my family's behalf, the intoxicating scent and sound of the sea finally won me over. Plus the fact that there was far more room for my cats and a really good shopping centre a short walk away. One of the bedrooms sufficed as my office, and the main bedroom was plenty large enough for me, although the noise of the traffic was disturbing. It took many months before I could sleep reasonably well without needing earplugs.

**

Soon after our move to Parklands, a painter, hired by my sister and brother-in-law came to give some of the rooms a big facelift in soft peach and white, and the lounge room a much softer shade of mint green. He was a very polite man, very skilled and patient in his job. One morning when he was there, the strong smell of paint drove me outside. I thought I would make a small attempt to weed one of the gardens. The soil was knotted together with twitch and was horrible to weed. But I persevered for a few minutes, trying different positions that would not cause me too much pain. Finally, I knelt down and did some cursory weeding.

"Oh, oh, *ohhhh!*" came some groans from the open dining room window where the painter was diligently working. I thought he was in severe pain, perhaps from a fall that the noise of traffic on the street out front had dulled the sound of. I tried hard to get up from my cramped position. The pain was intense but I managed to stand up by working my hands up my legs as I straightened up. *He's hurt*, I thought. *I must get to him quickly!*

"Oh...Bernadine..." came the painter's voice again, this time sing-song. I realised then that he had been singing part of the chorus from a well-known old song of Pat Boone's. This was one time when I was grateful for the pain and stiffness: had I been able to move quickly I would have caused embarrassment to us both!

Reilly sniggered when I told him later on. "I can just imagine the poor man's mortification, woman, if you'd asked him where it hurt."

"Well, I didn't get that far, so it didn't happen!"

"Lucky for you! Dat man sounded like he was groaning in agony!"

"That's what I meant! But I didn't think you had heard him."

"I did. I was at the other end of the house with Katie. We couldn't stand the paint smell. We heard da groaning though. Why, if he hadn't added da Bernadine bit, I woulda gone out to see what I could do for him."

"What could *you* have done for him?"

"Given him some urgent singing lessons!"

**

Reilly thought the house was great: he could chirrup and race up and down the hallway to his heart's content. I thought that was so sweet, but not so sweet if he decided that two a.m. was the right time in which to go hall-racing. One night I yelled at him to "cut that out!"

"Woman, have you no sense of adventure?" he called out.

"Not at two o'clock in the morning, I haven't!" I called back wearily.

My nights were still filled with pain. My GP had more or less told me I would not get any better; that I was going to get worse. Too much heavy work, domestic abuse, accidents and time were the main causes behind the condition, he said. I was officially diagnosed with osteoarthritis in my lower spine, and still had RSI problems as well. I was informed by the hospital that I had moderate to severe degeneration of the lower facet joints. I pictured myself in a wheelchair in a short space of time, and the vision was even clearer when I was forced into taking pain relievers before I could go outside to hang my washing on the line. Every simple task took on mammoth proportions, in part because I had to think of other ways in which to do them. Bending over, even slightly, was an effort, and by the time I had performed simple household tasks during the day, I was exhausted. I did not ask for home help, because I felt that by doing so, I was resigning myself to not getting better. Okay, so I had accepted home help some months before while under ACC jurisdiction, but the situation was different then.

I knew I could not live like this for much longer, and besides that, I was fed up with Reilly's comments.

"Ha, I can be as naughty as I like and you will never catch me!" he would call out, then do some rascally thing like leap about the furniture, seeing how far he could go without actually touching the ground.

At first I had thought this was because there might have been fleas in the carpet, but there wasn't. It was just Reilly being himself. Growing a little older had not slowed him down at all. If anything, he was still the bad kitten I had first brought home to Carter's Beach; the kitten who had literally taken my poetry evening by storm.

Other comments from Reilly were in the form of: "Youse acting like an old lady full of arthritis! Time youse did something about it, woman!"

"Huh!" I would respond. "I am definitely *not* an old lady, but arthritic, yes, I have to admit."

"Yez only gonna get worse, me darlin'!"

"Why are you talking like an Irish cat?" I asked him that day.

"Simple. Coz I have an Irish name! Didn't you tell people in the past that I meow and purr with an Irish accent, and so does Katie?"

"Well, yes..."

"And some of those people believed you, didn't they?"

"Well, I am a storyteller after all!" I defended.

"So! If Oi wants ter talk loike an Oirish cat, den Oi will!"

"Fair enough," I replied, too sore to argue.

I knew he was right about my situation, though. It was long past time I took a good hard look at my life. If I went along with what the GP and all the other specialists had said, I felt certain that I would indeed be in a wheelchair within a short space of time. I had read about a health product, one that had a four-fold effect; it was a natural pain reliever, it lowered the cholesterol level, improved the heart function, and helped with arthritic conditions. I decided it was worth the rather high cost. I had nothing to lose except some money in trying.

Just three days after taking the product, the difference was astounding, and life has looked up even further since then. I had read that in some cases, the product would actually reverse a chronic condition, and in my case it certainly did that.

The cats were really pleased for me, not only because I was a lot happier and could move about a lot more freely, I was able to play with them more often.

"Can't catch me!" Reilly called one day. I started to chase him down the passageway. He scampered to the dining-room doorway and peered around it. "Haven't seen you run in a big while, woman. *Big* being the operative word. What an amusing sight! All that flesh leaping and bouncing about!"

"What a rude cat you are!" I said between huffs. I was so out of condition, but it was a great feeling to be able to run again. I was not nearly as big as Reilly had inferred, but I had certainly put on some weight. Still, I knew that would gradually disappear as I became more active.

I even began to feel the urge to write articles again, and as such, placed an ad in a newspaper and received a good response.

"Oh no, back to the drawing board, back to the grindstone, eh? When will you *learn?* Didn't I say to you when we were about to move here dat I hoped you weren't gonna get into dat stuff again?"

"When will you learn to keep a civil tongue in your head, cat! It's only going to be a part-time journalism job. I am struggling to make ends meet!"

"Go with the flow, and trust in God," was his succinct reply.

A moment later I heard him taunting Katie.

"Go away, you beast! Mum, *Mum!* Reilly's picking on me again! Make him stop!"

Some things never change, I thought.

"Reilly! Leave poor Katie alone!" I ran up the hallway.

"What is that great thunder I hear?" Reilly called. "Katie, quick! Hide under the beds! Thunder is a-coming!"

I appeared in the lounge.

"Oh," Reilly snickered. "Oh silly me. It's only the woman running. You know Katie, I could have *sworn* we had thunder!"

I had to stop and laugh. Cheeky as Reilly was, you had to admire him for his quick answers and *joie de vivre*.

***

CHAPTER FOUR

"Enough Is Enough"

It was time for my cats to have their annual flu vaccination.

"You know I hate it woman, when you take me to those places!"

"Would you rather get sick with a very nasty flu that could end your life?"

"Oh, how very cheerful, I must say! How absolutely boring and depressing! How utterly *miserable* and degrading! I do *not* want to have a flu shot!"

"But you and Katie both need one. Hey listen cats, it only takes a few seconds and it's all over!"

"Didn't you listen to *me*, woman? Watch my lips..."

"Oh, I suppose cats do have them..." I countered.

"Watch my mouth," Reilly said. "This is what I am saying..."

"I shall say zis only once," I said in a mock French accent, reminiscent of the old funny television program "'Allo, 'Allo".

Reilly glared at me. Katie simply sat there next to him on the sofa and blinked owlishly. She never really *was* a cat for small talk.

"I think I liked you better when you weren't well!" Reilly snarled. "At least you didn't get cheeky, like you are now!"

"Oh? So at last you're telling me that you actually *liked* me?"

"I could go off you in a big way, I could, and real soon."

"But you won't, cat. Because I am too useful to you."

"Back to the...ugh, vaccinations. I do not like them! How would *you* like a needle stuck in your bum?"

"Not particularly," I said with a laugh. "Although I have had worse. A huge needle which the nurse actually broke, leaving it stuck in me. You can't imagine the pain!" I realised as soon as I had said it, that perhaps *now* was not the time to tell my cats of that extremely bad experience in National Woman's Hospital in Auckland some years before.

"Huh! And you think I wanna go through dat?"

"Well, your experience will be a pushover in comparison! I should not have mentioned it!"

"No, you should *not!* Katie, I think it's time you and I left home!"

"There is a lot of cat flu going about," I quickly improvised, knowing however, that what I said was true. "Would you rather get very sick and be put down?"

"Put down! *Put down!* Huh! What do you think I am? A mangy dog?"

"You can be pretty mangy at times, Reilly." I meant "mangy" in the sense that he could be disgusting and horrible.

"How dare you speak to a cat such as I, like dat!"

Only mildly moved, I agreed. "Yes, how dare I? How very naughty of me!"

My word, the health products were making such a difference to how I was feeling! So many things, which before had seemed too big - too hard to cope with, were now nothing to worry about at all.

"Wasn't it just?" Reilly smirked.

Katie said nothing, just yawned and blinked and walked away. She was quieter than ever and I felt disturbed by it. But I almost forgot about her quietness with the business of taking them both to the vet for their vaccinations.

**

Reilly was furious.

"I told you that I did not, I repeat, *did not* want *this!*"

He hissed and snarled at the vet, who looked at him in amusement.

"Hard to imagine such a beautiful cat acting as badly as this."

"He's just a bit of a prima donna," I said, watching the vet quickly give Reilly the necessary vaccination.

"A *what?*" Reilly hissed at me. "Just wait until we get home! I am gonna repay you for dis!"

"Don't be nasty, Reilly. After all, who would have you if I didn't?"

The vet looked at me oddly. "*Ha, ha!* It's as if you know exactly what he's thinking!"

"Most times I do," I said sweetly.

"Yeah, and I know what *she's* thinking all of the time! So there!"

"Okay Reilly, I happily agree that you cats are a most evolved species and you know exactly what I'm thinking."

The vet gave me another odd look. "If I didn't know better, I would say you had a secret language with your cats. I assume your other cat is the same?" He gave a slightly derisive snort but I didn't care. I was used to it.

"Well of course she is! We have conversations all the time, although I do admit Katie O'Brien isn't nearly as chatty as Reilly is."

The vet gave me another odd look, this time as if he'd better humour the potty cat lady. "No, she is certainly a lot quieter than he is." By this time Reilly was back in his cage, glaring at me, and Katie was on the receiving end of the vaccination needle. She gave a brief peep of alarm and pain and then it was all over. "Look at that. You are a good girl cat," the vet added, to my delight. Maybe my pottiness was cat-ching! "When you go home you can have a nice cup of tea."

I laughed. "Do you mean me, or the cats?"

"Er...all of you, perhaps?" Reilly snarled at his words and the vet added: "no, perhaps not all of you. Perhaps Reilly here, doesn't care for tea?"

"Cream, you fool!" Reilly snarled. "*Cream!* And don't you forget it!"

"Reilly likes cream, preferably whipped cream from a can," I smiled.

"Hmmm..." the vet smiled. "Does this cat...er Katie O'Brien, didn't you say?" At my nod of assent he continued: "does she like whipped cream too?"

"Oh yes, she does," I said, giving her a gentle stroke.

"I suppose she sits down with you to have a nice cup of tea and a piece of fruit cake?"

His sarcasm was not lost on me, but I was enjoying the situation.

"Of course she does. She likes dainty cucumber sandwiches too, partaken outside on the patio on a nice fine day." I was sure my eyes were gleaming with mischief.

The vet quirked an eyebrow at me. "Perhaps I should not be surprised if that were so."

"No," I agreed. "You should not be at all surprised. In fact, you are more than welcome to visit and have afternoon tea with us, out on the patio." I felt a delicious rising of laughter, but by then the vet was helping me out the door with Katie in her cage, while I emerged with Reilly, still growling in his cage.

"I'm gonna get yer for dis," Reilly said. I noticed however, that he wasn't as loud as before.

"Nice to know you're happier about the situation, Reilly," I commented. "I told you it would be all over in a few seconds."

"Yeah, but then you had to go on to say some hogwash about inviting the vet to afternoon tea!"

"I was only being polite, Reilly," I defended.

"And laughing at *him*, at the same time!"

By now the vet was quickly ushering another woman and her cat in, while looking sideways at me.

"...just had an unusual woman in with her cats that she has conversations with, and..." I heard him saying as he closed the door.

"Dat vet is a gossip, too," Reilly observed.

I agreed. Well, at least he referred to me as unusual, which is better than I have been described in the past! I was aware too, that the vet had not agreed to sometime taking me up on my offer to come to tea with me and my cats. But maybe that was for professional reasons, I told myself. In other words, not getting involved with clients, outside of business hours.

By the time we had returned home, Reilly appeared to have forgotten his revenge on me, but just in case it reared its head, I went to the fridge and retrieved a can of whipped cream. The distinctive 'pock' sound as I removed the lid had the cats running.

"Gimme! Gimme!" Reilly demanded.

"And me too!" Katie piped.

I squirted a small amount of whipped cream into their bowls and didn't mention the fact that the cream was their treat for getting their vaccinations over and done with. Otherwise the situation could evolve into their expecting the treat at any time, even to reward them for having eaten all their other food. They sat there, side by side at their separate bowls, for once in total accord, and slurped happily at the cream, even though it was only a small amount, given that they'd just had their vaccinations and I did not want the possibility of a bad reaction.

It was both an amusing and lovely sight to see them side by side, in harmony. I again felt the swift rush of pleasure that contained a many-fold feeling: of pride that they were *my* cats; of admiration in their beautiful colouring; the fact that they were at peace with each other (at least for the next minute or so!) and also for the immense feeling of privilege that they chose to stay with *me*.

Okay, so I know there are plenty of cynics out there who will say cats are full of cupboard love; that they only stay where there's going to be a good feed for them at least twice a day and a cosy place to sleep. While I know that this is true too, they also love company. Mine had proven that over and over. And I too, was more than glad of *their* company!

Reilly finished his cream and stared at Katie's bowl. I saw her watching him out the corner of her eye and was highly amused when she turned her back on him so Reilly couldn't see what was left in her bowl, and she proceeded to quickly lick up the last morsels of cream.

"Fancy turning your back on me, Katie O'Brien. How dare you?"

"I will if I want to," she said as she sat back on her haunches and washed her face.

"You're getting to be too smart for your paws. Since when did I say you could answer me back?"

"I did not know I had to get your permission," Katie answered him and blinked twice – rather provocatively, I thought. She really was changing her tune. It should have cheered me that she was sticking up for herself more, but instead I felt alarm bells ringing again.

She sauntered away in much the same way Reilly would when he thought he'd had the last word. Correction, when he *knew* he'd had the last word.

"Perhaps you're not feeling well, Katie?" Reilly called. "I've heard females can be like that! Perhaps you're going through *cat*-opause?"

"I am *more* than well!" Katie returned. "And I am far too young to be going through a mid-life crisis!" She leaped onto the sofa and, with eyes half-shut, began kneading the crocheted rug I had thrown on there. "In fact, I am *very* happy."

I had the distinct feeling Katie O'Brien was already distancing herself from us. Reilly of course, felt it too.

"If you think you can find a boy cat better than me, you've got another think coming!" he said smugly as he leaped onto the sofa next to her and yawned in his nonchalant way.

"Bighead, as always," Katie responded as she curled up into a ball. She looked so tiny that I wondered how she had the nerve to speak to Reilly like that. Even though he had long deserved some of his own treatment in retaliation. The point was - he was so much bigger than her, and his nature ten times more aggressive.

"Well of course," Reilly said. "Am I not a wondrous cat, all-seeing, all powerful etcetera?"

"I like the all-seeing a lot better," Katie said sleepily, and promptly went to sleep.

"Huh, I like that! I really like that!" Reilly snapped. "*Women!* You just can't trust them these days! *Huh, huh, huh!*"

I could see a storm was beginning to brew, but was unprepared for what happened next.

Reilly shot off the sofa, galloped up to me and bit my leg.

"Ow!" I yelped. "What was *that* for?"

"I *will not* have you females treating me dis way! Enough is enough, I say!"

"And herein lies the poet," I said, rubbing my leg and wondering why oh why, for the hundredth, no *five* hundredth time why I put up with Reilly.

Of course the answer came swiftly back, as it always did: because he is a cat in a million; he has entertained you in so many ways; he has given you company where before you had next to none; sure he has fire, but that's coupled with warmth of another kind. He is both Reilly the Dreadful and Reilly the Adorable Cat!

So maybe he was right in saying enough was enough.

***

CHAPTER FIVE

"Turning Up The Heat"

Shortly after that episode, overnight I had left my small pink panties on the night store heater. Forgetful of me to do that, but normally they would have been removed long before the heater was due to automatically switch back on. I commented to Reilly on forgetting my undies on the night store heater but he just gave a smirk and a knowing look. I put my forgetfulness down to my day starting at four o'clock in the morning; later on going to a church breakfast, followed by the service and a talk given by a man who travelled around talking to groups of people about community sharing and caring, and then followed by us all leaving the church and singing the final hymn on our way out. We congregated outside the new opportunity shop in the old vicarage adjoining the property, and listened to an inspiring speech given by a young and up-and-coming MP.

"So what's all that got to do with leaving your pants on the heater?"

"Gee Reilly, you can be so *basic!*" I said, my cheeks burning.

He smirked. "Maybe you're hot stuff!"

"Don't be so rude!" I retorted, my face hotter than ever. "All I was trying to do was give you my reasons for forgetting I'd left them there overnight. The rest of the day was full too, even apart from the church festivities."

"You *do* go on, woman. Well, get on with the story, then. You can even write about it for the church magazine! Heh, heh, *dat* will guarantee some comment! Maybe you could even write about from some rural aspect! Hmmm, let me see now...wait a minute... let me think of a bright headline for dat rural paper yez writing for now. Hmmm...yeah, yeah...I see it now. 'Rural Writer In Da Hot Seat!' Your opening paragraph could be: Rural writer Amber Jo Illsley is in the hot seat once again, this time for her actions built on the old 'burn your bra' protests. But in this case, it's 'burn your pants'! How's *dat* for a good opening line, eh? See? It would look even better in da church magazine! Guaranteed reading, heh, heh. In fact, I could do your stories for you! Of course, you would have to establish exactly *why* you burnt your pants! And den it gets real interesting..."

Responding to his remarks with a brief "don't be so crude, Reilly," I told him that after church that day I took my friend Karen to her parents' house where we had a light lunch and I sorted out a few problems they'd had with their computer. Then I returned home to the phone ringing almost non-stop, it seemed, with visitors in between, and a message left on my answer machine when friend Gary and I went to a restaurant a short walk away, to relax over a wholesome meal.

The telephone message was from my friend Elma. She'd phoned earlier. Another friend arrived – Michelle, the daughter of close friends Kevin and Shelley. While Michelle was visiting, more calls came in and soon I was feeling as if there was 'not enough of me to go around'.

I said as much to Reilly.

"Well of course there isn't, you silly woman! You need a secretary!"

"Who would do *that* work for me?"

Reilly appeared to huff on his claws and give them a rub against his chest.

"I would, of course. I told you before that I could write your stories for you."

"How? You can't read or write!"

"*Nonsense!* Must I keep on reminding you that we cats are a highly-evolved species and can understand the rudiments of any language? Have you ever heard a cat purr in another language?"

I grinned. "Yeah, you and Katie."

"What do you mean?"

"Remember the time I told you about several years ago when someone asked me why my cats had Irish names, and I said because they're Irish cats?"

"Oh yes, I remember now. I reminded *you* about that not so long ago!"

Reilly acted in a lofty manner, half-closing his magnificent eyes and pretending that whatever I said was all rather a bore, really, and so very ordinary. That look of his could have been very demoralising, except that I knew it was *intended* to affect me that way! I thought I knew my cats pretty well by now. But I had to constantly remind myself that just when I thought I could predict what my cats were going to say and do next, they proved me wrong. And so, as I have said in the past, the only thing really predictable about cats is their *un*predictability.

"Well then, I told them that you meowed and purred with an Irish accent – that's when they asked me how I knew you were Irish."

"Yeah, and that's an *accent*, woman! A real Irish *accent!* Highly evolved as we are, we still have accents pertaining to our relative countries. Unless, that is, we leave that country early enough and develop an accent from living in the next country of choice for some time."

"Fancy that now," I said, bemused, particularly as his speech had been very clear and without slang. "The more I talk to you cat, the more remarkable I find you."

"That's because I am far too profound for you to take it all in at once," he said with a smirk and stalked away around the corner into the bedroom, where I heard that evil snickering of his. I felt as if our conversation was left unfinished.

I also felt sure I would love my cat a great deal more – if only he wouldn't *snicker* like that, when he thought he'd had the last word!

It seemed like he hadn't finished with me for this round, however. He stalked back out of the bedroom. *Round Two coming up*, I thought.

"You didn't get around to finishing off your story about your pink pants, woman."

"I didn't, either," I said, wondering what was coming next. "You kept interrupting me. It was just that when I plucked them off the heater the words 'done to a turn' or 'fried to a crisp' came to me."

"Looks like you're in the hot seat again, woman. *You* got back into journalism. *Dis* is a taste of what is to come. Burning your knickers overnight! Oh, let us wonder what da rural writer will do next! Start frying sausages on the night store heater maybe? Bacon too, maybe? Eggs to go with da bacon? Hmmm...now *there's* a thought! I do fancy a nice bit of fried bacon...maybe wid some lamb's fry ter go with it, and not to mention the eggs..."

"Then don't mention them!" I said wildly.

He gave me one of his special looks, which could have been deemed 'old-fashioned', and stalked back into the bedroom and snickered again. Or maybe I should get a little of my own back on him and say: should that be s-nickered? Mind you, a remark like that was best kept out of Reilly's earshot otherwise he would have something else smart to say. He is the smartest-mouthed cat I have ever known.

"Woman, you're *nicked!*" he called from the bedroom. Then he chirruped in glee.

How did he know the lines I was thinking along?

"How many times must I tell you what an evolved species we are?" he called. "We *always* know what you humans are thinking!"

"God help us all!" I retorted, and went on with some household chores.

"There is no need to be sarcastic, woman. I was merely stating a fact."

"And so was I," I replied. "And I'll say it again. God help us all – that even our secret thoughts are privy to the spying of cats."

"Spy? *Spy?* We don't need to spy! Only when we're in the mood for some fun. We just *know* things."

"Such a know-it-all," I responded.

"You'd better believe it, woman. Now be *quiet*. I want to have a nap if you don't mind."

As I said, a smart-mouthed cat.

**

The work I did in journalism this time round was not nearly as demanding. It was for a small nationwide rural newsletter, issued by a large real estate firm. The work came up only every three months, but petered out after a year or so. That suited me fine too, as I was becoming more involved in writing books. *To everything there is a season,* I thought several times after that job finally ended, due to the change in company policies, which mainly meant downsizing.

I began my involvement with internet marketing; it was shaky ground but interesting, and that continues today.

"Where the wind blows, so do the internet programs, eh? Like leaves on a tree, they are there for a season then fall off, to be replaced by new leaves, supposedly better ones, but they too, fall off eventually and get swept away."

"How did you know that, cat?" I said, surprised at his interest.

"I hear you muttering away to yourself, woman. Why don't you get back to work on your books full time? That's where your heart is."

"Oh what a profound cat you can be," I said, while sending out email advertisements for a particular program. It was quite hard work and so often fruitless but I was determined to make it work for me. I knew that one day it would. Perseverance was the key, as I had reminded myself in the past.

**

It was my nephew Brett's 21st birthday and I had been invited to the party. My sister Sandy said if I wanted to bring anyone, I was welcome to. I thought of taking Reilly but he would have tried to steal Brett's thunder, so I dropped the idea as quickly as it had formed. I asked Big Mike if he would like to go and he said yes, adding that he would have to bring Mickey, his small dog. He hadn't been very well, Mike added, saying that he would leave him in his car and would check on him regularly.

Mike called around to my place and sent Mickey for a run into the garden. Then, when he figured his dog had run around the garden enough, he called to bring him inside. Mickey decided that the outdoors was far more interesting than indoors though, and Mike's repeated "Mickey, come *here!*" fell on deaf ears. Eventually though, Mike brought him inside.

"Thought I'd give 'im a good run around outside so he doesn't need to go to the toilet!" Mike announced, pacing around my lounge room.

I glanced down. "Stop right there!" I said quickly. "Don't move at all!"

"Why?" Mike asked, beginning to move again.

"Because you've trodden in dog poo and have walked it all around!" I snapped, despairing of the man.

There, in clear footprints in doggy-doo, was proof that Mike had indeed been in the garden, although thankfully not for the same reasons as Mickey had. The smell wafted up and I ran quickly to get a bucket of hot soapy water and disinfectant.

"Aw, I think I was being so good too," Mike said. He looked like a wounded puppy and I had to forgive him. But I sure was glad we were going out.

Reilly was not amused at all. "Dat man offends my sensibilities. Should I say, dat...puke, puke...dog of his offends my sensibilities."

"Well you don't have to worry now, Reilly. The mess is cleaned up and we're going out."

Mike rolled his eyes, quirked an eyebrow and tossed his head back. Those actions spoke volumes about what he was thinking.

"Amazing how a giant corncob can do all dat in one movement."

I smiled and wisely chose not to say any more to Reilly for the time being.

**

The party went very well as I knew it would. Mike brought his dog inside for a few moments to show him off to people who ooh-ed and aah-ed over him and commented on his one eye.

"I call 'im a one-eyed Cantabrian," Mike said, his comment resulting in laughter.

On the return to Parklands, Mickey made his presence felt – or smelt would be the better word. He had bad wind. I felt like diving out of the car even while it was still moving, to escape the stench.

I told Reilly all about it the next day.

"I always knew that excuse for a dog was a little windbag!"

"That's not nice."

"Nor was his wind, from what you've been telling me!"

"Can we change the subject?"

"Gladly, since *you* raised it in the first place."

"I'll raise *some*thing, if you're not careful!" I warned.

"What, your hat, in deference to a fine cat such as myself?"

"No, I'm not wearing a hat! I'll raise the roof! You know I love telling you stories, and *especially* after you've asked me for one and then you twist it around to make it sound like a chore and a bore!"

"What a long bit of dialogue for a little woman, *woman!*" Reilly smirked. "Anyway, you really can be quite grubby, the things you come out with."

"Well, thanks very much!" I exclaimed, indignant.

"You're welcome, woman. Haven't I always maintained what an obliging cat I am?"

"No, definitely not always. Have you forgotten so soon - Reilly the Terrible, Reilly The Awful...?"

"Haven't *you* forgotten something?"

"What?"

"Reilly the Magnificent, The Grey Wise One, The Caped One, Reilly The Wonderful...and so on. Really, there are such a lot of eloquent titles; it would take far too long to name them all."

"*You've* forgotten one *very* important one!" I snapped.

"Oh?" He gave a bored yawn, curled a forepaw around and appeared to be huffing on it, as if polishing his claws.

"Yeah, Reilly The Egotistical!"

"Who's gonna love me if *I* don't?"

"You know *I* will," I said, falling into his trap yet again.

"And so you should too, woman, and don't you forget it!"

"As if I would!" I snarled.

"No need to get tetchy. I'm just reminding you."

He stalked away as if our conversation had never taken place, while I just stood there, exasperated and infuriated.

Shortly afterwards he returned, sat at my feet and looked up at me imploringly.

"Katie's no fun anymore. Wanna tell me a story?"

"Only if you do not interrupt me."

"As if I would!"

"As if I would, as if I would!" I said, mocking him for the times he had said the same thing to me.

"Are yer gonna tell me or not?"

"As it happens, I do have another story to tell you..."

"Get on with it then. You take so *long* to get going!"

I took a breath and counted to five and hoped my outward breath would not produce smoke.

"My sister Sandy told me about the time she had to take a man to hospital for his regular check-up. When Sandy arrived at the man's house, the man's cat was missing and the man was really wound up about it."

"Like a spring? Was he going *boing boing* around the house as if he was on a pogo stick, going '*here* kitty kitty...*here* kitty kitty'?"

"No he was not!" I said firmly. "I thought you were not going to interrupt?"

"I don't recall promising you anything like that. Now, get on wid da story, will ya?"

I took another deep breath.

"Watch it woman. Yer buttons will pop off your chest if you keep taking deep breaths like that."

I glared at him. "Anyway, as I was saying, the man was really wound up by the time Sandy arrived. He had looked everywhere for his cat and wanted him to be put inside the house, in case he ran away while they were away. Sandy found him, sitting underneath the car. She tried to entice him out…"

"Who, the man or the cat? Was the *man* under the car? No *wonder* he had to be taken to hospital!"

"No, the cat was. Stop interrupting me, Reilly, or I won't finish the story!"

"Get on with it then."

"She tried enticing the cat out from under the car and when that didn't work, she asked the man if he had any meat she could entice the cat out with. The only meat available to use for coaxing the cat out from under the car was a frozen chicken leg."

Reilly snorted and looked at me as if to say: 'are you mad? Even you humans know it's not safe to eat frozen chicken!'

I looked at Reilly sternly, almost willing him to try to interrupt me again. He didn't; he just looked impassively at me.

"Sandy suddenly saw the situation as very amusing. The cat eventually came out and was quickly put inside, and the frozen chicken leg put back in the freezer. No bite had been taken out of the chicken leg, of course. Time was very short and as the man had a wooden leg, she had difficulty in trying to get him into the car."

Reilly couldn't resist it. "He stuck his leg out the window?"

"No!" I laughed. "In the end he had to take his leg off and Sandy tossed it into the back seat while the man literally hopped into the car."

"So, what's the punchline to this story?"

"None really, except that Sandy thought the whole incident very amusing. And I know I would too."

"The man is upset; he's limping around looking for his cat; he's running late for his appointment; the nurse offers to try to get the cat out from under the car; she does her coaxing with a frozen chicken leg, and then once the cat's inside the house and the chicken leg returned to the freezer, she throws the man's leg into the back seat of the car? Is that it?"

"Well, I guess so."

"Here's a good punchline for *you*, woman: When your sister throws the leg into the back of the car; what she hasn't noticed is that the rear window is open and the foot sticks out at an odd angle. They drive off, then fairly soon afterwards get pulled up by several cops in cars with blue lights flashing and sirens wailing as 'looking very suspicious' because some old duck of a woman peeping out through her lace curtains has seen them at a stop sign with a foot sticking out the window and she thinks they have a body in the car, so she rings the cops, giving them the registration plate number. The woman might be old, but she has excellent vision."

"Whew!" I exclaimed, seeing how the story could have unfolded, given a shift in the circumstances, namely the wooden leg – well, at least the foot - sticking out the window.

"Next thing they know, there are reporters sniffing around; and we know what reporters are like don't we?" He gave a derisive snort and gave a wicked chuckling sound at the look on my face.

"That's not nice!"

"And nor would be the situation, with the scenario I have just given you! Then, as you would know, where there is a reporter, there is often a photographer...oh silly ol' me - you did *both*, didn't you? Two people in one, heh, heh. As I was saying, there is often a photographer present, but in this case, there could be several from different publications, all clicking and snapping away, taking pictures of the foot sticking out the car window, and making a journalistic meal of the nurse and her patient. Imagine what the tabloids would say? 'Did the nurse perform surgery in the car? What *kind* of surgery did she perform? Was she even qualified to do so? Or was it surgery of *another* sort...if you get our meaning! Who, heh, heh, *foots* the bill? Read all about it in this week's exclusive story!' Then imagine how it would look in The Press - how they would turn it into a joke, and how a not-so-nice journalist could twist the facts even further? Now, here's another possible headline: 'Give Them an Inch and They'll Take a Foot...'"

"You're out of date with the measurements. We've been metric for years and years," I said sourly.

"Who cares? Why spoil a good story?"

I sighed. "All I wanted to do was tell you the story you asked for, Reilly. Now you have turned it into a big scenario that would not only hit headlines nationally, but probably would internationally, making our policemen and policewomen look like a bunch of fools. And where would be the old duck of a woman you spoke of earlier?"

"Gossiping to her cronies about how she had, single-handedly caught the nurse with the foot sticking out the window. Of course by then the story would have been embellished even more. The patient sitting in the front seat would actually have been in cahoots with the nurse, and there is still a body in the car, with the foot sticking out the window."

"And what would the motive for all this be?" I asked, trying not to sound sarcastic.

"Who knows? *You're* the one telling the story, woman!"

With that, he dashed away, chuckling. As usual, I was left feeling infuriated with my cat.

"The old woman's vision couldn't have been *that* good, or she would have seen that the foot was artificial!" I loudly pointed out, but Reilly had vanished. I did think however, that I heard him sniggering somewhere close by.

"Try not to let him get to you, Mum," said Katie, who seemed to have appeared from nowhere, as she often did. I knew she was right. "I was listening to all the things he said."

"I try not to Katie, but you know he has a point. You can see how stories can get twisted all out of recognition!"

"Particularly when Reilly has a hand, or paw in them," Katie said succinctly.

She was right again.

***

CHAPTER SIX

"Dented Egos"

It was a lovely day in late summer. Magpies were weebling and warbling in the big pepper tree at the side of the back lawn. I was sitting on the patio, enjoying the feeling of the sun on my face and the warmth seeping through my clothing. Both cats were with me, each sitting on a white plastic patio chair, as I was too. They both had their eyes half-shut, enjoying the heat from the sun, but had their ears twitching at the sounds and antics of the magpies. Reilly began chattering.

"Not worth trying to take on those fellows," I warned him. "You know they're big birds and can get nasty."

"They're on our patch."

"Who cares? It's a lovely day and their sound is beautiful."

Reilly yawned as if he hadn't been that interested in what the magpies were doing, anyway.

"Tell us another story, woman."

"Okay." I thought for a moment. There were so many things I remembered; so many amusing incidents that I had put to the back of my mind and it was only when a similar thing occurred that I remembered the earlier incident. In this case I remembered an incident due to a dent in the wall that sheltered the patio from prevailing winds.

I told the cats about the time I flatted for a very short while with Jeff in Pine Avenue. Jeff was a very moody person whom it was only possible to share with because he was away for most of each week, working as a bus driver for a tourist company. And so, mostly he just visited and stayed elsewhere in the meantime. On this particular occasion when he visited he was in a good mood. He told me about telephoning a bus company about an extra driving job and was nervous about making the call.

"You've told us about him before. We know all about him, remember? He moved in for a little while and then used to visit quite often and was very moody after he'd been on a trip. In fact, I bit him one day when he was becoming extra nasty, and he threatened to tell the authorities!"

"Oh yes, that's right, of course you remember," I conceded, thinking about the fact that Jeff was taken away by the police for threatening them. I never did hear what happened over that episode, but oh, how lovely was poetic justice that day!

"Why would a big bloke like him be nervous about phoning up for a job?" Reilly wanted to know. "The way I see it, he shouldn't have been nervous of *anything!* Then again, he was a particularly tetchy chap, wasn't he?"

"Still is, the last I heard of him, which was some time ago."

"Anyway, woman, on with the story."

"Yes, well, Jeff was nervous as I said and not only that, he dialled the wrong number and got the pronunciation of the contact guy's name wrong."

"'Police Department here,' came a strong, masculine voice. But Jeff wasn't thinking straight and asked: 'is Huge Dent there please?'

'Huge dent? Do you wish to report a car accident, sir? I'll just take down a few details...just a moment sir.'

"And Jeff, suddenly realising he'd made an awful blunder, quickly said 'oh, sorry, wrong number' and put the receiver down, his face aflame. 'I thought that was how you pronounced Hugh – as in huge,' he told me. Yeah, the man's surname really *is* Dent. Embarrassing, eh?"

"Must have made a big dent in his pride." Reilly smirked at his pun.

"That wasn't all, cats. Jeff told me about the time when he was a policeman himself – I think he was in Auckland at the time, waiting to nab someone. The guy was in the shadows in a bus shelter, trying to light his cigarette and his lighter wouldn't work. He kept flicking away at it and while doing so Jeff who, in a dark coat and also in the shadows moved forward quietly. Suddenly the lighter worked and in the flame the suspect saw Jeff, who quietly said: 'evening, sir.' Jeff told me the look of fright on the suspect's face was priceless. Jeff, at 6ft 3″, well-built and fit, would be a formidable sight for a small weedy crook."

Reilly yawned. "Yeah, for sure. I like dem sort of stories. Got any more?"

"You look tired, Reilly," I remarked. "Don't you think, Katie?"

She turned her big green eyes onto Reilly and purred. "Oooh, yes I do. Worn out, really!"

He narrowed his eyes at her and looked as if he would pounce on her but a stern warning from me changed his mind.

He yawned nonchalantly. "I ain't really tired, yer know. I'm just giving myself some more oxygen."

"How about this one then? Would you like to hear about my friend Bob, when he went to Sydney for a holiday?"

"Fire away."

"I told Bob that I hoped he stayed away from King's Cross."

"Sounds like royalty."

"Royalty it ain't, my friend. King's Cross is a very notorious part of Sydney where the prostitutes, their pimps, transvestites and what have you hang out."

"Uh-huh, on wid da story."

I looked at him suspiciously. Suddenly he didn't seem tired at all. "Bob told me that was the main reason for his intention to go there!"

"You're kidding us! Didn't you tell us he's in his eighties?"

"Yes I did."

"Looks like there's life in the old dog yet!"

We three had a quiet snigger together there in the sun, before I resumed my story.

"Anyway, when Bob returned from Sydney he phoned to tell me he was back home. 'I hope you kept away from that awful place, Bob,' I said to him.

"'I had every intention of going there, and I did!' he told me.

"Oh dear. I hope you didn't get any propositions."

"'Actually, I did,' he responded brightly. 'I went for a nice walk just to see the sights and I intended to *not* make eye contact with anyone but somehow there was this one tall, beautiful girl – really beautiful she was, and she had a very cultured voice. Unusually deep too, I thought. 'May I help you, sir?' she asked me. I replied that I thought I was way past help, didn't she think? And I walked on. I heard her call out that no one was past help and she would be willing to help me in any way I cared for, but I just carried on.'

"Oh dear. I think the very beautiful 'she' might have been a 'he', Bob," I had said in an amused tone.

"'Huh, I hadn't thought of that! But you could be right!'

"I think I am."

"'But who cares? It's all an experience, anyway.'

"*Experience*, Bob? I sincerely hope you didn't take him/her up on the offer?"

"'Of course not!' he'd retorted. 'What do you think I am – daft? I may be old and wrinkled but there're still a lot of brains left under my thatch.' I'd chuckled at Bob's droll humour and thought of his amazing thick silver white hair. When in need of a good trimming, it truly was a 'thatch'. Soon after, we'd ended the conversation. The mental picture of Bob being propositioned had amused me for days afterwards, given the character of a man that he is.

Reilly smirked at me. "I think you were secretly hoping he had a dirty story to tell."

"Don't be rude, Reilly!" I snapped. "You know I am not like that!"

"Well then, my guess is that you'll be getting pretty desperate by now."

"You are most definitely a horrible cat," I informed him. "You have said some dreadful things to me over the years, but that just about takes the cake!"

"Dreadful, yeah, but don't ya still love me? Aren't I your cute, loveable boy cat?" he wheedled.

I smiled, taken in yet again but also relaxing again in the sunlight. The magpies were still warbling and weebling, although not so much now. Perhaps they too, enjoyed the odd story or two. "I guess you are, Reilly."

Katie yawned and made a slightly derisive noise. Reilly spun his head around to face her, but then decided it was too nice a day to make the effort to pick on her.

"Dat's me, Reilly, a dreadful, adorable cat!"

"Yeah, so I've heard before," I replied, suddenly tired and rather despondent. Reilly's words had hurt. Sure I got lonely at times, but it was far preferable being lonely and single, than what I had been in the past – terribly lonely...picked on, and married.

"What's the matter with you now? Aren't we cats good enough for you? Haven't I been a good cat and kept those undesirables away from you? Haven't I alerted you when I suspected that certain men taking an interest in you weren't kosher?"

"Yes, yes, all of that Reilly," I agreed tiredly.

"Maybe it's time I found you a man, but it would have to be one of *my* choice! You haven't had much luck trying on your own, have you?"

That hurt too, but I knew he was right.

"Quite frankly cat, I am not really in the market for a man."

Reilly gazed straight at me. "Please let me know when you are and I'll check him out for you."

"Patronising cat! Anyway, the ones you're talking about were the ones pursuing *me*, not the other way around."

"Remember what I said before about keeping undesirables away? Remember how I got rid of that awful man at Carter's Beach?"

"Which awful man?"

"You mean, there was more than *one*?"

"As you well know, lots of them were awful," I responded, remembering some of the unpleasant suggestions made to me. "But which particular one are you talking about?"

"The one I bit; the one who was gonna complain to da authorities about you keeping dangerous animals on the premises, or some such thing," Reilly said.

"Oh yes, I remember him well," I grinned, cheering up. "I was immensely pleased with you that time, Reilly. And also when you got rid of another one for me when you were just a kitten, a tough little guy too, I might add. Well then, find a good man for me if you can, but I won't hold my breath. Remember, my friend Carmen and I took a three and a half hour train journey from Krattigen in Switzerland down to Geneva; she was hoping to find me a man while we were there seeing the sights, and it didn't work. Not that I'd expected it to of course, but it was an amusing thought of Carmen's, all the same, and we'd had a good laugh about it."

"You find men amusing?"

"Some of them," I replied. "I remember one chap in particular when I was living in a small haunted flat in Westport..."

"Is this gonna be another story?"

He reached over and bopped Katie awake.

"Ouch! What did you do that for?" Katie piped.

"The woman's gonna tell us another story. Do yer wanna hear it or are you going to sleep the day away?"

"I can listen quite happily with my eyes shut," Katie primly responded.

"Youse is a clever ittle wittle puddy tat, den," Reilly sniggered and sat back in his chair.

"I am so glad you think so Reilly, at long last," Katie said with a secret smile, her great eyes wide with innocence, and then closed her beautiful eyes again.

Rounds one and two to Katie, I thought with pleasure.

"As I was beginning to tell you, I was living in Westport at the time, in a small, haunted flat. In the main street one day, I met this man, who is brother to a woman I had became friendly with at our church. The man was determined to find a pioneering wife..."

"Why? Are you *dat* old?" Reilly smirked.

"Don't be so cheeky. No, it was the man who had archaic ideas about women. I had tried to avoid him after he more or less proposed to me in the street when and where he was introduced to me by his sister."

"You mean, *he* was desperate?"

I looked sternly at Reilly. "I don't think that's very nice, cat. I think the real reasons were that I was single, unattached in any other way, healthy, clean and a Christian woman."

"Oh yeah, and a good worker. You told me about him. It seems to me that being healthy and a good worker were his main criterion."

"I think so. Anyway, one day when I thought he'd (I shall call him Hank) already returned to his hometown, I was out in the back yard, dressed in stretch cut-off pants and a tank top, and wearing my little red gumboots while mowing the lawn. I was suddenly aware of being watched, and looked up to see Hank there, staring at my hips. My heart sank. 'Hello,' I said offhandedly.

'Hello to you, too. I'm so pleased to see you again,' Hank said. 'I was admiring your hips.'

'Oh yes?' I'd said coolly.

'I was admiring your slenderness and yet strength. You seem to me to be a good pioneering woman. You know I'm looking for a pioneering wife.'

'Right now I don't feel very pioneering,' I'd retorted. 'I'm hot, sticky, need a wash and a cup of tea.'

"His apparent compliments were wasted on me. I knew them for what they were worth. Zilch."

"Did he offer to make you the cup of tea?" Reilly enquired, his great golden eyes blinking in amusement.

"Of course not. I'm supposed to be the pioneering sort, able to turn my hand to *any*thing!"

"Fix his truck perhaps? Do an oil-change maybe? Clean and re-set the points? Change the spark plugs? Put a new gearbox in? Change a worn tyre?"

"Probably all that too! While he told his mates about how he had the little woman trained! Huh!"

"I love it when you get mad," Reilly chirruped.

"You do?" I promptly glowered when Reilly smirked at me.

"On with the story, woman! Even though I've heard it all before, *dis* one I like to hear again and again...wid a reasonable gap in between, of course!"

"Well, as I was saying, I'd told Hank I was hot and tired and needed a cup of tea. I ushered him into the lounge room, had a quick wash and change of clothes and made a pot of tea. I commented that my friend Keith was due to visit at any time."

"Oh, I remember dat big man well! And was he?"

"Was he what?"

"About to arrive at any time, woman. Dat memory of yours gets bad at times. I, of course, remember what happened next. But I want to hear it again."

"If I have said it once, I'll say it several times more, you are a very rude cat and I do not know how I put up with you!"

"Dat's coz ya love me! Now, on with the story!"

"Well, as I was saying, Keith was due to arrive..."

"You already *said* dat!"

"Stop interrupting me! I told Hank about how tough Keith was. But of course Hank could see that for himself on the previous time he had visited and had been at my flat for about half an hour when Keith had arrived. Keith acted very macho and protective and I almost laughed."

"*Laughed?* When you had two big men to choose from?" Reilly said gleefully.

"I wasn't choosing *either* of them!" I retorted. "I almost laughed because Keith looked taller and tougher than usual and his voice had become even deeper than it already was. Hank was sitting down when big Keith strode purposefully in and said: 'yeah, gidday.'"

"Did Keith have an FJ Holden?"

"Good grief, no! Why should he? That wasn't his kind of car!"

"As in that old talking kind of song produced by an Australian band. You know...Don't You Let A Chance Go By...or whatever it was called."

"Oh yes, I see what you mean. Yes, all macho as in that song, and very amusing it was too. Hank looked terrified of him. It was all I could do not to laugh. Why, it was even better than the telly!"

"Yeah, I've heard that about women. They just *love* men fighting over them."

"Fighting? No one was fighting over me! But I sure was glad that Keith had turned up when he did."

Anyway, as I told Reilly, *this* time round, the mentioning of Keith's name had Hank very worried. I had even joked that the enormous watch-clock on my wall used to belong to Keith and he wore it on his wrist. That would have made Keith at least twenty feet tall. But Hank hadn't worked that out, and looked even more terrified. As we sat and drank our cups of tea I told Hank about the fights Keith had been in and won. None of the fights had been instigated by Keith, either. Hank looked increasingly worried and kept looking at the big watch-clock. I was aware of his repeated glances and said: 'Don't worry, he's not here yet, but of course will be soon.'

"And was he? Which I remember, of course. But I like to hear it again and again. Lucky for you dat I do."

"Yes he was," I replied, trying to ignore the fact that even while Reilly wanted to hear the story again, he liked to remind me that he *had* already heard it! I'd told Hank about how tough Keith was. But of course Hank could see that for himself the previous time he'd visited. Keith had turned up, acted very macho and protective and I had almost laughed, as I had told Reilly before.

"Laughed? When you had two big men to choose from?" Reilly repeated gleefully. "*Two* of dem? Who's a greedy little woman, den? Who's a greedy, *seductive* little woman?"

"I wasn't choosing either of them, as I said before, and nor was I being seductive!" I snapped, my patience sorely tried. "I almost laughed because Keith looked taller and tougher, and anyway...I've told you all this before, cat. And actually, I'm getting a bit fed up with telling it over and over."

"Yeah, I have heard dis story before, several times in fact. And I've heard that about women. They just *love* men fighting over dem."

"So you said before, too."

"I suppose a bit of repetition never hurt anyone. I remember Keith well. He came to my birthday party, didn't he?"

"Yes," I said, momentarily distracted from the story I had to repeat to Reilly every so often. "And he held you while you very suspiciously checked out your mincemeat and cream cake. *And* it was only when Keith was about to leave, that he realised it wasn't actually your birthday for another month! That's because we always seem to argue on St Patrick's Day, which is your birthday."

"Of course it's my birthday! And you say *I'm* cunning!"

"Well, it saved an argument on your real birthday, by having it a month early. Getting back to my other story...Anyway, as I told you *this* time round, the mention of Keith's name had Hank very worried."

"You're just a naughty little woman!"

"Well I must say - it was rather amusing in a bizarre sort of way. Hank finally left just before Keith arrived. I couldn't help but notice that Hank's little truck was driven away at great speed. For all I know, he could have got a ticket for speeding."

"It would have served him right. Did he ever get a pioneering woman?"

"A few years later I heard there was one, but the relationship didn't last long."

Reilly gave another of his derisive snorts.

"One day Hank's niece came to see me, after I had moved to Motueka to be editor of one of the several newspapers there. She told me that her uncle had said: 'when Amber comes to live here, the first thing I'm going to get rid of is her car.'

"Of course I was furious when I was told that. Young Francie said she knew I would react like that and that she knew I was not the sort of person to put up with that sort of nonsense. 'But I hardly know him anyway!' I'd protested, outraged.

'Oh, but Uncle Hank is like that. If he makes up his mind he wants something, or some*one*, he goes all out to get it...or *her!*'

'Well, he didn't get me!' I'd said darkly.

'No,' Francie had said. 'I told him you were too strong a person for him; that you wouldn't put up with his old-fashioned, possessive and controlling ways.'

"There you go then woman, another man for the chop," Reilly sniggered and gave himself a quick wash.

"So to speak," I said, remembering the incident, and also remembering that I had told Reilly all about that one on another occasion. He gave me a superior look, as if to say, 'I've heard all this before, but since I am a strong, patient and caring cat, I will listen yet again.'

I remembered also, Keith telling some of his family members in the local pub that I always attracted the oddballs, even without trying. One of his sisters looked up at him and said: "yes Keith, do you know what you are saying?" and he had replied that yes he did know what he was saying. However, I think it was only his sister asking him, that made him instantly realise that he was tarring himself with the same brush of 'oddball'. So he tried to save face by saying that I seemed to be a magnet for all the down-and-outers. Which only served to make his sisters look at him with widening grins.

They could of course, have told him to stop now while he was – only just – still ahead.

"Too late for dat," Reilly observed, reading my thoughts.

I wholeheartedly agreed with him.

***

CHAPTER SEVEN

"A Long Time Gone"

For several months now, Katie had become steadily more and more withdrawn. I could see it was affecting Reilly too. He seemed almost confused by Katie's show of independence and her standing up to him so often. If Reilly felt confused, I felt both sad and confused. I knew what a bully Reilly could be, but I thought that after a few years, surely Katie would have become used to his ways by now and would have learnt to stay away when he was in one of his belligerent moods.

But Katie had chosen another path in life. She was teaching herself to become more independent and literally cutting herself loose from us. I did not want her to go away, and I knew Reilly didn't either, despite the way he acted towards her.

He began to change tack, wheedling his way around her. She would gaze at him from those great green eyes and obligingly give him a wash. Perhaps if Reilly had done more of the giving, Katie would have stayed around. I loved her so fiercely, but the old saying about loving someone enough to set them free is true. We have to put their needs first.

One evening Katie wanted to be let outside. I opened the door for her and she ran out, then did a quick turn around and rubbed up against my legs.

"I love you Mum, and I know you have always loved me," she piped. Then off she skipped happily, her neat little body, in the last rays of the sun gleaming with good health.

"I love you too, little Katie O'Brien," I said. A strange feeling of loss came over me. It was a warm, balmy evening when cats love to go out and play and explore. A light sea breeze brought the tang of salt, mixed with a sweet-scented shrub. Ten minutes after letting her outside, I had a deep premonition that all was not well. I went out calling for her, but she did not respond. I asked the neighbours, some of whom looked at me strangely because Katie had been gone for such a short time. The feeling of premonition persisted. Somehow I knew I would never see her again, but I still persisted, just in case someone, somewhere had seen her. Over the ensuing days I telephoned the SPCA and Cats Protection League, placed advertisements on notice boards and in newspapers, and telephoned the council in case one of their workers had picked up a dead cat answering Katie's description. I was glad that they had not. I had learned only a few years before that local Councils keep a book in which they write the description of any dead pet found on the road, and at what location. It seemed a gross thing to have to do, but it was very practical, and at least it gave cat owners closure for their missing pets, had those pets been killed on the road.

I walked around the street for months afterwards looking for Katie, and several times went back to our old place, even though she hadn't cared for the place there. I phoned Keith on the West Coast and asked him if, by some remote chance, had he seen a little cat answering Katie's description, but alas, he had not.

Reilly was moody and bored.

"Huh, I've got nobody, apart from you, woman, to pick on anymore!"

"I'm sure you could find someone easily enough," I said sadly.

For a year after Katie disappeared I would wake in the middle of the night, thinking I had heard her sweet, plaintive little meow, calling for me to come and rescue her. But it was only a dream each time: the dream of wishful thinking. Each time I had a dream like that, I would step up my efforts to find her. But all to no avail. I missed her dreadfully.

"Hell woman, you've still got me! Aren't I still your lovely boy?"

"Yes you are Reilly," I agreed, and I took him to the beach.

He didn't like it.

"Dis is not as good as Carter's Beach. There are *far* too many people! And it's *far* too cold!"

"I thought you were tough enough to withstand any sort of cold weather," I commented. "Don't you want to go for a swim?"

"Certainly not! You know how people laugh at me when I go swimming with you! Think how much worse they'll be here!"

"I thought you didn't mind the attention. Why should they be any worse than they were at Carter's Beach?"

"Because, woman, they're city folks here and besides, there are a lot more of them! No thank you very much! I do not, I repeat *not*, want to show off my swimming prowess in front of all these people!"

"You could become famous," I pointed out, trying not to shiver from the cold easterly blowing through the open car window. There were just a few stalwart people going for a walk on the huge New Brighton pier. Normally it was a most pleasant walk – less than a kilometre for the return walk in the fresh sea-scented air, with a wonderful seascape all the way round. And at the beginning of the pier, a beautiful library built in the shape of a ship, with a restaurant and café as additional attractions.

"Cold - very wet and cold in fact and not to mention famous, with all dem people ogling me? I think not!"

"Oh Mummy, look at that strange pussycat, staring out the car window!" came the voice of a very young girl. "He looks like he's talking to someone!"

"How unusual," said the mother, who was dressed in a designer track suit. She glanced at me, with my long hair blowing in the cold breeze. "The owner seems rather unusual too, to say the least."

Then don't say it, I thought. The woman didn't realise how clearly her words were carried on the breeze. I was aware of her snide tone.

"I think the cat thinks he's a doggie, Mummy," said the little girl. I must say - I much preferred the little girl to her smartly dressed mother, whose long fingernails were painted in deep coral, matching some of the colours of her tracksuit. I guessed that her lipstick probably matched the nail polish exactly, and huh, she probably used designer toilet paper too! They walked past slowly, looking back all the while until my car had passed from their line of vision.

I looked away and sighed, forgetting the designer woman and her nice little girl. "I think we should go home Reilly. I have to agree with you, it really is too cold down here today."

"Yes, home to Carter's Beach."

"Oh, if only we could, Reilly."

"Why can't you? You're a lot better now. What's to stop you?"

"I am too tired to shift again. I simply cannot bear the thought of shifting again...at least not for some time. You know cat, it's not just the sheer effort of physically sorting everything out and packing everything up and then the massive task of shifting, but there are so many other considerations to take in as well..."

"Like what?" Reilly interrupted.

"Telephoning so many places to get them to update our information..."

"Woman and her cat Seamus O'Reilly are now moving house. Please update your databases with our new information. We are moving to Carter's Beach on the West Coast! Phone us on... etcetera..."

"That would be nice Reilly, if it were as easy as that," I interrupted. "But there are times when you literally and metaphorically cannot go back."

"Why not?"

"Because it is never the same. We think it will be as it was when we left, but it never is. People move on, or die, children grow up and landscapes change. Old buildings are demolished and new ones erected. It would almost be like going back to a new town altogether!"

"Didn't I hear you once say that when you went to Westport for the first time, it was as if you went back fifty years in time?"

"Yes I did say that, but what I said before still stands. Many of the people we knew then will have moved on. New people will have moved into the area, and there would still be little or no work for me."

Reilly appeared to sigh.

"Then why go out to work? Why not retire from work altogether?"

"Because, cat, I would get too bored, and anyway I am too young to retire!"

"Find a rich man, then. You could stay at home and wash dishes and his clothes, and play the part of hostess whenever he brought home his business acquaintances. You could put another log on the fire!"

"Oh how droll, how absolutely dreary and *boring!*" I retorted.

I would rather stay poor, than put up with that other sort of loneliness. I thought of Reilly's other remark about putting another log on the fire. Like the old song – and cook me up some bacon and some beans, etcetera, although I would not have thought that was the sort of fare requested by a rich man...unless, poor soul, that he was tired of lobster, caviar, full banquets and the like!

"How would you be lonely?"

At my look of surprise, he sniggered.

"Woman, you keep forgetting that I can read your thoughts! Now, back to this loneliness business. You could invite the vet to tea, and maybe start up something good."

"I'm sure that a vet on the coast would be much too busy for the likes of me as a girlfriend! It looks like we'll be staying here for a while yet, cat."

"Rats! It's too noisy and I can't go across the street."

"You could, but I would not recommend it." I thought of the vehicles whizzing by, and thought too, of the morning when I was fed up with the traffic noise and decided to do a quick count of traffic. I chose a 'light' day, when there would be less traffic, a Tuesday morning between 10.30 and 11 o'clock. In just a half an hour I had counted a hundred and thirty-five vehicles, which included buses and large trucks, as well as utility vehicles, motorbikes, taxis, cars...and just one bicycle, the latter with a person riding it, of course, and even *he* was whistling loudly.

When we first moved to that house I figured we would be there for around two years or so, certainly no longer than three years. I didn't mention this to Reilly at the time, though. He was 'chomping at the bit' as it was to move, and we had only been there for a short while. The fact that he no longer had Katie to pick on, or sometimes to simply enjoy as a fellow cat only served to increase his restlessness and boredom.

That all changed one day when Shelley and Kevin, who had recently returned from their stint much further down the South Island, asked me if I could put them up for a short while, until they found somewhere else to live. They were staying with Kevin's parents, which was not working out so well because the new sleeping quarters were far too cramped.

I told Reilly.

"Is that fat brown rat of a dog coming too?"

"Well of course he is. And he is not a fat brown rat of a dog! Inky is the dearest little dog I have ever known!"

"Huh, well, if he *has* to come here, he has to, and there's not a lot I can do about it."

But I could see a sneaky look come over Reilly's face, and I began to feel sorry for Inky, even before he arrived.

My friends moved in over a weekend. We'd made arrangements to share the chores and costs and it all worked out very well. Kevin provided much of the entertainment. A naturally very funny person, on several occasions when dressed in his light blue cotton knit nightshirt, he would tuck the hem of the nightshirt between his legs, dangerously fasten a safety pin in the hems to form a makeshift leotard and do pirouettes, in his version of ballet dancing. On one particular evening when I was stretched out on the floor watching television and Shelley was sprawled on the sofa, Kevin came a-leaping and a-prancing in to the room, clad in his blue nightshirt, tucked up to simulate a 'well-endowed' male ballet dancer. On his final leap, he landed in Shelley's high heeled shoes that she'd kicked off earlier; the momentum of Kevin's leaping carrying him a few steps further, his heels hanging out the ends of the shoes. It was one of the funniest things I had seen in a very long time and I screeched with laughter. Reilly, who was observing the goings-on in a bemused manner, flung up in the air in fright. Inky barked madly. Reilly landed back down on the floor and glared at Inky. Shelley laughed and I continued laughing.

"I could have been injured!" Kevin wailed.

Which only made us laugh all the more.

"What a stunning show, Kevin!" I said. "I'd love to see you do that again!"

"Huh, a tall man pirouetting around in women's shoes. It just isn't done," Reilly muttered.

"It is in *this* house!" I informed Reilly. "We just saw it happen!"

"Pardon?" Shelley said.

"Reilly just told me that pirouetting around in women's shoes isn't the done thing!" I replied.

"Now I believe everything, you mad Irish washerwoman!" Shelley exclaimed.

"My act has been *spoilt!*" Kevin complained.

"No it hasn't!" I retorted. "It was wonderful! I haven't laughed like that in a while."

"Yeah, and gave me a nasty fright in the meantime!" Reilly snarled, his tail swishing.

"I didn't think anything could frighten you, cat," I remarked.

"Well it did, so *there!*"

"Probably because you haven't heard me laughing so loud in such a long time."

Shelly looked at me quizzically. "Anyone would think you could understand what he's thinking."

"That's because I do!"

"And I understand *her!*" Reilly joined in.

"I know you do, Reilly. I have to be careful of my thoughts even, when you're around!"

"Now I've heard everything!" Shelley exclaimed. "If we're here for much longer, I guess we'll hear Reilly talking too. Does he talk to Inky?"

"Of course he does. They have quite good conversations sometimes."

"What about?" Kevin asked, his blue eyes gleaming with mischief. "War in Afghanistan, the royal family, or what fiendishly expensive car they're going to buy next?"

"Good heavens, not all that," I protested with a grin. "They leave the car buying to *you* guys, and they're not interested in war, unless it's between themselves. If you listen carefully, you can hear what they're saying."

Both Shelley and Kevin turned their blue eyes onto me, in a most disbelieving way.

"Who? The Royal family, out to buy their fiendishly expensive new cars, or the dog and cat?" Kevin's eyes were this time showing a mixture of mischief and puzzlement.

"Oh, I thought you were talking about the *animals* buying new cars!" I laughed. "Anyway, as I was saying, if you listen carefully, you can hear what Inky and Reilly are talking about."

"Sure Amber Jo, we'll expect it when it happens!"

"Reilly, stop that! That's not nice!" I said.

"I didn't see him do anything," Kevin said.

"He told Inky he's nothing more than an oversized, fat brown rat of a dog, like he did that time at Archer Place in Carter's Beach."

"I thought that all he did was meow and chatter in a funny sort of way while staring at Inky."

"That was Reilly telling Inky those things I just told you about! All I can say is that I am sure glad Inky is good natured!"

Both Kevin and Shelley looked at me in a way that spoke volumes: w*e know that you're potty Amber, but we still like you!*

**

Inky settled in as well as Kevin and Shelley did. He was going blind and was inclined to walk into things. One day he walked into Reilly.

"Huh, not only fat and brown - but you're also going blind!"

"I can't help that. I am a senior dog you know, and you should have respect for me."

"Senior? Don't you mean old?"

"In China, senior people are well respected. The older you are, the more respect you get."

Reilly sniggered. I wished Kevin and Shelley were around to hear it. Maybe then they would start to believe me when I said I could hear what the animals were saying. Such a wonderful thing, until they started talking about *you!*

"So dat means you should receive da utmost respect in every way! Oh, bring on the waiters; bring on the maids! Chop! Chop! Chop suey, even, since we are on the subject of China!"

"Sarcastic sod of a cat," Inky whuffed.

"Oooh your Highness, would you care for some grapes, some pate on crackers, caviar, perhaps? Gee, I sound like my woman, when she's in a sarcastic mood."

"That's not nice way to speak about your person."

"I don't care. Whaddya gonna do about it, fat rat?"

"Your respect for me was very short-lived!"

"I went off the idea. Besides, we don't have royalty here as such, as they do in Britain. We're in New Zealand."

"We are? Oh my goodness me, I hadn't noticed!"

"Go away, fat slug of a rat."

"I'll have you know I am a very highly esteemed dog!"

"Dog, schmog, who cares? Dogs make me want to puke, but lucky for you that hasn't happened with you yet. In fact, I quite like you! Now I'm hungry. Let's grovel around our humans."

"It's not suppertime, yet."

"Has that ever worried you before?"

"No."

"Okay, so let's grovel!"

With that, Reilly came wheedling around me making such a fuss I wondered at first if he was sickening for something.

"Ooh yes! It's called hunger!"

"But you already had a snack earlier!" I protested.

"That was then and this is now. My tummy is empty and it needs filling, *now!*"

"Oh, you are so demanding, cat," I said amusedly.

"Inky gets like that too. In fact he's doing it now," Shelley said.

I glanced over at Shelley, who had been out visiting and had returned home at the end of the animals' conversation. Inky was gazing up at her in such a beseeching way, his brown eyes woeful.

"He does it very well," I remarked.

"Yes, he seems to be even better at it since we came here," Shelley said with a sweet smile.

"I wonder if my cat has been having an influence on him?" I said, tongue in cheek.

"I shouldn't be at all surprised," Shelley replied. "Hmmm... remember that time in Westport, when you had come over from Christchurch and were staying with us?"

"Which time was that?"

"The time you came and sat on our bed when Kevin was already up and getting his breakfast. Inky was on the bed with me...you remember...."

Remember I did. Shelley had not long before told me that Inky had had some surgery on his anal glands, and he 'broke wind' some times without realising it and then wondered where the strange noise came from. Shelley had said it was such a funny sight.

This particular morning I sat on the end of their bed in my old nightshirt and talked to Shelley while Kevin was busy in the kitchen and Inky whuffed and huffed and snuffled around on their big bed. I was amused at the crinkling up of his nose as he chewed and bit at 'livestock' on him, real or imagined. He was curled into a wonderful shiny, stocky chocolate brown circle and as he reached around a bit more to bite at another spot at his rear, the movement caused him to break wind in a 'foof' sound.

Inky, being part Pointer and part several other hunting dogs (plus a very small breed which kept him short and stocky with a curly tail) immediately stared fixedly at his rear end, where the sound had come from. In fact, he eyed it with such deep suspicion that I laughed. Then I began to choke as a not-so-nice smell assailed me.

Gasping, I commented to Shelley that I now knew exactly what she meant and it was no wonder Inky was eyeing his rear end with such suspicion!

"Dat is disgusting!" Reilly said, sitting and looking at me in an aloof manner.

"Disgusting? Funny, more like!" I said.

"Eh?" Shelley looked at me, puzzled.

"Reilly thought that was disgusting."

"You'd never get me doing a thing like that."

"You'd be sneaky," I said.

I saw a light dawn in Shelley's eyes and then she grinned. "Okay, I get it. You're talking to Reilly again."

"I am too! I do wish you could hear some of the things he says!"

"Yes, and we could make a fortune from him too," Shelley said with a grin. "I have to say though, that he *does* seem to be having an influence on my dog."

I didn't care to ask her if she thought it was a good or bad influence. I suspected the latter.

"I am already a star in my own right," Reilly said loftily. "I don't actually need any more fame, as you have inferred. Although if I had to put up with more fame, some nice smoked chicken or pickled chicken would be nice. That would have to be one of the perks of the job."

"Yes, Reilly, your ego is big enough for several film stars!"

Shelley smiled at our exchange, eyeing Reilly's swishing tail with amusement. "I'm off to bed. I'll leave you and your cat to discuss fame, and whatever else you were talking about."

"Reilly being sneaky. I was going to remind him about the Siamese cats one of my cousins had."

"Not that Garçon?"

"Yes Reilly. Garçon. The cat who waited around doorways and if he didn't like the person on the other side he would wait until they had just come through the doorway then leap on them and literally attack them. He was a worse cat than you, even."

"Well, I like that! Thanks very much!"

"It seems to me Reilly, that wherever the wind bloweth, there blow you."

"No, you silly woman. It's *Inky* that has all the wind!"

Inky chose that very moment to sidle past. He burped and as he went past to head up the hallway into Shelley's and Kevin's room, I heard another 'foof' sound. My eyes went crossed and I reeled.

"Ugh! Flamin' heck! I knew rats smelled bad, but not *this* bad! Just as well Katie ain't here! She would have been sooo disgusted!" Reilly snapped.

Any amusement I had felt at the past few minutes' exchange fled, with the mention of Katie. I missed her dreadfully.

Kevin arrived home. I heard Shelley telling him shortly afterwards that he had missed a good exchange between Reilly and Inky.

"What, did they fight?" Kevin asked.

"Oh no, they just had an interesting conversation."

"What, did *you* hear it too?"

"No, I kind of worked it out from the responses that Amber Jo was making to the things Reilly said."

"So you did hear him?"

"Well no, not really, but I could imagine the things he might be saying."

"If we live here much longer we'll get pottier as the days go by...that is, *you* will Shelley, not *me!*"

***

79

CHAPTER EIGHT

"I've Been Very Lonely..."

"I'm lonely without Katie," Reilly said one day soon afterwards.

"But you have Inky to chat to now," I reminded him, surprised that he would have even admitted to missing Katie.

"It ain't the same! I feel as if I am stooping beneath myself when I talk to him!"

"Good heavens! Why?"

"I'd like to see *you* have conversations with a fat brown rat!"

Since I am the kind of person who would treat most things where animals are concerned as something unique and edifying, having a regular conversation with a large brown rat would not faze me at all. And I told Reilly so.

"You're a weird woman, if I may say so."

"I'll have you know that I even had a pet rat once. Only it was a black one, not a chocolate brown rat."

"Tell me about it," said Reilly, whose eyes were beginning to close as he listened to me. Oddly, he hadn't been so cheeky to me of late, when I wanted to tell him a story, or when he asked me to tell him one. He had even eased up on his very bad habit of interrupting me with wisecracks while I talked.

"You'd really like to hear about the rat, or are you just trying to work your way around me?"

"What, *moi?* Work my way around you, woman? You should know that an esteemed cat such as me would *never* stoop to such levels!"

"Sometimes you talk such rubbish, cat!"

"Oh woman, I must have caught the habit off you! Now get on with the story!"

Oh, I should have known his improved behaviour was too good to last!

"I was just a kid..."

"Were you *ever* a kid? How long ago? A hundred years, wasn't it?"

"Sometimes, Reilly, you make me feel as if it was *two* hundred years!" I snapped.

"Dat's nice, innit," Reilly said in a mock Cockney accent. "You should be grateful for being able to live so long!"

I took a deep breath and continued. "Anyway, I had this pet rat when I was a child and we were living on a farm in Golden Bay, up in the Tasman District. I think the rat had eaten some poison and was a bit sick. So I took pity on it and used to get up in the attic to care for it. I don't think Mum was too impressed, but having said that, I think the other family members had reasonably accepted that I was the kind of little girl who was going to attract all sorts of creatures and try to care for them..."

"Some drongo men, included, when you got older!"

"I'm a caring person!" I defended hotly. "Besides, I don't necessarily go looking for creatures to look after...they seem to find *me!*"

"So I have noticed," Reilly said wryly. "You are a magnet for weaker vessels."

I ignored his comment. "Anyway, they were rather aghast when this big black rat first appeared in the kitchen and I said in excitement: 'oh what a lovely rat! Can I have him for a pet?'"

"Aghast might be a word, but I would probably have said: *stunned.*"

"Alas, even though Mum actually agreed that I could, much to my delight, I did not have the rat for long. One morning some weeks later, Dad put the can of cream out on the stand ready for the dairy collection that day and got a shock when it was returned. My rat had apparently managed to climb in before the lid was put on and had drowned. Dad put the lid on, not realising that my rat had got in. Oh, I was so sad."

"I just bet your dad was too, losing all that cream."

"I'm sure he was. I loved cream, but I loved my rat even more."

"Think of it this way woman, you may have lost that rat, but now you have an even bigger one, a fat brown rat!"

"Inky is not a rat. He is a lovely sturdy little brown dog," I coolly informed Reilly. My big cat sat back on his rounded bottom and looked at me evilly. "And what's more, he does not belong to me."

"Well den, if you ever get da urge to have another rat, you have two choices."

"Oh yes?" I said suspiciously.

"You can either get your rat 'fix' from Inky, or allow some of dem drongos to hang around you. I can see they are little more than human rats! Mind you, I could sharpen my teeth on dem. Dat would be very handy!"

"Thank you very much, I'm sure," I said, not amused. "I was very lonely after losing my rat."

"Gee, life sure is tough when even a rat is better company than none! What about your brothers and sisters?"

"Of course I had them, and they were great. But the two eldest siblings were already away working, and I always felt as if I was the odd one out. So I often went away by myself, eeling in the creek, or else climbing the tallest trees on the farm. I think I must have had several guardian angels at once. Maybe even they despaired of me, as I was always an adventurous kid, and would wander off from home as soon as I was able to walk. And when my little sister Sandy started to walk, I would take her by her hand and we would go for a walk down to the beach. The neighbour used to be horrified. These two little wee kids, floundering around in the surf..."

"Once upon a time you were a little kid...about a hundred or so years ago, and now you is an odd little icky widdy woman."

"There's no need for that nonsense talk, Reilly. Besides, I am not a widow." But I was hardly aware of what I was saying, as I had been thinking of the phrase 'I've been very lonely' – relating it to a very bizarre young man I'd met some years before.

**

"Here's another lonely story," I said to Reilly a few minutes later.

"Do I want to hear this?"

"It's quite amusing."

"Oh do go on then, amuse me, woman."

"Some years ago my dad was in hospital in the Nelson area. My sister-in-law and I were visiting him and when we were sitting out on the front veranda talking to him, this young man came along. He was visiting someone there too, but really, he should have been admitted to a psychiatric ward."

"Why?"

"He kept saying he would like to go into hospital, because it was free rent and a bed and food."

"What a very bad attitude!"

"A very bad one," I agreed. "Considering that he probably would have put on a big act to get into hospital and in the meantime deprived a genuinely needy person from a hospital bed and treatment. His whole attitude was weird and we were glad when he went inside the hospital, presumably to search out his family member or friend."

"So, what was so psychiatric about him?"

"Wait, there's more..."

"Like the TV infomercials...but wait, there's more!" Reilly interrupted.

"That's right, cat. There's more to come. A couple of years or so later I was in Christchurch with my friend Lou. She had offered to buy me dinner at a Greek restaurant in the heart of the city and I had readily agreed."

"Hungry for Greek food, eh?"

"That too, but I enjoy Lou's company. She's very bright and amusing. We'd been to see examples of the Chinese Buried Warriors, on show at the Christchurch Museum. I had come over from Westport and she had flown down from Nelson. The Buried Warriors were amazing!"

"How could you see them if they were buried?"

"They *were* buried, for over two thousand years, and that's why they were called that. They were first discovered in, if I remember rightly, 1974 and there were around eight thousand or so of them, plus chariots, horses and so on. The soldiers were known as the Terracotta Army. But there were just a few at the museum, of course, and I was told that they were replicas."

"Of course. They should have been called The Chinese Uncovered Warriors!"

"Yes, but that would sound as if they didn't have any clothes on, and they were in full battle regalia."

"Were you disappointed?"

"At what?"

"That they had clothes on!"

"Reilly!" I snapped. "Don't be rude! Do you want to hear this story or not?"

"Of course I do! Only you keep getting off the subject."

Inwardly I fumed, but I was secretly glad he was getting back to his old self. Reilly the Egotistical; Reilly the Overbearing One; and Reilly the Wondrous One I could cope with. Reilly the Moping One I could not cope with very well. It *so* went against the nature of the big cat I had known all this time.

"Now, where was I?"

"Ogling the Uncovered Warriors," Reilly smirked.

I glared at him, and then resumed my story. "Anyway, we went to this wonderful Greek restaurant afterwards. The whole atmosphere was magic; there were real Greek people dining there, a sort of home away from home for them, and a band made up of real Greek people. The music was traditional and fantastic..."

"Mandolins, guitars and accordions and things?"

"Something like that. And the vocalist was terrific. He was a small guy with a strong voice. Suddenly this strange man appeared; he'd come up the stairs from off the street, stood in front of the stage with his arms outspread, his body tilted to one side and said in a very loud voice: 'la la LA!' I tell you, the effect was quite stunning. Everyone in the restaurant, including the band, looked as if they weren't sure if this guy was for real. Suddenly, in one sweeping motion the guy sat down in the spare seat at our table, with his head suddenly in one hand and said in dramatic deep tones, 'I've been very lonely.' Because of his distinctive looks, I recognised him immediately as the same man who, a few years before I had seen at the hospital just out of Nelson where my dad was, talking about getting free rent at the hospital."

"Who, your dad or the other man?"

"The other man, of course. My dad was in hospital quite legitimately, as he was ill, and..."

"They seek her here, they seek her there..." Reilly began singing.

"Don't interrupt!" I snapped. "Well, Lou and I sat there rather stunned. I said something like 'that's a shame' and then the guy in one fluid motion again..."

"Leaves his motions about, does he? It's a wonder dey didn't kick him outa da restaurant! What a *filthy* man!"

"Don't be disgusting! Anyway, where was I?"

"The man was leaving his fluid motions at your table..."

"You *dirty* boy cat! Well, the man leaped up in one fluid motion and, with arms outspread again, sang in a very loud voice: 'La, la la la LA!' then *whammo!* He was back at our table with his head in his hands saying: 'I've been soooo lonely. You don't know how lonely I have been in my life!'

'We all get like that at times,' I'd tried to soothe.

'Awwww! I have been SO VERY LONELY!' the man wailed.

I heard a funny noise at the next table and saw that the young couple dining there were almost crying with laughter. The young man at that table asked me chokingly if I was okay and I said yes, that I was pretty well used to this kind of thing.

Lou couldn't stand any more and said so.

"I can't stand this! I'm going down to the table where that guy is sitting by himself!" And she promptly did so, leaving me to fend off the weird man as best I could.

I turned around to see the other restaurant patrons all looking at me, and those who were not outright laughing, were sniggering behind their hands. Probably the weird guy was the best entertainment they had had in a long while.

'Chicken!' I called to Lou.

'I'd rather be a chicken down here than put up with that!' she retorted.

There was more sniggering from the patrons.

Boing! Up the man leaped again, almost as if he had springs in his shoes. 'LA LA LA LA!' he carouseled very loudly in front of the band, then again the same thing happened.

He zoomed back into the spare chair.

'I have been soooo lonely, you would *not* believe!' He wailed again, putting his head into his hands. I found myself gazing at his blackened, broken teeth, those few that he had left in his mouth, that is. Somehow I was not surprised at his loneliness.

'Still lonely, even *now?*' I said drolly and heard a spluttering sound. The young man at the next table was now openly crying with laughter.

The weird guy suddenly seemed aware of what was going on. 'What's wrong with *him?*' he said, swinging around to stare.

'You made him cry,' I said. This only made the young man at the next table even worse. By now his head was almost in his plate. His girlfriend was also laughing and when I turned around the entire restaurant-full of people were laughing, including Lou who was at a safe distance, and still sitting with the young man who'd been dining on his own.

'Chicken!' I called out to her again.

Everyone laughed again.

'I'd still rather be a chicken than come back there!" she called. 'It's much safer down here!'

'What's wrong with everyone?' said the weird guy. 'Don't they realise how lonely I have been?'

'Oh I am sure that if they didn't know before, they most certainly do now,' I said dryly.

I heard a lot of snickering behind me. The young couple at the table next to us were convulsed with laughter. Then the lead vocalist stepped off the stage and came to our table.

'Is this man bothering you? Is he making some trouble for you?' he asked in a strong accent.

'Not particularly,' I said. 'Nothing I can't handle. I'm fairly used to this sort of thing.'

'If he bothers you some more, please to tell us and we will toss him out of here.'

I looked at the very slender Greek man of short stature and highly doubted if he was capable of tossing a rat out of there, let along a man of above average height. Hmm...thinking of rats though...the 'lonely' guy did come into the category that Reilly had been making reference to earlier, but in looks rather than anything else! That fact did not put me off rats, however.

'Perhaps I should have bought something, do you think?' the weird guy said, becoming normal.

'If you had booked a table, it would have been different,' I said, trying to be kind. I did not want a scene, but nor did I want this strange man who had obvious psychiatric problems, staying here at my table, when Lou should have been sitting there with me.

Eventually he left, but we never forgot the situation.

I mentioned to Reilly that I had told the story to Kevin.

"I just bet he enjoyed that!"

"Oh yes indeed he did! You'd never guess what Kevin did one day!"

Reilly appeared to look shocked. "*Nooo!* What?"

"Well, he and Shelley had invited me to go with them to this 1960's type restaurant in the main street of Westport. You know the sort of restaurant..."

"Should I?"

"Aren't you all-knowledgeable, all-seeing?"

"Of *course* I am!"

"There you go then, you'll know what I'm talking about. It was the kind of restaurant that has red Formica-topped tables, old condiment sets supporting a battered menu folder that looked as if it hadn't been changed for forty or more years, and a general atmosphere of time having stood still. Oh yes, and there was the traditional plate of diagonally cut slices of fresh buttered white bread."

"Do please go on," said Reilly. And he wasn't even being sarcastic, for a change!

"We ordered our fish and fries and coleslaw, and out the plates came – huge plates they were too. The food was delicious – exactly the way I remembered it years ago when I was a kid."

"About a hundred years or so ago."

"Not quite that long," I said, amused this time. "I was chatting away about this and that and suddenly Kevin's eyes filled with mischief and he quickly assumed the same dramatic pose that I had demonstrated when telling him the 'I've been very lonely' story some time before. 'I've been so verrrry lonely!' Kevin said, quite loudly. I automatically let out a great burst of laughter and everyone stared. I could have crawled under the table."

"Dat would definitely have aroused da suspicions of management," Reilly observed.

I agreed wholeheartedly.

"But that wasn't the end of it."

"Flamin' heck? How lonely can a person get?" Reilly's sarcasm was returning.

"*Very*, apparently. I was in bed early this particular evening. Shelley had gone to their bedroom to read and I was also reading. My bedroom door was open a little and next thing I knew, Kevin had come in and thrown himself across the end of my bed in an 'I've been very lonely' pose. Only this time he continued on and landed on his shoulder on the floor. My bed was on castors. The bed ended up askew with that end of my mattress coming off the bed. I shrieked with laughter, of course."

"Oh I remember dat incident well. I thought something nasty had happened to you. All that shrieking gave me a fright, I can tell you."

"Shelly called out and I could barely answer her as I was still laughing."

'I could have been badly injured!' Kevin wailed, rubbing his shoulder. It seemed that Kevin quite often could have been 'badly injured' with his antics.

Shelley had entered my room and wanted to know why my bed was at that funny angle and why was the end of the mattress off my bed. When I explained that Kevin had been 'feeling very lonely' she laughed too, knowing exactly what I meant and told him it served him right for coming into my room like that.

'But my shoulder is very sore!' Kevin wailed again.

'I'll give you something to cry about if you're not careful!' Shelly had said. "Get out of Amber's room!'

"Loneliness can be a dangerous thing," Reilly commented.

"Amen to that," I said, grinning at the memory.

***

CHAPTER NINE

"The Tooth Of The Matter"

A few months after Shelley and Kevin and Inky had first moved in to board with me they found a place to rent – a lovely home within walking distance of my place.

"I'll miss them," I said to Reilly. "Even though they don't live far away."

"No more fat brown rat of a dog to tease."

"So, you actually admit you teased Inky?"

"Yeah, I cheerfully admit it! I get bored, woman, *bored!* A cat such as I needs a decent amount of stimulation! And I needed a substitute for Katie. Gee, I miss her!"

"Oh Reilly, do you really?" I melted towards him.

Reilly straightened up and started washing a front paw. "Naw, not really. I just said that to get you going!"

But I had seen the look on his face. I missed Katie dreadfully too. I still looked for her and still went driving by my former flat, just in case she had decided to return there. No one had seen her – not that I expected to receive good news, but I lived in hope.

So once again, Reilly and I were on our own. It had been several years since this was the case – except for the short stint between her leaving and the Jenkins family arriving, and it took some getting used to again.

I pondered going through the motions of getting another cat to keep company with Reilly, but I couldn't bear the thought of a similar thing happening. That is, getting a new cat and loving him or her only to find Reilly doing the same thing: that is, bullying the other cat so much that he or she eventually left.

**

One of my teeth started to niggle at me. I'd had problems with this one on and off for several years and had numerous expensive trips to the dentist as a result. This time it had become a bit loose.

"Forsooth," I said to Reilly when the pain was becoming unbearable. "I've almost lost a tooth!"

"Ain't dat da truth!" Reilly smirked.

I say smirked because that's truly what he appeared to be doing. So I commented on it.

"Oh boy, you sure know how to *smirk*, cat!"

He looked at me with one eye half shut. "What do you mean? We cats are *renown* for being able to smirk!"

I grinned, happy to score a point for a change. "Ain't dat da truth!" I said, mocking his speech.

Reilly harrumphed in his cat way and stalked off.

"Huh! The woman can't even talk properly!"

**

Eventually I had the tooth removed. Odd how such a small part of one's body can be missed so much! My face was swollen and I felt miserable. My friend Gary's daughter had asked me to dinner, but I had to decline, due to my face feeling so sore.

"Oh please come anyway," said Gary's grandson Jason. "We'd love to see you. You could take some pain relievers."

But I knew that they would wear off and I would feel miserable again.

Then Gary arrived from the Coast.

"Are you coming to Robyn's for dinner?"

I told him I had already phoned their house to decline. Gary said I looked terrible but that my old tooth was probably feeling a lot worse! I always did appreciate his droll humour, even knowing that there were times when he tried to 'bait' me! 'I like to hear your Irish accent!' he'd tell me. I apparently had one when someone was trying to wind me up and I was not in the mood for nonsense!

"Are you sure you won't come on over? We'd only be a few hours."

Much as I liked his family, I felt that 'a few hours' would stretch a few more and it would become an endurance test. Having endured dinner parties and barbeques that went on and on for hour after hour, I resolved never to go to anything else that I couldn't drive myself home from when I'd had enough of it, or at least be with a person who was gracious enough to understand when I finally wanted to leave.

After half and hour or so and a cup of tea, Gary left. I felt mean that I hadn't gone to the dinner, and disappointed too, that I would miss out on lovely food and pleasant company, but another stab of pain in my face convinced me that I had made the right decision.

**

But it wasn't too long before I was back to normal. I decided to hold a small dinner party. By that time, I had a Chinese girl student boarding with me. As is the custom when Asian students come to this country, they give themselves anglicised names. My student called herself Michelle, and was a pleasant girl, despite her colossal appetite.

Our dinner party was small – just four of us. I had cooked roast chicken with all the trimmings, and had invited Big Mike and another friend, Gavin. I knew the men would have plenty in common as they both have a strong interest in computers.

The dinner was going really well; I was in full flow with telling a funny story and as is a habit of mine, I was avidly gesturing with my hands. I leaned forward a little in my delight in my story and wondered at the instant sniggering, which developed into raucous laughter from the men, and giggling from Michelle. I glanced down towards where Mike, with much amusement was pointing and there, like a small white mountain topped with gravy, was an addition to my left breast. I had accidentally leaned into the mound of mashed potato topped with gravy, to one side of my plate.

"Woman, dontcha think they're big enough as it is?" Reilly demanded. He was sitting under the table and had leaped out when the laughter broke. "Climb every mountain, ford every stream..." he began to sing.

"Stop that, Reilly!" I said as I carefully wiped the mashed potato off my bosom. The others were still laughing, and laughed even more when they saw the wet patch left behind. I glanced up to see Michelle wiping tears from her eyes and by then Gavin had risen from his chair and had walked away from the table. I asked him a few minutes later why he'd got up from the table the way he did.

He told me bluntly that the reason was "because I thought I was going to piss meself with laughing, and thought I might have to make a quick exit."

"I didn't think it was that funny," I'd commented.

"No, but *we* did! It's one of the funniest things I have ever seen!"

"Yeah, right," I said drolly, and then smiled at the mental picture of how it must have appeared to the others.

"Climb every mountain..." Reilly was singing again.

"Don't be cheeky, Reilly!" I snapped.

"What's that cat of yours saying now?" Mike had asked, giving the others a wink.

"He's singing 'Climb Every Mountain'," I said, rather unwillingly. Which only resulted in more laughter.

I didn't have another dinner party for a long time after that.

**

While thinking about sharing a meal with friends, I remembered another incident. I told Reilly about the time on the West Coast, long before he was born, when friend Keith invited me to a barbeque.

"How long will it be before we get to eat?" I'd asked warily. Having already had several experiences of the Great Kiwi Barbeques when the wind turned cold, the people drank too much before they started to do the cooking, and everyone stood around shaking with cold for hours, pretending they were having a great time, and then by the time the food was finally cooked, it was either black on the outside and uncooked on the inside, or else it was all well and truly overdone.

"Oh, I think they'll be starting the cooking as soon as we get there," Keith said easily.

Somehow I was not convinced. "Maybe I should take my own car, so I can come home when I'm ready."

"Naw, don't waste petrol when I'm already going out there! I'll pick you up at five o'clock."

Reluctantly I had agreed. It was still early in the afternoon but as the time wore on, the thought of going out to Cape Foulwind to share in a barbeque with a lot of people whose main aim in life is to go to pubs and talk about rugby and horse racing is not really my 'thing in life'.

When Keith returned, I asked again if they would start the cooking as soon as we got there, and justified my questioning by telling him about previous 'barbies' that had been little more than an endurance test.

"Stop worrying. You know everyone who'll be going. You'll have a great time!"

"Hmmm..." I'd muttered, concerned still.

The venue was too far away for me to walk home if I wanted to, but I decided I might as well try to make the best of it. Almost as soon as we arrived, Keith announced: "We're just going up the road for a few quick ones and then we'll be back." Interpretation: "We guys are going up to the Cape Foulwind pub for a few drinks which could easily stretch into several hours, and then we'll come back here to start the barbeque."

My heart sank. I knew I should have listened to my instincts.

The women were chatty enough, but some of them were hard as nails, and had language to match. I felt I had nothing in common with them, but I tried my best to enjoy myself. In the meantime, the sun went down and the sandflies and mosquitoes whined around us. I felt that most of them landed on me, as I have fair skin, and maybe tastier skin, since it wasn't pickled - as these women's skins appeared to be from all the heavy drinking they did!

There were six children running around. They began to fight and were tired and hungry. A breeze blew cigarette smoke my way. Since I cannot bear the smell of it, I tried not to breathe, telling myself to be thankful we were sitting outside where mainly only the mosquitoes and sandflies could get to us! The children became very overtired and excitable. I knew there would be tears in a moment or two, and there were. One child ran hard into another one, hitting him in the nose. His nose bled profusely. Another woman and I got blood over us while we tried to mop up his tears as well as his blood.

Nearly five hours later, the men arrived and they began cooking the meat for the barbeque. We ate at around 11pm and I was not amused. They looked as if they still had several hours' worth of socialising in them, but I had well and truly had enough.

"I want to go home," I said to Keith.

"But you haven't even been here long," he protested.

"Correction, you mean *you* haven't been here long!" I snapped. "I've been here for nearly five hours! You can always come back here if you want."

Keith told me I got a steely look in my eyes when I was angry. He decided that perhaps it *would* be a good idea to take me home.

"*I* could have told him dat!" Reilly said with glee.

"You could have, cat, but you weren't even born then!"

"Well, I *would* have told him, if I had been born."

"I always knew you were an Irish cat!"

"What's *dat* got to do wid da price of a barbie?"

"Nothing at all. It's just the way you come out with things sometimes."

"I must have caught it off you, woman."

"No you didn't! Now cat, I have just remembered another interesting incident that happened on the West Coast. I was living at that same haunted flat, too."

"No wonder you wanted to go out all da time."

"It depended on where I was intending to go to. If it was to an Arts Council function, then I would gladly go, but not to functions where there were too many people drinking and you could hardly see because of the pall of cigarette smoke."

"What about this other story then," Reilly said, yawning.

"Are you sure you want to hear it? You look tired."

"I am tired, but I will listen to you on the proviso that you make me a nice snack."

Since it was almost time for dinner anyway, I readily agreed, and fetched him some cat biscuits.

"Dis ain't exactly the Ritz fodder, but it'll do I suppose."

"Good, I am glad of that. I want to tell you this story while I think of it."

"Is it true?"

"Of course it's true!" I said. And it was.

Keith had asked me if I would like to go with him and his friends to a raft and boat race up the Buller River. What will I be doing? I wanted to know. Keith told me I could help keep an eye on his son, who was wont to getting into trouble. I didn't really fancy the idea of being an unofficial child-minder while everyone else had a great time, but it was a lovely day when we set off, and anyway I liked these particular friends of Keith's.

Keith and his friends had built a raft, while other contestants had used a varying assortment of old dinghies, colourful rafts, aluminium punts, and so on. Keith's and his friends' raft was pretty straight forward, and looked sturdily built. It was made from strong timbers lashed with light but very strong nylon rope over 44-gallon drums, and it floated extremely well. It needed to, as there were several men on board, including Keith, who is a well-built man of around six feet in height.

Being a former naval man, the job of captain appeared to naturally fall to Keith. I could hear his deep voice echoing orders down the mighty Buller River, while I kept an eye on his son Tony, swimming in a shallow part of the river. I was bemused to find myself the minder of wallets, watches, cigarettes and the like.

"I am fully aware of why women generally carry handbags around," I said wryly, as they were about to embark on their adventure. "It's not just to carry our own bits and pieces. It's to carry men's gear as well!"

Tony began swimming out of his depth and that worried me, as he wasn't a strong swimmer and I knew how deep the river was. I called to him and he eventually and very reluctantly came out, shivering and complaining.

"I wanted to go on the raft," he said. "Dad always gets to do the best things and I miss out!"

"Now that's not true, Tony," I corrected him.

I could see a tantrum coming on and changed the subject. Soon afterwards word came through that they had arrived at the finishing point. As prearranged, I drove one of the men's cars up to the Berlins Hotel, Tony complaining as I drove - where we had to hang around because the *hangi*, which should have been well underway, had only been started a short while before.

At first the atmosphere was enjoyable, with friendly bantering about the race. I don't know who won, but no one seemed to care very much as it had been a fun thing...for the others taking part anyway!

The evening began to wear on. Some 'bright spark' decided that since the *hangi* was a long way off being cooked, they would boost the fires by adding kerosene. The food, which was incredibly tender, should have been delicious, but had an overwhelming taste of kerosene and was therefore, disgusting to taste and I immediately felt sick. I'd started eating a piece of pumpkin and that's all it took for me to start feeling sick. I offered my tender slices of meat to a dog, but he looked sideways at me in a very mournful manner, whined and wandered quickly away, his tail between his legs and his back hunched over.

"I don't think the dog likes it either," I'd commented. "I hadn't even started eating this, but someone must have given him some to try before I came along."

I moved away from the *hangi* to sit upwind of the breeze that had sprung up. Alas, another smell assailed me. Someone had been sick. I suspected from eating kerosene-flavoured food.

Keith took me home early as I'd had a political meeting to attend. We'd arranged to meet at the pub afterwards, not that I liked going to pubs normally, but there were times when it was a nice change. I attended the meeting and tried not to burp throughout, but the burps sneaked up, strongly flavoured with kerosene. I felt quite ill, and was glad when the meeting was over. At the pub I asked for a drink of orange. It too, seemed to taste of kerosene.

When I went home soon afterwards, the smell seemed to be all around me. I suspected it was coming out through the pores of my skin. My stomach lurched and I made a hasty trip to the toilet to be sick, immediately feeling better afterwards.

"Maybe some of that special-flavoured meat got stuck in the gap left when da dentist took out your tooth?"

"Good heavens no! I had the tooth taken out years later! In any case, I hadn't even started on the meat."

"So many stories, woman! It's a wonder you don't get confused with what happened exactly when!"

"Not usually. I get mixed up with what happened in what city sometimes though, if I've been doing a lot of travelling."

"Is all what you've told me in this session the truth?"

"Of course it is, Reilly! Nothing but the tooth...er, truth."

"I swear you're getting barmier as you get older."

"It's the company I keep!" I retorted.

"Yeah, left over from the wild and woolly West Coasters!"

"I've been away from there for years..." I began.

"Yeah, *too* long! My sentiments, exactly! When *are* we going back there?"

"One day, Reilly," I said sadly.

"One day, Roger Phipps!" Reilly snapped, using a line from an old television ad. "One day, sometime in the next twenty years!"

"Play your cards right, cat, and it could be sooner."

"Is dat da truth?"

"And nothing but the tooth," I said with a grin.

"As I said, getting barmier as you get older."

"It's the *current* company I keep!" I returned.

Reilly looked gleefully at me.

"Ohhh, I've been *sooo lonely!*" he chirruped, sing-song, and darted away outside.

***

CHAPTER TEN

"Que Sera, Sera"

Even though the Jenkins' arrival had somewhat tempered the loss of Katie, I still missed her terribly. If I awoke in the early hours of the morning, thinking I'd heard her – even if it was only in a dream, I would get up and go for a wander outside, softly calling for her. She never came home, of course, but I was ever hopeful.

"What are the neighbours gonna say if they see you wandering around outside in your night attire?" Reilly asked me after I came back inside early one morning.

By this stage, Shelley, Kevin and Inky had moved into their new rental property a block or so away, so I didn't have to whisper quite so softly outside anymore.

"If they hear me calling Katie, they will correctly assume I'm outside calling my cat!" I retorted.

"Mumsy-wumsy's little bittle cat has run away!"

"Well Reilly, tell me you don't miss her and I'll tell you that you are a lying cat."

"Naturally I am a lying cat; I lie around a lot."

"Finally you admit how lazy you can be!" I said with grim humour, shivering a little in the cool of the wee small hours.

"You distracted me, woman! We were talking about Katie. Of course I miss her! I miss not being able to assert my authority around her! And *you* are no fun!"

"Well, thanks very much, I think! I'm going back to bed."

"Er, didn't I hear you mention something about getting a snack for me?"

"You heard nothing of the sort!" But at his beseeching look, I gave in. He got cat biscuits.

"Rump steak this ain't, but I guess it's better than nothing!"

"Anyone would think that rump steak was a regular part of your diet!"

He stopped munching for a few seconds to stare up at me in disgust.

"You mean it ain't? Why not?"

"Because, dear cat, my financial resources will not stretch that far."

"You have da mince and a sausage, and I'll have da steak."

I glared at him and returned to my room, getting into bed and lying in the darkness. I could hear Reilly munching on his biscuits. The sound echoed clearly in the still of the night. It seems to me that the wee small hours are the loneliest hours of all; when there is little or nothing to distract you from your thoughts, hopes and dreams. I hoped and dreamed that I would find Katie – or even better, that she would return to me of her own accord.

My mind in full gear again, I sat up, leaned over to switch on the bedside lamp, and grabbed an old envelope and a ballpoint pen. Katie was still weighing on my mind. This poem is for her.

A Plaintive Meow

I see her so clearly
in my mind's eye;
her silken fur rippling
in the day's soft breezes;
her great green eyes nearly
fixed on some distant
horizon that only she can see,
while I can merely look on
in sadness, with the realisation
that Katie O'Brien was simply lent –

only lent to me for a time:
a time in which I
savoured her ways dearly,
revelled in her endless love
even knowing her going was nigh.
I see her now –
frolicking with Reilly when the latter thought
I couldn't see them:
Katie' O'Brien's fur - black smoke beauty.
Why – even now
I still hear her plaintive meow.

**

I think I must have fallen asleep for a moment or two because the next thing I felt was Reilly landing on my bed.

"What's this? Have you written something about that icky cat Katie? Put the light out, woman, and save some power!"

If there was one thing Reilly was good at – it was as a leveller! My brief sojourn into sleep had allowed me to dream a little of Katie - of the sun glinting off her beautiful coat, and the sun casting incredible delicate lights into her jewel-like eyes. In my alpha state I was exclaiming over the Master Creator's handiwork.

Reilly soon brought me out of that lovely state.

"Come on woman, get the light out and get some sleep. You know how haggard you feel in the mornings!"

"And *you* don't make me feel any better!" I snapped. Tiredly I switched off the bedside lamp and snuggled down under the duvet. Reilly sat on my legs and rode them like a wave while I made myself comfortable. "Get off my legs, Reilly."

"I'm going, I'm going. Dis is not conducive to sleep!" he grumbled. I felt him move to the far corner of the bed, and soon I was back in a world of dreams – dreaming that Katie returned and told me: 'I'm okay Mum. I just needed to move on in life. I'm staying with a nice lady who has been very lonely since her husband died. She is very kind. I will always remember you Mum, and what you did for me...'

**

I awoke feeling happier – as if a burden had lifted.

"All smiles now, huh? Last night, correction, early hours of this morning you looked like you was gonna cry."

"Your language needs some improvement," I said lightly, ignoring his comment.

"Dis is dating back from when I was in da Bronx."

"Don't be ridiculous, Reilly! You were never in the Bronx!"

"Dat got you going, didn't it? But I was so there. We cats have ancient memories, you know, like elephants."

"Oh Reilly, you are much larger than I thought!" I exclaimed.

He looked at me suspiciously. "What's dat supposed to mean?"

"I thought you were a cat, but now I must revise my thoughts entirely. Now I realise that you were an elephant all along."

"Try picking up an elephant, you daft woman! Better still, have one drop his daily bundle of recycled vegetable matter on your feet and see if it's cat-sized!"

"You are a foul cat."

"Fowls and cats only go together when I am stalking one. Yummy yummy, chicken for dinner!"

"Go away Reilly. You are too smart-mouthed for me to cope with this morning!"

"You have to get me a new girl cat!" Reilly said suddenly.

"What?"

"You heard me, woman! I want a new girl cat, so I can have a girlfriend again. You realise, do you not, that it is a little unbecoming for a cat such as I, to be unaccompanied by a beautiful girl cat?"

"Oh Reilly, won't I do?" I said with a grin.

"No, you're far too big, and not nearly furry enough!"

With that smart answer made, he scampered off outside.

**

I thought long and hard about Reilly's request for a new girlfriend. I wondered why he didn't try to find one of his own, but on the other hand he may have thought: why bother going out looking for himself when there is a perfectly good human at home who can make the effort on his behalf? Oh yes, it would be a similar situation to when I first brought Katie O'Brien home from the animal shelter just outside Motueka. Wee Katie, hungry, dirty and malnourished. I remember well the bonding session we had, lying on the lawn in the warmth, with ever such soft rain beginning to fall on us. It was a magical time.

But again, I thought about the pain of losing an animal; the pain of getting another cat; loving and nurturing her, only to have her leave just as Katie did – fed up to the back teeth of Reilly's bullying ways. I thought too, of how Reilly was beginning to be a real ratbag again. It proved just what a big buffer Katie was, despite her small size and very dainty, feminine and gentle ways. Perhaps it was time I found a tough female cat – one who was a match for Reilly. But then the images of the two fighting in a cartoon-like circle came to me and I dropped the idea.

For now, it was just Reilly and me. Besides, I was still grieving for Katie. I also needed to get my health back to normal. I was well on the way, but there was work to be done on me.

**

For years it had been at the back of my mind that I should begin to learn Spanish. One day while reading the classified ads in the local newspaper, an advertisement for Spanish lessons almost leaped out at me. Without thinking too much about it, I telephoned and made an appointment for my first lesson. For the next seven weeks I studied hard with the tutor and for many months after that I listened to Spanish tuition tapes.

"Amiga, I would like some dinner if you don't mind, por favor," Reilly said one day.

"Oh Reilly, you can speak some Spanish!" I exclaimed.

He sat on his haunches and huffed on his claws.

"Gracias, Senora."

I stood there in the kitchen, looking down with great pride at my cat.

"I am so proud of you, cat," I said, smiling.

"So you should be. Not only am I an Irish cat, but I can spikka da language of da other nations. So...what about some dinner, por favor?"

"Most certainly, with mucho gusto!"

**

Big Mike arrived and we got on the subject of singing. He was visiting a singing tutor to help with his computer problems and I'd mentioned to Mike that I had always wanted to learn to sing properly. I had been in church music groups, music hall, an operatic society and repertory, but had never had proper singing lessons. Mike told the tutor – whom I was already friendly with and next thing I had my first singing lesson arranged. I was thrilled and yet very nervous.

"What about my Spanish lessons?" I wailed to Mike.

"Never mind. You can still do them and one day you'll be able to sing in Spanish!"

That hasn't happened yet, although I do have Que Sera, Sera in my repertoire of around 70 songs so far.

I worried if I would be able to keep up with everything.

"You should take a leaf, literally, out of your own book, woman."

"What do you mean?" I asked Reilly, who this day was sitting out on the patio table, sunning himself.

"What do you mean?" I asked again.

"Que sera, sera. Whatever will be, will be."

"I have always said you are a very smart cat, Reilly," I said, lightly sarcastic.

"And have I not told myself a hundred times, nay, a *thousand* times that you are a very wise woman?" Reilly countered.

"Not within my earshot, you haven't!" I retorted.

"Woman, you're getting to be a deaf little thingy. Listen harder next time, or get yourself a hearing aid!"

I resisted the urge to make a rude finger sign.

Reilly sat up and looked at me with his eyes half shut.

"You are a rude woman!"

"How do you know what I was thinking?"

"Not only getting deaf, but also losing her memory, fellow creatures." Reilly looked around at an imaginary audience and gave a theatrical sigh. "Yes indeed, human beings may be a lot larger than us, but they exhibit so many *weaknesses!*"

"Mow the lawn for me and weed the garden, and go and do the shopping and pay the utility bills. Then you could go and make my bed for me and vacuum and wash the floors. *Then* see if we human beings are supposed to be such weaklings!" I snapped.

"Oh, but woman, remember that time in Carter's Beach when I wanted to do the shopping and those nasty people tried to shoo me out of the store? Imagine *that!*"

Reilly looked around again at his imaginary audience and I found that I was beginning to see them too!

"In the end, I more or less told them they didn't stock anything worth having anyway!"

I laughed at the memory of that time a few years before.

"It *was* rather funny!" I chuckled.

Reilly stopped looking at his imaginary audience and looked at me, positively gleeful.

"It's all a matter of being patient and letting things happen as fate decrees it."

"What do you mean?" I asked again, falling into his little trap.

"Que sera, sera. Whatever will be, will be," Reilly sang, continuing on with the rest of the song as he leaped down from the patio table and swanned around on the big back lawn.

Shucks, I didn't even know he knew the words!

***

CHAPTER ELEVEN

"'Tis But For A Season"

It was as if Reilly suspected something was up, even before I did. He seemed in an unusually good mood on this particular day.

"What's up?" I said, suspicious of his elated mood.

"What's up, Doc?" he mimicked. I had some old songs playing on a CD, and he began to sing along with them. "Oh, I am soooo lonely..."

Was he being smart again, giving me a dig over the story I told him about the deranged man at the restaurant some years before? But no, he didn't seem to be, because he kept on singing in his pussycat way. "Oh darlin', please please, come back home... you mean so much to me baby..."

My heart clenched. Was he singing for my sweet Katie O'Brien? Or was he singing for his new love? I frowned as I watched and listened.

"You get to me girl...*ah-hum* - you really get to me..."

Shucks, perhaps it was *me* he was serenading?

"Not on your Nellie, woman! I am singing in advance!"

"Advance of what?" I realised this time that he had picked up my thoughts.

He smiled in a special secretive cat way.

"You will soon see, little woman, you will soon see. There are some things good, and some not so good. The last one I said comes first."

I had to be content with that mysterious answer.

**

Big Mike arrived, upset because Mickey was looking really ill.

"Mickey's not well," Mike said, unnecessarily. His little dog was in a terrible state, giving little moans every so often.

"Have you taken him to the vet?" I asked, stroking Mickey. I was terribly concerned about Mickey. His one eye already had an opaque appearance and he didn't seem keen on doing anything. Which was most unusual for Mickey.

"I've taken him there. The vet said his liver's failing..." Mike's voice broke on a sob. My heart went out to him and his little dog that Mike had bought from an animal shelter about eight or nine years before. As Mickey was about eight years old, possibly more, at the time of Mike's new ownership, Mickey was indeed an old little doggie. "But I've given Mickey some medicine and hopefully he'll get better," Mike added.

I knew Mike was clutching at straws.

He said he had until four o'clock that day to see if the new medication was working, but it was plain to see it was not; and Mickey was still suffering badly. Mike was too distressed to phone the vet so I did it for him, and had a good talk to the very kindly young man on the other end of the phone. I was almost afraid to face Mike after I hung up the phone. When he saw my face, Mike broke into sobs afresh. My heart felt like a huge lump of lead to see such a big man's shoulders shaking with grief.

Even Reilly was quiet for a change.

We put Mickey outside in some cool grass in the shade. That helped him a little as he was overheating.

Reilly sat next to him, and it was most unlike Mickey, for he did not bark at him. Indeed, he seemed almost pleased to have some animal company.

"Well lambie dog, you is on my territory now, and as you see, I ain't gonna growl. I can see you ain't too well and are due for that big cool grassy place in the sky."

Mickey lifted his head and gave a small *whuff*. He understood.

"I'll reserve a nice place for you, cat," Mickey said softly. Why, it was almost too soft for me to hear but just for a few seconds a slight cool breeze sprung up and lifted his words. It was almost my undoing. I felt that terrible ache at the back of my throat when tears are imminent. I would not let myself cry. I needed to be strong for my friend Mike.

"Hey that's great, old friend. But give me a few years yet, eh? I've got a lot of living to do!"

"My living's about done, cat. I've been everywhere with my dad Mike. We've done a lot together and I've had a great life, but my mortal body's giving out and I'm so tired."

"Next time ya come back to dis earth, ya better come as a *cat!* You can go even *more* places as a cat!"

"I'll have to talk to God about that," Mickey said softly and tiredly.

"Tell Him not to be too eager to see me upstairs, eh?"

I was glad Reilly was being his old self. I couldn't bear it when he was too sympathetic! It was pulling too hard on my heartstrings as it was, seeing Mickey like that, and knowing that this day was his last on this earth. I thought back to the times when he and Reilly were at loggerheads over territorial rights. I wished for those times again.

I went inside and looked at the clock. "It's time, Mike," I said softly.

Mike carried Mickey out to the car and handed him to me when I got into the passenger side. We drove the short distance down to the vet's rooms and carried him inside. The vet was kind and gentle and said again that Mickey was very old and that the medication he'd prescribed was a last resort, hoping it would save Mickey's liver from further deterioration. But that it was not to be. Mickey passed away very quickly and peacefully. My heart pounded with sorrow. The vet passed us tissues. It was so hard not to cry. When Mike went back to Mickey lying there on the sterile table and listened with his head against Mickey's tiny, curly flank because he thought Mickey was still breathing, I had to turn away.

Hope dies oh...so *hard*, I thought sadly.

Arrangements were made to have Mickey cremated so his ashes could be scattered in a place where he loved to run and explore with snuffles, snorts and general great excitement.

We left.

"That was one of the hardest things I have ever had to do," Mike said a few minutes later, his hands clenched hard around the steering wheel. I agreed absolutely.

**

Reilly looked from one to the other when we returned.

"He's gone to that nice cool green place in the sky. He's gonna reserve a place for me...but not for a long time yet," Reilly said.

"I know, I heard him talking to you about it," I said as I began making us a cup of coffee.

"Pardon?" said Mike.

"Reilly's just been telling me that Mickey's gone to a nice cool green place in the sky and he's going to reserve a place for Reilly."

"Oh sure, sure," said Mike with a small laugh. His eyes were red with weeping.

We talked about Mickey as if he was still there, and I decided that it was a good thing to do. Because in so many ways, he *was* still with us. Even Reilly thought so.

"Dat doggie is nothing more than a runty lambie-dog!"

"He is *not* a runty lambie-dog!" I retorted. "Curly little fellow, I would have said."

"Pardon again?" said Mike. "Oh yeah, Reilly's talking to you again, I can see! How come *I* don't hear 'im?"

"That's because I know cat language," I said, smiling.

Mike rolled his eyes. "You get dafter every day."

I didn't mind him telling me that. After all, it kept his mind off Mickey, even for those few seconds.

"I'm going to get another dog," he said suddenly.

I felt alarmed. "Oh please don't Mike. Please give yourself a bit of time to grieve for Mickey."

"What will I do by meself?"

"You can do heaps. You've got friends and family, and your computer jobs."

"It ain't the same."

"I know, I know."

"You *could* get a cat!"

"Reilly just said you could get a cat, Mike."

He rolled his eyes again. "Sure, and you *know* I'm allergic to them!"

"You're not too allergic to Reilly!"

"I would be if he bit me," he said, some of his old humour returning.

"He doesn't bite you because you don't try making a play for me," I said bluntly.

"Oh, don't I? Yeah, well, you're not really my type, you know!"

"His type is very tall and skinny, while you, woman, are short and...er...hmmm...definitely not fat, but you do have a rather large deck! Why, you could launch jet fighters from it!"

"You are such a rude cat! By the time you're finished with me, you'll have my chest as big as the Titanic!"

This time Mike laughed out loud. "'E wouldn't be too far out, at that!"

It reminded me of the time when my American friend, also called Mike, sent me a very large t-shirt. When I lifted it from the wrapping, I was amused to see the word CONCORD in bold letters on the front. Big Mike, who had been visiting when the mail arrived, had laughed. "Concorde is right!"

"Well, thanks very much! It's a different spelling anyway, and that's where California Mike is from!"

"It don't matter! It looks funny! Are you really gonna wear that down the street?"

"Tell him, woman! Flaunt yourself with the Concord t-shirt. Let everyone know you have a big deck and are proud of it!"

"Mixed metaphors, my cat," I said sternly. "I will not flaunt myself in this t-shirt!"

I really didn't mind the digs. After all, it got the subject away from Mickey and eased the hurt for a while.

"Lose some weight woman, and wear the shirt and fly, baby, fly! Well, it's da Concorde, right?"

"Different spelling as I said before, cat, and anyway, I'm still only little, compared to some."

"How you can talk to that cat, I will never know."

"But you talk to Mickey all the time!" I said, then wished I had not mentioned Mickey's name. Mike's eyes welled up with tears. "You can still talk to him," I added gently. "Mickey will never be gone while you have such wonderful memories."

"Ain't dat da truth!"

"Yes Reilly, it *is* the truth!"

Mike rolled his eyes, the tears almost forgotten again. "If I've said it once, I'll say it again, you get dafter every day, girl."

"Dis is one time when I have to agree with da giant corncob. You *are* a daft woman!"

"I'm surprised you don't think of *me* as some kind of vegetable," I said with an edge to my voice.

"What are you on about now?" Mike asked with a grin. "I don't think of yer as a vegetable at all!"

"No, maybe not, but Reilly thinks of you as one!"

"He does?" Mike's eyebrows lifted in disbelief. "Oh, and what sort of vegetable does he think of me as?"

"I've told you in the past, actually. A giant corncob."

"Well, that's bleedin' well nice, innit!" Mike said with a snort.

"I thought so too," Reilly said with a smirk.

"Reilly is being very smug about it," I told Mike, who was beginning to look warily at me.

"Of course I am smug about it! Dat's what da big man is, when he's got his yellow raincoat on with da hood over his head! A giant corncob! Butter him up, hehehe, and sink your teeth into *that*, woman!"

Reilly's puns could be most annoying at times.

"Reilly wants me to butter you up and sink my teeth into you," I told Mike, with tongue in cheek.

"Oh yeah? I don't think you'd find me very tasty."

"Shall I get Reilly to try you out first? He's done it to others in the past."

"Not bleedin' likely! I'm bleedin' well allergic enough to cats as it is!"

"I would imagine anyone would be very allergic to a sudden bite from Reilly!" I said, trying not to grin. "I can think of a few people who have been bitten by him. It was so entertaining... besides, it gave *me* a rest!"

Reilly looked up at me in a considering way, seeming to ignore my comment.

"Actually woman, I have been thinking about it, and I think you would make a very nice butternut, you know, one of them squash things."

"I'm surprised that you haven't likened me to a pumpkin," I said dryly.

"Now that you mention it..."

"That will be enough of that!" I snapped.

"I should tape you sometime Amber Jo, and play the tape back to you," Mike said.

"Why?"

"You should listen to yourself!"

"My statements will sound disjointed because you can't hear what Reilly's saying to me."

"Oh sure, and pigs will fly!"

"They do too, if you put them in special crates and put them in the back of an aeroplane!"

"Roly poly, roly poly..." Reilly began to sing. "Anyone for pumpkin pie?"

I think he was giving me cheek again.

But at least we were off the subject of Mickey. However, that was short-lived as Mike announced again: "I'm gonna get another dog."

"It's up to you Mike," I said. "But won't you give yourself a bit of time?"

He looked mutinous, so I thought I would leave the subject alone for a while. Once Mike had made up his mind about something, he would pull out all stops to get his way.

**

If I missed his little dog sorely, it must have been nothing in comparison to the loss Mike felt. He arrived at my place a few days later with a pretty little burgundy cardboard box with Mickey's name beautifully etched on it in gold paint. I knew what it was immediately and tried hard to stem the rush of tears. Mike broke down again when he saw how upset I was, but quickly recovered when I offered coffee and cake.

We made arrangements to take Mickey's ashes to The Groynes, a beautiful park on the outskirts of Christchurch city that had provision for exercising dogs. Mickey had a favourite spot where he loved to run. It was by the little stream that meandered and chuckled its way through the park. My friend Pierre was visiting from down south, and another friend Elma said she would like to take part in the ceremony, so the four of us travelled out to the park after church on one lovely Sunday just after lunch, which had followed a most enjoyable church service.

Mickey's ashes were sprinkled along the riverbank and in the water and we had a prayer time while we all said our final goodbyes to little Mickey. It was a moving time and although sad, it was also coupled with relief that Mickey was no longer in pain.

"I have never been to a dog's funeral before," Pierre announced.

"A first time for everything," I said lightly, hoping Pierre's announcement didn't upset Mike too much.

Fortunately it didn't. We went looking at a new housing estate and enjoyed ourselves looking at the beautiful open homes displays. I wished one of the houses could belong to me, even knowing it could not be so - at least not for some years.

***

CHAPTER TWELVE

"Along Came Chloe Arabella"

I missed Mike's little dog Mickey so much – in fact a lot more than I would have thought. But I think also, that the loss had an added edge because it wasn't so long since Katie O'Brien had left home.

"I thought you said there were good things and there were bad, cat," I said to Reilly a week after Mickey's funeral.

"The bad thing was Mickey clearing out to the green grass in the sky."

"But I didn't think you liked him much," I said.

"Like? Smike? That's *your* opinion, woman! I liked baiting him... oh that was wonderful! Besides, he really *did* look like a runty sheep! He wasn't bad for...oh must I puke yet again...a *dog!*"

"Okay, now that's *your* opinion!" I countered. "So what's the good thing that hasn't happened yet?"

Reilly looked at me with his eyes narrowed to slits and a smug look on his face. "How should *I* know?"

"Didn't you tell me that you cats are all-powerful, all knowledgeable, all-seeing, etcetera, etcetera? Which, if that is so, means that you can see into the future and you will be able to tell me what the good things are, that are about to happen."

"You *do* talk a lot, woman!"

"You're pretty good at it yourself, cat."

"Now, back to what you were rabbiting on about before."

"Which was?"

"See, I told you that your memory is not as good as it should be!"

"But you keep on distracting me!" I protested. "Now, where were we?"

"In the lounge room on this lovely fine day, when we should be down the beach, preferably at Carter's Beach."

"My God, you sure are a trier, cat! You try my patience all the time!"

"Get on with the story, woman, and stop rabbiting on! Rabbits, rabbits! There are far too many of dem in this country as it is!"

I took a deep breath and counted to twenty this time.

"So, what about these good things about to happen?"

"Okay, I'll tell you. You're gonna get a new cat."

"I am? Sez who?"

"I sez, and what's more, she's gonna be my new girlfriend."

"If you say so, Reilly!"

My good humour suddenly restored, I wondered what cat would be sucker enough to be Reilly's girlfriend. I thought suddenly of Katie and felt another pang of loss. But I believed in the dream I'd had, that she had gone to stay with a lonely widowed lady. I could only wish the very best for Katie: that she would have a happy and comfortable life. I had done my best for her, but also knew that I couldn't send Reilly to a good home and still keep Katie. I did not want to inflict Reilly on anyone else. Besides, bad that he could be, I still adored him. Who knew anyway – Katie may *still* have wanted to leave home, whether or not Reilly was there. Besides, that old knowledge reared its head again; the knowledge that it would be a rare person who could put up with Reilly's wicked ways. Okay, so I am a rare person!

"*Rare* isn't the word!" Reilly startled me in my reverie.

"It's very rude to read people's thoughts," I said sternly.

"Then you shouldn't be such an open book, woman! Anyway, I was simply displaying some of those all seeing, all knowledgeable, all-wise ways we cats have."

"So, if rare isn't the word for me, what is?"

"Oh woman, I shouldn't like to swear in front of you!"

I counted to twenty again.

He scampered off out the open ranch slider door and chirruped around the big back lawn. Two magpies, which had been sitting warbling in the large pepper tree, screeched at him, warning him away. Reilly stopped for a moment, sat on his haunches and stared up into the tree.

"If youse birds think youse gonna scare a cat such as me away, youse got another think coming! Why don't cha try me out, eh?"

He chirruped and frolicked, goading the magpies. One flew down in an attempt to dive bomb him. Reilly lifted a paw up, Garfield-style and took a swipe. The magpie screeched its outrage at the loss of several feathers and flew away, his mate flying off with him.

"Dat will teach you to get smart with me!"

I laughed. Much as I liked the sound of magpies warbling in the trees, they could become quite a pest and were no favourite with farmers.

"Seagulls however, could be another matter," I said with a grin.

"Show me a seagull that thinks it can outsmart me, and I'll prove dat seagull is a liar," Reilly said as he slouched back into the lounge.

"Anyway, back to this new cat you've told me I'm getting. Who says I want another cat? Why, *you* are like six bad cats rolled into one!"

"Flattery will get you everywhere, woman! The cat will be here soon. Take it from me, woman. Out of the goodness of my heart, I wanted to warn you."

"Warn me? I don't think I like the sound of the word 'warn'! Why, I should have been warned when my friend Lou told me she had this cute little kitten and would I take it off her hands, because it was already picking on her dog Tessa! *You* were that cute little kitten, although I should hesitate over the word 'cute'! Small you were, but tough as nails!"

"As I said, woman, flattery will get you everywhere! Oh, I am soooo flattered."

"If you remember Reilly, Tessa was a big dog – a spaniel and German Shepherd cross. Fancy you picking on a big dog like that! Tessa was their watchdog for their hotel! She could have picked you up and eaten you in one tiny gulp!"

"Oh, but aren't you just glad that she didn't! Haven't I been your lovely boy cat? Haven't I stopped you from having some very lonely days and nights?"

"Yes, yes, to all of that, but you have also left me scarred for life and I have lost some friends because of you."

"Then dey weren't worth having as friends in the first place! And anyway, what about that bloke on the Coast that I bit because he had a few bad plans for you?" Reilly said bluntly.

"Well yes, I agree you have had your uses in the past!"

"Huh, *uses*, eh? You ungrateful woman! I don't know now if I should organise a new cat for you!"

"*You* organise a new cat for me? That'll be the day! I'll get my own cat if I want one, and I am not sure if I want any more cats. I miss Katie too much, and if I got a new one, I have no guarantee that you won't bully that one as well."

Reilly leaped onto the sofa and curled into a ball.

"Oh ye of little faith. We shall see what we shall see."

A few minutes later, I heard his contented purring as he slept.

**

A few days later Mike arrived with a rush and a roar up my driveway, as was his usual practice. For such a big man, he could move very quickly, inside his car and out of it.

"Did you get the Buy, Sell & Exchange?"

The Buy, Sell & Exchange newspaper is what its name suggests, a newspaper where people placed ads, paid or free. The newspaper itself was loaded with literally many hundreds of advertisements for almost anything you could imagine.

"No, did you?"

"As a matter of fact, I did. There's a cat in it!"

"Really?" I said, amused. "What has this cat done? Rolled itself up inside the newspaper, ready to startle a wary purchaser?"

"Nope. There's one advertised in it I think you'll like. It's a sort of Persian smoky grey cat, one of those ones with a flat face."

My heart melted. I had always wanted a cat of that beautiful colour and with the cute little grumpy face.

"Hmmm..." I began.

"Why don't you ring up and see if it's still available?"

"I might."

"Do it now, while we're talking about it," Mike said bossily.

To get his request over and done with, more than anything else, I telephoned the number given in the advertisement and left a message. The problem was that I was already madly interested in the cat and when I thought of a lovely grey cat with a 'squashed-in' face, my heart melted even more.

Later on in the day I received a call. The young man on the other end of the line said that a lady who was going overseas had first advertised the cat and that she would need to put the cat put down if no one was interested. I knew that was often an advertising ploy, but didn't say so to the man. He and his partner hoped the cat would get on with their dog, but after just three weeks, it was not to be. So they wanted to give her away to a good home.

"What's the cat's name?" I asked, already well smitten.

"Smoky."

We made arrangements to visit the people the next day, which was Saturday. When we arrived, this adorable looking cat greeted us with a meow and chatter. She had the plush coat of a Blue Cream Shorthair Persian, blue-grey with speckles of cinnamon throughout, and a velvety finish. She almost looked like a toy cat. Her eyes were enormous speckled gold jewels.

We chatted to the very nice people and they had agreed to let us have the cat, as, according to them, we seemed very keen on her. I hadn't known it showed so well!

Unfortunately, the cat had other plans for the time being. She did not want to go with us that day, and so arrangements were made for the young couple to bring her to me. Which is what they did. The cat got out of the cage, looked around the lounge and sat down and began washing herself.

"This'll do me," she said.

"She's settled in already!" the young woman exclaimed, but also looked sad as she was obviously already very fond of the cat. I picked up the cat, gave her a cuddle and kiss and thanked her for coming to share my house with me and one other cat. I gave the people a signed book of my poetry as a small thank you for the cat. They went home happily enough and I was left with this cute little round cat who looked as if she had no trouble twisting anyone around her little plump paw!

I gazed at her, glad for the moment that Reilly was still somewhere outside. I needed a few moments just to stare at this newcomer and get her used to me, as well as the other way round. She still had Reilly to contend with. I thought she looked as if she should be deemed a purebred and had asked the nice young couple, but they said they didn't think so; that the first owner would have told them if she were.

I firmly decided that Smoky was far too inadequate a name for a cat such as her. I thought hard and decided that Chloe was to be her first name, but she needed something wonderful and elegant to go with it. I walked around the house and thought hard, and then the name came to me.

I returned to the lounge where the cat was beginning to explore her new surroundings.

"Welcome to your new home, Chloe Arabella," I said softly. "I hope you'll be very happy here."

"Hmmm, about time I was given a decent name!" The newly-named Chloe Arabella blinked her huge eyes at me and turned sideways at the noise outside. She looked so comical at that angle: she reminded me of a little monkey, except for her huge eyes, which side on looked like big speckled gold marbles stuck firmly into eye sockets.

Reilly bounded in and came up short when he saw Chloe sitting there. She hissed.

"Who do you think *you* are, big cat!"

Reilly looked very smug, and arched a look at me. He appeared to be grinning from ear to ear. I could imagine him thinking, I *told* you so!

"My name is Seamus O'Reilly, but you may call me Reilly, for short."

"Hi there, Reilly for short. What a funny name! My new mother has just given me a wonderful new name."

"Oh yeah? What's that? Furball? Flathead? Flatface?"

"Certainly not! My new name is Chloe Arabella!"

"What happened to your old name?"

"It wasn't suitable for a cat such as me. Anyway, who do you think you are, coming into this nice house without so much as an 'excuse me'?"

"I come in here whenever I like, because I *live* here, oh smoky one! Say, did you get the number of the bus?"

"What bus?"

"The bus that stopped suddenly and you ran into the back of it!"

"If you think that statement is going to rock me, you are in for a surprise! I think you are just jealous of my very good looks!"

"Hmmm...well, I suppose for a female, you are not bad looking. Mind you. Most cats *are*, in my opinion!"

"It seems to me, that you are a very opinionated cat!"

"I take that as a compliment."

"It wasn't meant as one."

"That's not at all nice! HISSS!"

"HISSS!"

I thought that now would be a very good time to remove Chloe and take her to my room for a rest. I was sure she must have been quite stressed out by the upheaval just over three weeks before of moving from her old home to a new one with a big dog in it, then having to move again and having to face Reilly. I thought however, that she had done remarkably well. Perhaps Chloe Arabella would prove to be a good match for my big cat. I left her on my bed and that pleased her no end.

"Say, this is nice! I think I'll sleep here every night."

"You may have to share it with Reilly," I cautioned.

"Oh, I can handle *him!*" she said airily.

I sure hoped so. But all the same, I wouldn't want her getting *too* bossy! One bossy cat in the house was more than enough to handle.

I returned to the lounge.

"Well, woman?"

"Well, what?"

"Didn't I tell you that in a few days you were going to get a new cat?"

"Yes you did indeed."

Reilly sat on his haunches, huffed on his claws and said: "Am I a clever cat or *what?*"

"You are a very clever cat, Reilly. Now, let me get on with dinner."

"What's for dinner?"

"I haven't decided yet. Maybe bangers and mash and peas, and some gravy to go with it."

"How boring! What about frying up a lot of tasty chicken so I can have some too?"

"What about Chloe having some as well?" I added.

"Oh yes, well I suppose she could have some. What do you think of her?"

"I think she will be a match for you, Reilly."

"A match? Hmmm, okay, we'll just see how far she goes. Personally, I think she's a bit too cheeky, for a cat who has only just arrived. She will have to learn her place in this house."

"And where is that place, cat?"

"Under my paw!"

"Sort of under your thumb?"

"Dat's what I mean, but paw it is!"

"We will just have to wait and see, won't we?"

"Yes we will, woman."

He chirruped, and scampered off outside again. He was clearly happy enough with the new arrangements. Or maybe Reilly saw

Chloe Arabella as simply a new challenge? Whichever way it was, it looked like life was going to become *very* interesting!

A few days after Chloe had moved in, her previous people phoned to ask after her. I told the young man that she was settling in, although we hadn't had much sleep since! He then told me he'd found out that she was indeed a purebred – a Blue Cream Shorthair Persian, but apparently her breed wasn't recognised when first owned by the lady travelling overseas. This of course put Chloe Arabella into the 'senior' age bracket, but I for one, was not going to mention that to her! One does not remind a lady, even a cat one, about her age...

***

CHAPTER THIRTEEN

"It's a Matter Of Taste"

If ever I thought that the two cats would get on well together quickly, then the thought had to be dismissed – also quickly. Chloe Arabella lived up to her purebred reputation of being demanding and lazy. She also pretended to be innocent in ways, yet she could prove just how bright she was too, when it suited her.

Reilly was not amused.

"If you think you are going to be queen bee around dis joint, den youse have another thought coming!"

"Queen bee? Who said anything about being queen bee? I *am* Queen of this house, *that's* who I am!"

"Queen, green, smeen, spleen! Youse is a flat-faced lazy tart of a cat, and the only one who will be doing any queening around here, is *me!*"

"You a queen? Oh my goodness me! How an innocent cat such as me can be fooled! Here I was thinking that you are a *boy* cat!" Chloe's huge gold eyes took on a soft green cast. "Perhaps there is something you need to tell me, Reilly?"

He looked very suspicious. "About what?"

"Are you a boy cat, or something in between?"

Chloe blinked a couple of times, almost innocent. But I was fast getting to know her.

This time Reilly looked furious. He squatted down, his bottom wriggling, ready to pounce on Chloe. She looked at him disdainfully and he apparently gave up the idea of pouncing on her, at least for the time being.

"I'll have you know that not only am I known as the Caped One, the Wise One, etcetera, but I am da king around dis joint!"

"Hmm, Caped One and Wise One. Are you sure your name isn't Michael Jackson?"

"Why? Certainly *not!*"

"Oh, that is a shame! Because you could put on a white glove and be called the Gloved One as well!"

"Sure I could! In fact you *can* call me that. It could refer to the fact that I have to give people a regular royal wave." Reilly began to huff on his claws. "Some of us have it, and some don't. That's life, kid."

"I know one thing you *do* have."

"Oh? And what is that, fat lazy cat?"

"You have a huge ego!"

"If I don't have a problem with that, then neither should you. Listen here cat, if youse wanna stay in dis house, youse better be on your best behaviour!"

"That's for me to decide."

"I wouldn't get too cocky if I wuz you! The woman still misses our other cat, and if you aren't nice, she just might give you to someone else."

"She wouldn't do that."

"Wouldn't she just? She can be a tough woman when it suits her!"

"Nonsense! I've seen the way her big blue eyes go all soft and mushy when she looks at us."

"Soft and mushy maybe, but don't let dat fool you."

"I'm not so easily fooled, buster."

"You're another one of dem females dat looks all soft and big-eyed, and can be tough as nails underneath."

"We have to be. Physically, we are not as strong as you males, so we have to make up for it in other ways."

"You can say dat again!"

"We have to be. Physically, we are not as strong as you males, so we have to make up for it in other ways." Chloe looked smugly at Reilly.

"Youse is just *asking* fer a bopping, scatty cat!"

"Come on then, buster. See how affected I am by your street talk!"

"Be wary, I warn you. I wuz raised in da Bronx!"

Well, I had heard that many times before and was most amused that he was using it on Chloe. She was certainly good at sticking up for herself, but I worried that she might go too far. All the same, it was most entertaining. I could have sat and listened to their exchange for hours and hours. But it was better to keep them apart when it looked like Reilly was going to pounce. I knew from past experience that his teeth and claws were very sharp. And I didn't want him to sharpen them still further on Chloe.

Chloe sat on her round bottom and began to wash herself. I thought of the old quote that a cat lover had said once: "When in doubt, wash." Maybe Chloe was a little in doubt and was trying to act nonchalant, but on the other hand, er, paw, maybe she was doing what she appeared to be doing, washing herself as if she no longer had a care in the world. If it was the latter, then I was really glad, because it meant she was settling in well and was relaxed with us.

But being the kind of cat she was, she would also need some mental stimulation, and she was certainly getting that from Reilly!

Chloe yawned and lay down in a trusting way. I felt myself relax a little.

Reilly suddenly pounced and whacked her just as the cartoon character Garfield would do to the much-maligned Odie the dog.

"That is most uncalled for!" Chloe protested as she leaped to her feet and backed off to a respectable distance.

"Dat is just to show you dat you can't just come into dis house and think youse can take over dis joint! I told you I was raised in da Bronx!"

He ran away with a snigger. Age had not slowed him down, nor had it improved his egotistical ways.

"Think you can stand being here, Chloe?" I asked gently.

She turned her enormous eyes on me. "I like to think of that cat as a challenge! Bronx be damned! I couldn't care less *where* he was initially raised! If *you* can put up with him, then so can I!"

"Good on you, girl. Katie, the cat we had who ran away, adored Reilly but she got tired of his bullying ways. Katie was too gentle for him, but she did at least assert herself unexpectedly from time to time, in the last few months before she left."

"She left it a bit late, then, didn't she?"

"Most likely. But she wasn't as tough as you. All she wanted out of life was to love and be loved."

"Sounds rather ideal. Oh yes, I could handle *that* very well! I do expect to be waited on you know. We purebreds are very sophisticated cats and should never be expected to forage for our food."

"Hmmm, you'll get waited on, just as Reilly always does!"

"Then we should all eventually get along very well, shouldn't we?"

"I expect we should," I agreed, bemused.

They say that cats are the most egotistical of all animals, and once I might have argued that, but after Chloe's conversation, I would now agree. She was, in her statements at least, another Reilly – just a female version. It remained to be seen if she would want to go on walks with us, or go to the beach. Somehow I didn't think so. She was too fond of lying around on my bed, or in a sunny spot wherever it might be. But I allowed that I could be proven wrong.

∗∗

I took my breakfast back to bed, as is my usual habit. Toast and coffee, and a good book to read for a while, is my idea of luxury. But I had barely raised a piece of raspberry jam-spread toast to my mouth when there was a strong protest from Chloe. She walked slowly up to my face, staring all the while and then said: "so where is *my* piece of toast?"

"I didn't know you liked toast," I said, amused.

"That's because you never asked me! I also like fresh raw carrot, and the scent of toothpaste!"

"Then we should have absolutely no trouble in getting you to the vet for a tooth cleaning and scaling operation, eh?"

Reilly, who was sitting on the corner of the bed, sniggered.

"I knew you would be a weird cat. Fancy liking raspberry jam on toast, and carrots and toothpaste."

"Some us like to be individuals. You like whipped cream in a can, so *there!*"

"How did you know that?"

"We cats are all seeing, all powerful, etcetera. Haven't I heard you say the very same thing before?"

"You may well have done, but I certainly do not, I repeat *not*, want you stealing my sayings!"

Chloe chose not to answer him, but simply came closer to beg some toast from me. I gave her a small morsel and she happily munched that. Then I gave her another piece, and another.

"*Real* cats don't eat toast!" Reilly snapped. "Maybe it's something to do with da bus you ran into! You forget what you are supposed to be."

"Reilly, that's not nice. Listen cats, it's a lovely day and I want some peace. I have things to do."

"Such as what?" Reilly snapped. Clearly he was not in a good mood. I think jealousy may have come into it a little, seeing Chloe right up by my face. But I had never discouraged Reilly from getting close to my face. Indeed, it had been some time since we danced together – Reilly draped over my shoulder, but that was not my fault. Reilly had not indicated for quite a while that he would like a re-enactment of those times, and in any case, I had not felt well enough for it. Now that I was well on the mend, I intended to initiate a little dance or two with him.

"Housework, some writing, feeding you cats and doing some grocery shopping," I replied.

"How droll, how exceedingly, boringly *droll!*"

"Not if I am buying cat food and whipped cream for you and Chloe, Reilly."

"Gimme, gimme. All for *me*, and none for Chloe."

"You are a selfish cat. I'll be buying for both of you and that is that."

"May I remind you that Chloe has already had her breakfast? Toast and jam! Hey, I thought that was supposed to be for *tea!* Oh yeah, dat's right, marmalade. That's great, then I get the good stuff! Toast and marmalade for tea, sailing ships upon the sea... tra la, tra lee!" Reilly sang.

Reilly jumped off the bed, still singing "Toast and Marmalade For Tea", and soon I heard him munching on some cat biscuits while muttering in between mouthfuls: "dis ain't filet steak, but it's better dan nothing!"

The last time I heard him say something similar, he had mentioned rump steak. This time it was the more expensive filet steak. I think he was trying out subliminal messages on me. I felt it was about time to try out some of my own. Filet steak, alas, was almost *never* on my menu.

"When we move house Chloe, you'll have a nice garden to run around in and you'll be able to have your own territory."

Reilly came dashing back into my bedroom.

"Move, *smoove*! Who said anything about moving house?"

"Why, Reilly, are you moving out? You didn't tell me!"

"I will move when you move, and it had better be back to da coast!"

"I'll make sure we're near the coast. Chloe, would you like some more toast?"

"I don't mind if I do."

"Hey, you're a poet, woman!" Reilly announced. "Toast and coast. They go together!"

Chloe delicately munched the small piece while Reilly looked at her in disgust.

"Are you a cat, or what? Some sort of namby-pamby?"

"I am a purebred cat, in case you haven't noticed."

"One who couldn't see properly, despite the saucer eyes, and ran into the back of a bus!"

"Stop it, Reilly. Get out of here and go and do something useful."

"Such as what? Scare the neighbours, scare the dogs around here, or scare Chloe? All of it sounds old-hat and pretty *boring!*"

"Maybe you're getting old, Reilly," I suggested.

"That is utter, absolute *rubbish!* I'm as good as I ever was! Anyway, Chloe is older than me."

"I have never told you my age," Chloe responded.

"Quite old, I would say."

"You are a very rude cat! And what's more you are tough and arrogant!"

Reilly positively beamed with pleasure. "Dat's me, and don't youse forget it! You are the one whose gonna go to the vet, what's more, especially since you like the smell of toothpaste! Why, going to the vet should be a doddle for you."

"Perhaps I am more resilient than you, Reilly, and can withstand pain a lot better."

"Pain? Don't talk to me about pain! *You* are just a stupid cat, if you can put up with unnecessary pain."

"Stoical, is the word, Reilly."

"Stoical, smoical...what the hell does *dat* mean?"

"Coming from the Bronx, Reilly, I guess you would not know," Chloe said silkily. She proceeded to wash herself again. I again was reminded of how like a little monkey she looked side-on, but when she turned her gaze to me, I was struck afresh at how amazing her eyes were. My eyes travelled over her plush coat with its shades of soft blue-grey and cinnamon. As she moved to catch a little more sunlight, her coat had a velvet appearance. How amazing, how infinitely clever our Creator is, I thought.

"Yeah, He made *me*," Reilly said, picking up my thoughts.

"He did indeed, and what a wonderful creation you cats are. I am so blessed to have you both." I meant it most sincerely, although there were many nights when I wondered if Big Mike's instigation into me getting a new cat was more of a mixed blessing.

**

That night was a good example. I went to bed at around my usual time of 9.30pm, and read for a while. Both cats were on the end of my bed, and for a change were not swapping insults.

After an hour of reading I switched off the bedside lamp and soon afterwards Chloe got off the bed and went out to the lounge to sleep on the sofa. At around two am she howled.

And I mean *really* howled. I had already gone through quite a number of these incidents but no matter how often, they always had the power to make my heart feel as if it was standing still, and lift the hair on the nape of my neck.

"We're in here, Chloe!" I called.

"*Howl.* Where am I?"

"We're in the bedroom and you are in the lounge! Come back to bed, Chloe!" The sound of my own voice woke me properly. Never a good sleeper, I knew that would be the end of sleeping for the next few hours.

"Stupid cat!" Reilly moaned. "Just when I was having a good sleep too. Not only is she stupid, but she also *shows* it!"

"I really thought you wanted a new girlfriend, Reilly," I yawned.

"There are girlfriends, and there are girlfriends."

"What is that supposed to mean?" I was not in the mood for Reilly's silly little riddles. I just wanted Chloe back in my bedroom, safe and warm on my bed so we could all get back to sleep.

He looked at me as if I, too, was rather dense and therefore did not warrant speaking to. I did not care for the look he gave me. After all, I was the one who fed and housed him, and attended to so many of his needs for love and companionship and here he was in the half-light, throwing an evil look my way.

"It means, woman, some girlfriends are the ones you love and leave; some are those you keep for their usefulness, and then there are others that barely warrant speaking to."

"So which category does Chloe fit into?" I yawned again.

Reilly flung me another evil look. "If you are such a clever little mummy, maybe you could tell *me!*"

"Why Reilly, don't *you* know?" I teased.

"Huh! I like that! First I have to explain to her the differences in girlfriends, and then she tries to twist it right around as if I don't know! *Huh! Huh!*"

"Well?" I asked; amused despite the fright Chloe had given me and the fact that I knew I would not be able to get back to sleep for several hours. "Do you really know which category Chloe fits into? Not that she should fit into any category...that's *cat*-egory to you, Reilly!"

"Huh, I think she could be useful to me some time in the future. She's certainly not my ideal of a girlfriend. Maybe if I stretched her face back out she would look more like a cat. And therefore a lot better looking."

"You are becoming more of a chauvinist every day, cat," I said. "And I didn't think it was possible!"

"Anything's possible with me, woman. You should know that."

I guess I just needed reminding.

***

CHAPTER FOURTEEN

"More Than Just A Dream"

Chloe's howling in the wee small hours of the night left me feeling ragged.

"Why don't you stay on my bed?" I asked her.

"Because Reilly is there, and perhaps you don't know it, but I feel the bad vibes from him every night. That's why I go out into the lounge room."

"You mustn't let him intimidate you," I said, glad that Reilly was outside, glaring at some magpies that had interrupted his dozing on the patio table. I hoped he was sufficiently involved in out-staring the magpies to not pick up on my thoughts and words.

"I try not to. I could say something fierce to Reilly but it would wake you up," Chloe said sweetly. "And I would not want to do that to you."

"I have no doubts that it would wake me up! But Chloe, your howling in the middle of the night or at least, the wee small hours of the morning are guaranteed to wake me up even more smartly than anything you would have to say to Reilly, while on my bed!"

"I have a lot of bad dreams," said the little round cat.

My heart went out to her. I forgot how she had been when she first arrived – a seemingly typical aristocratic purebred.

"Is that why you wake up almost every morning in such a state?"

"Yes."

Chloe looked down at her velvety paws, almost as if she was ashamed to speak it aloud.

"Oh dear. That is really sad. Can you tell me about your dreams...nightmares, I would have said."

"Oh I don't know..."

"Come on Chloe," I coaxed. "While Reilly's not in here to interrupt us. It would help me understand why you sound so terrified in the middle of the night, or in the early hours."

She gazed up at me and paused, about to say something, and stopped. I waited.

"There was a time you know, when children tormented me in the house where I used to live. They used to push me under the blankets and hold me there so I could hardly breathe. It was only because I was so strong that I could get out. The lady of the house got angry with me for tearing the sheets, but I could not speak to her as I speak to you, and tell her exactly why the sheets were torn."

"I suppose the children looked innocent, as if they knew nothing about it?"

"Oh, you *do* understand! That's exactly what they used to do! I *hated* those children! I really wanted to like them, but every time I started to like them a little, one or all of them would do something nasty to me."

Chloe looked at me so gratefully for my understanding that I felt a surge of anger towards those horrible children and their mother.

"I understand all right! I will never understand however, not in a million years, why people can be cruel to animals!"

"Unfortunately, because they are bigger and love a power game, and also have nothing better to do...that's why they do it. They also do it because they have a very nasty streak and are bullies."

"You are very forgiving, Chloe," I said gently, pleased at her tone, which was soft.

"Not *that* forgiving! The woman had some dogs, and they also tormented me, but I had my revenge in small ways!"

"How was that?"

"I would wait on top of the fence when one of the dogs was going by, and would rake my claws across his nose! Then I would quickly disappear into the shrubbery so I couldn't be blamed. I would then run along the back of the house, get through a bedroom window and lie on one of the beds, as if I had been there all along."

"That was very crafty of you."

"Crafty? Oh yes indeed, I *had* to become very crafty! It was *me* against all those people and their two big dogs."

"Why didn't you leave?"

"Because I didn't know anywhere I could go to. I mean, who wants a stray cat?"

"But you are so beautiful Chloe," I said, meaning it absolutely. "And *I* wanted you!"

Chloe preened for a moment or two. "Thanks, much appreciated. But you are different from most people."

"I have been told that many times," I said wryly.

"Well, anyway, the woman of the house was leaving for overseas and her kids were going on a long holiday with relatives, before joining her in her new country. She found new homes for her dogs but didn't want me. I was very sad in one way but not sad in another. At least I wouldn't have to put up with them all again. Then I heard her read out her advertisement she was going to put in the paper. The advertisement was about *me*. In it she said that if a new home couldn't be found for me, I would have to be put down. *Put down!* Can you imagine it? After all that had been dealt out to me, *this* was to be my end?"

"Oh Chloe," I said sadly. "I hardly know what to say."

I needed to hear more, so I would fully understand her, and glanced out the window to see what Reilly was doing. He was still engrossed in out-staring the magpies, which were playing a little game of their own, in stringing him along by flying just out of his reach, then dive-bombing him. I thought it would be a good idea to keep a 'weather eye open', just in case. In groups of three or more, magpies were a force to be reckoned with. Their beautiful bell-like warbling early in the mornings belied the other side to their nature.

Chloe signed deeply. "Well now, a nice young couple answered the advertisement, but they had a dog! A young Doberman who was nice, but so full of energy and was always knocking me over! I tell you, I got really fed up with him."

"Maybe he was doing it on purpose?"

"No, I don't think so. He was just young and very exuberant and sometimes couldn't see me because of my colour. I used to try to hide down the side of the sofa, which was a bluish grey colour, but sometimes the naughty dog would leap over the sofa and catch a paw on me. I tell you, that big paw could really hurt!"

"I would imagine so." I felt so sorry for her. Her eyes looked bigger than ever. Even if it was a ruse to really get my sympathy, it didn't matter. There was no doubt she had been through a lot. Her nightmares were testament to that.

"But before the new people came to take me, the woman and her family and the dogs went away one long weekend. Oh, the peace! It was wonderful, but then at nights I started to wonder where they were, and if they were going to come back and feed me. They had left biscuits and water for me, but that soon run out and I was getting pretty hungry. I would wake at night after imagining being locked up in the house forever with no food and water, and howl with fright. But then some friends of theirs came to stay for a few days while the advertisement was in the paper for me."

"I understand now why you still do that, Chloe. Have nightmares, I mean. But in a while, they will stop; because within yourself you will know that never again would anyone ever do that to you. You will always have us with you."

"I hope so."

For a moment she looked so forlorn. I picked her up and cuddled her, nuzzling into her thick, beautiful fur. She smelled delicious, of rain-washed foliage and sun-drenched earth. I have always found it interesting; the anomaly that cats can smell of both at the same time.

"Thank you for telling me all these things, Chloe," I said into her fur. I looked up, catching sight of Reilly outside. "Shall we watch and see what Reilly is doing?"

"I don't mind if I do," Chloe purred. "I find him quite amusing, really, when he's not being so chauvinistic."

I knew that was a very good sign for the future.

**

Reilly was in his element. He knew what the magpies' strategy was, and strung them along, even as he knew they were trying to string *him* along! One magpie flew a little too close. Reilly swung a paw Garfield-like, and whacked the bird hard. The magpie shot up in the air, squawking angrily. Some feathers drifted down the earth.

"You lot *bore* me now!" I heard Reilly call. He bravely, or foolishly, depending on how you looked at it, turned his back on them and walked in through the open ranch slider door. He stopped when he saw us there, Chloe in my arms and purring.

"I hope you saw how I out-witted those pesky birds!" Reilly said happily.

"We saw, Reilly. I only hope they don't turn on you one day when you are not expecting it!"

Reilly sat in the middle of the lounge floor and huffed on his paws. "I am Reilly the Wonderful and Reilly the Great! I am *never* caught unawares!"

"Never is too strong a word, Reilly. Saying 'never', is like saying Murphy's Law does not exist."

"Whaddya on about, woman?"

"Murphy's Law – the Law of Cussedness, if you like! When you make a profound statement like you just did, there may come a time when you have to eat your words!"

"I *never* eat my words! If ever you think there is a need for it, then I shall eat my hat!"

"But you don't have a hat," I reminded him.

"Who cares? I have a *cape*, remember!"

"I have not seen your cape since we were at Carter's Beach. Besides, it was not a cape, but one of my tea towels draped over you."

"Carter's Beach? Now *there* is a jolly good subject to be on!"

Naturally, I thought. Reilly had, as he often did, drifted away from the main thrust of the conversation. He was so good at that, and at the same time, turning it to a subject he was particularly fond of, namely, Carter's Beach.

"We'll talk about Carter's Beach on another occasion," I said.

"Why not talk about it *now?*"

"We may indeed be moving house soon," I said warily.

"Really? Back to the West Coast, I hope?"

"Maybe not at this stage," I said carefully.

"But you *promised!*"

"Yes," I agreed, "if it was possible to do so. But I still need hospital treatment, and I can't get it if I'm back on the Coast."

"Why not?"

"Because, cat, I would have to travel all the way back over here again - a four-hour drive to the hospital. I would have to stay somewhere for a couple of nights and who would look after you cats in the meantime?"

"Lois in Waimangaroa would look after us, just like she did in the past! Reilly said triumphantly. "Well, she minded *Katie* and me, that is. Besides, I wouldn't mind eyeing up her chickens again! Yes, I'm sure she would *love* to have us come and stay with her! Hey ho, hey ho, it's off to the West Coast we go!"

"I don't think Lois is there any more," I responded.

"What? How *dare* she move away! She *knew* I liked her!"

"She also knew how much you liked looking at her chooks!"

"So where will we go?" Chloe asked.

"Away from here," I said simply.

"Yes but *where?*" Chloe insisted.

"Near the beach," I replied.

"But we're already *near* the beach!" Reilly exclaimed. "And what's more, I don't like dat beach much! I went down there one night..."

"What...by yourself?" I was aghast. *Anything* could have happened to my Reilly!

"Of course, you silly woman!"

"But you might have been *hurt!*"

"By a passing sea egg maybe? Or a sea lice, already half dead? A sand biscuit, even! Maybe a floundering mermaid, washed up on the beach, trying to lure me into taking her back out to sea? Or maybe a bit of driftwood could have lifted itself out of the sand and thumped me on the head! Whaddya think I am, woman, *stoopid*, or something?"

"The word is stupid, *Stupid*," Chloe said silkily. She smiled a secret smile. It was hard to imagine the emotions she had displayed a short time earlier; the sadness of this little round cat with the great speckled gold eyes.

"I know dat. Dat's coz I *told* you earlier, I was raised in da Bronx! But you didn't believe me."

"I believe *anything* of you now Reilly," Chloe said sweetly. "Especially the bit about being raised in the Bronx."

Reilly was aware of her sarcasm and chose to ignore her statement. "So where are we going then? What beach are you talking about? Is it really Carter's Beach? *Great!*"

Reilly had cleverly brought the subject back to exactly where he wanted it.

"I have to talk to God again about it," I said.

"I hope He tells you to go back to the Coast, where you should have been years ago, instead of all this traipsing around," Reilly said.

"May I remind you that I needed to get well again and it was you, who told me how terrible I looked, and it was *you* who told me I shouldn't go back to journalism again! That chapter of my life is over, so now we get ready to move onto the next one!"

It was true. I had been feeling for a while that it was time for us to move again. I meditated on my reasons, wondering if it was the gypsy blood in me that caused the restlessness after a year or two of being in different places. But after thinking deeply about it, I knew it wasn't that. It was simply a new chapter in my life unfolding; my health had improved a great deal and coupled with that, was the thought of having to spend another winter in the house.

I felt the cold terribly still, and the easterly that blew often, chilled me to the bone. I was still not as active as I would have liked to be, so on some days I would go for a walk around the block. The easterly would have me numb within a short time, and although the scent of the sea often came with it, it just wasn't the same as being on the West Coast. It could be cold there too, but never, ever did the temperatures reach the extremes that it did on this side of the South Island.

Additionally, the sound of the traffic, apart from just a few hours between one and four in the morning, was almost incessant.

***

CHAPTER FIFTEEN

"A Dog In The House"

However, these thoughts of moving took second place when Mike arrived unexpectedly one evening. He was elated.

"I've come to show you me new dog!" he announced. "Would you like to see her?"

I think my mouth was still open, as was my front door, and in waltzed an incredibly active little white dog with a curly body and hair in her eyes.

"Blimey! She must have got out me car window!" Mike exclaimed.

The little dog took one look at Chloe, yapped furiously and chased her out the ranchslider door. The dog went yapping down the back lawn and my heart gave a real lurch. I prayed that Chloe was too fast for Sarah and that she, Chloe would soon return. For the moment, I did not care if Sarah *didn't* return! Although I had to admit though that she sure was cute.

"Aw, I'm real sorry about that," Mike said, looking shame-faced. But he was still elated. It wasn't that long since Mickey had died and I really hoped that the new dog wasn't simply a replacement for Mickey.

"I sure hope Chloe comes back!" I exclaimed worriedly. "She's just getting used to the place and still has nightmares!"

"I suppose she told you all about them?" Mike said, with an edge of sarcasm.

"As a matter of fact, she did," I firmly replied. "Well, your doggie is really cute, even if she *is* a yapper. What's her name?"

"Her name's Sarah...don't ask me what her full name is coz I can't remember, it's so long. She's a Westie – a West Highland Terrier," he said proudly.

"I didn't think you could afford a purebred dog," I said slowly.

"Aw, I couldn't really, but the lady said she would let me pay her off."

I wondered what Sarah thought about being paid off.

Reilly entered the room.

"What the hell was that ruckus?"

"Mike's got a new dog."

"Oh yeah? Another runty dog, is it? Some silly little thing that thinks it is ten feet tall? Something new for me to get my teeth into, eh?"

"I think Sarah will have other ideas about that!" I said with a grin. My thoughts turned to Chloe. "I'll have to see if Chloe is okay. I wouldn't want to lose her!"

"Naw, she'll come back when she's ready," Reilly announced.

"Oh, you have faith in her then?" I asked, carefully watching Reilly's reactions.

A guarded look came over his face.

"Well, I concede that she is better than a...sheesh, oh, must I puke...a *dog!*"

"Why is it that the mention of a dog makes you nauseous?"

"Ask a silly question woman, and you'll get a silly answer! Because they make me feel sick! Sometimes sick with glee when I can chase them, sometimes sick with other things! They *smell* bad too! Now that makes me feel sick! *Me*, with my handsome, delicate and sensitive nose!"

"Well then, you should keep your handsome, delicate and sensitive nose out of other people's business!" I informed him.

"You and that bleedin' cat!" Mike said. "Still talking to him, eh?"

"Naturally," I said, watching Mike as he went to the ranchslider and began to call Sarah back inside.

"Dogs, smog, bogs...they smell awful. I am going to take my leave. How dare dat dog come onto my territory?"

"You'd better ask Mike that," I said with grim humour. Goodness knew to where Chloe had run away. I hoped it wasn't far and that she would come back when the coast was clear.

Mike looked at me with a disbelieving smile. "Ask me what?"

"Reilly wants to know why your new dog is on his territory."

For once, Mike didn't give me that look that said: I know she's daft and thinks she can understand cats and they can understand her, but I'll humour her!

"I'm really sorry about that, truly. But I didn't know she'd be so quick! Friendly little thing isn't she?" Pride in his new dog was back in his voice.

By then Reilly had left the room in disgust. But I had to agree with Mike. Sarah was indeed very friendly and leaped onto my knee. For a small dog, she was solidly built and her claws dug in hard. I told her so too, but she just looked up at me with her coal black eyes peering at me through her fringe of long hair and yapped...very loudly. My ears sang.

"She likes you!" Mike said, pleased. I was rather pleased too, as I always am when an animal likes me. Mike spoiled my brief pleasure by adding: "But then she likes everyone!"

Sarah jumped down and, with wagging tail, ran over to Mike and jumped onto his lap. He looked down at her with a fond expression in his eyes. While I was glad to see him happy again and not fretting over Mickey, I was concerned for Chloe.

"I'm going to look for Chloe," I said shortly.

I called and called her, going down the street looking for her and calling her. When I returned, Mike was about to leave.

"She'll be back. They always come back."

"No Mike, not always," I replied. Katie was proof of that. I still hoped that she would return one day, but after that dream I'd had, I knew that she wouldn't.

**

Chloe did not come home that night, or the next day. I rang the SPCA and also Cat's Protection League. No cat answering her description had been brought in. I left Chloe's and my details with each of the associations.

The next day Mike phoned me.

"Did Chloe come home?"

"No," I replied sadly. "I've just been out looking for her again and now I'm going to write an advertisement and do a letterbox drop."

"That's a good idea. I really am sorry about that," Mike said. "I just didn't think."

That was half of many people's trouble, I thought sourly. They often didn't think before they acted, and other people had to pick up the pieces. But in this case, I had to concede that Sarah had, of her own volition, come into our house without so much as a 'do you mind?'

My sour mood eased after typing out an advertisement in large bold print, and making fifty copies of it. Surely *someone* had seen her somewhere close by! She was such a distinctive cat with her beautiful soft coat, scrunched in face and huge speckled gold eyes. I had suggested in the advertisement that people check their garages, in case Chloe had been accidentally locked in one of them.

Just going for a walk and putting the leaflets in mailboxes restored my faith in Chloe's return. I missed her so much, and as I often did when I was upset, I wrote a poem, this one for Chloe.

Chloe Come Home

*I've seen the wanderlust
In your eyes, Chloe
I've seen too
How much you trust
Me...*

*So where did you go to?
Did you climb backyard fences,
Go over stumps and stiles;
Or see an open gate and go through?*

*Who did you meet
Along the way?
Trembling Torties, Tiger Toms
Or beautiful Persians, soft and sweet?*

*Now you're back again
But the faraway look
Is still there in your
Big gold and speckled eyes,
But is a rumbling purr
Your only refrain?*

*Tell me Chloe, kitty dear,
What sights did you see?
Trucks and cars and furry things,
Birds and butterflies, far and near?*

*I think you want to go
Again – to exciting new places
Beyond my vision;
Places perhaps contained only in
My mind's eye;
Chloe, I know you're ready to leave,
But kitty,
Please tell me it isn't so.*

**

It's true...I had felt there were times when Chloe wanted to leave, even though she had been with me for just a short while. The thought 'here we go again' often entered my mind, but I dismissed the thoughts as soon as they arrived, with the knowledge that Chloe was made of sterner stuff than Katie O'Brien. But Sarah was the catalyst for putting my thoughts into action...and not an action I liked.

I hoped my new confidence in her return wasn't just pie in the sky.

It wasn't.

At around eleven the next night I heard a distinctive meow. To my delight, it was Chloe, looking a little worse for wear and also rather thin. I picked her up and cuddled her. Even Reilly seemed pleased she was back.

"About time you came back, Chloe. The woman was missing you!"

"Did you miss me too?"

"Of course not!"

Chloe leaped out of my arms and nuzzled up to Reilly. "Didn't you miss me a teensy weensy bit?"

Reilly's eyes closed until they were little more than slits. The gold of his eyes was barely discernable in the artificial light. "Maybe a very small amount. I had only the woman to pick on! Now, where were you?"

"Oh, that white dog gave me such a fright! I ran away without thinking that all I needed to do was climb a tree and stay there until the dog had gone."

"Yes, but where did you go to? It's four nights since you ran away!"

Chloe began to purr. "So nice to know I was missed! Actually, I ran into an open garage down the road and found a nice pile of carpet to sleep on. Alas, a man came home and gave me another fright when he drove his car into the garage. Then he closed the big garage door down and I couldn't get out again until tonight.

146

I was so *hungry*! I heard someone outside talking to another person about getting a leaflet in the mailbox about checking the garage for a cat that went missing. They opened the door and out I ran. A lady called out: "oh, the poor little cat! That must have been the one that went missing!" She sounded so nice that I came back to let her pet me. She gave me a big drink of milk and some tasty food."

"That was nice of her. But you still feel very thin," I said. My heart felt light with relief, knowing my cat was home safe. And relief that Chloe had at least had something to eat and drink during her time away.

"Perhaps I could do with a rather large snack," Chloe wheedled.

"What about me? Don't I get one too, for being so supportive during Chloe's absence?" Reilly licked his mouth in wonderful pink sweeps of his tongue.

Both cats looked up at me with their big eyes and blinked owlishly. I melted.

"Of course you do, my beauties!" I exclaimed.

Reilly spoilt the moment a little with his announcement: "Glad to see you are still appreciating our good looks."

But secretly I smiled. Before, Reilly had not considered Chloe to be particularly good-looking. With a few words he said the opposite. I was pleased.

"I wrote a poem for you, Chloe," I said with a smile. "And it was I who wrote the advertisement about you and went around the neighbourhood, doing a mail drop."

"Oh, that *is* nice!" She blinked several times; her enormous eyes reminiscent of Katie's. "Thank you for going to all that trouble."

Reilly of course, had to go one better.

"Huh, the woman has written *several* poems about me! *And* I have already been published!"

"Becoming notorious, are you?"

I was glad Chloe was already getting back to her usual self.

"Notorious? Don't be foolish...the word is *famous!* How many times must I spell these things out to you?"

"Actually, I wasn't aware that you had spelt anything out to me."

"That's coz you wuz not listening!"

"There goes that bad vocabulary again."

"I already told you I wuz raised in da Bronx!"

"I have decided Reilly, that you are nothing more than a curmudgeon cat! Although a bit better tempered."

"Really? Shucks Chloe, dat's da nicest thing you have said to me in a while."

"Play your cards right Reilly, and I will say many more things of the same ilk."

"Ilk? Dat's a big animal like a stag, innit?"

"That's an *elk*, fool!"

Reilly appeared to grin widely.

"Just testing your knowledge, Chloe Arabella. You are a little bit brighter cat dan I first thought."

We all went to bed and as I lay there in the warmth I thought of Reilly's words. Oh yes, Chloe was and *is* bright indeed! This little round cat had obviously been through a great deal. It appeared that being a purebred cat was no guarantee of a cushy life, even thought it was apparent that the woman owner did not realise her cat was now deemed a purebred in her own right. Chloe confirmed that in ways other than what she had already told me. She couldn't bear blankets over her head; in no way would she crawl under the duvet and/or blankets, as most cats like to, even if she was very cold. Several times on cold days I attempted to put one of my crocheted blankets over her back, but she simply crawled out from underneath.

I read a story once, in which the main character mentioned how much cats liked un-made beds. It is absolutely true. They can burrow in amongst the blankets and make a nice cosy nest for themselves, or they can crawl under the blankets and leave an obvious lump. That was my often-used excuse not to make the bed! Cats have a way of making you feel guilty if you disturb them while they're sleeping.

"Of course we do! And so you *should* feel guilty."

148

"Reilly, you were listening to my thoughts again!"

"Perhaps you should keep your thoughts to yourself a bit better den," Reilly said succinctly.

"You shouldn't be such a nosy cat!" I retorted.

"A cat such as me has the right to know what is going on in dat blonde head of yours, woman! Why, who knows what you could be plotting! You could be plotting to overthrow us cats, for instance."

"Why would I want to do that, when I love you so much!"

"Dat's what *you* say, but how would we know what you *really* think, except for da fact dat we *basically* know what you are thinking, despite what I said before and we are smart animals... da smartest in da universe too, I might add."

"Not smart enough to improve your language though!"

"Why should I? It's my day off, woman."

"What's dat...er, *that* supposed to mean?"

"It means, woman, dat I can talk how I like when it's my day off, same as you humans wear what you want on your day off, and basically do what you want."

"But I hear you talking that like *every* day!"

"Heh heh, naturally, coz *every* day is my day off, stoopid!"

"You are an exceedingly rude cat, and there are times when I really do not know why I put up with you!" I said angrily.

Reilly turned to Chloe with a wicked gleam in his eyes. "You see, Chloe Arabella, da truth is coming out now! I was right! She just *may* try to overthrow us."

"Don't be daft, cat," I said. "That's what people do to governments!"

"Dat's what *I mean!*"

I sighed. "I really do not know what you mean, cat, and I am getting rather fed up wid...er, *with* this conversation!"

Reilly crouched down as if to spring up on me. "Woman, *we* are the government around here."

"Who is 'we'?"

"'*We*' is me and Chloe, dat's who, I say to you. And there you have some poetry again, woman."

I put my hands on my hips and struck a belligerent pose.

"And who and where am I supposed to be in the scheme of things, if you two are the government?"

Reilly sniggered, very loudly and turned to Chloe again.

"You see Chloe? It's just as well we are in charge, well me at the helm, of course, because dis woman here doesn't even know who she *is!*"

He chortled merrily and ran outside. Chloe mumbled something about me leaving myself wide open for Reilly's baiting, and casually followed him outside.

***

CHAPTER SIXTEEN

"Rolling in Clover...or Something"

Sometimes I felt that I had two cats gunning for me, instead of just one. Or perhaps that was just me...feeling a bit down on that particular day. I was feeling outnumbered.

"So go and get yourself a man," Reilly said as he ambled through the open doorway. "That should cheer you up a bit."

"I am not in the market for a man," I told him sternly. "But even if I were, I would not tell *you!*"

"Foolish woman!"

"Foolish? Why? I thought I was being sensible, actually!"

"No, dat's not what I meant...I meant foolish because you know jolly well dat I can read your mind."

"I think dat...er that you are not only a curmudgeon cat, but a very nosy one as well."

"So...I shoulda been a journalist! I could do a burglary and write about myself...with another alias of course. 'Reilly Catches Yet Another Cat-Burglar', the headline would read."

"Biffed yourself one left hook under the chin, eh?" I said, amused.

"I am not amused, even though *you* appear to be!" Reilly sniffed.

"I thought you said you can read my mind? Earlier on in the piece you said, quote, 'but how would we know what you *really* think?' Make up your mind, cat. Either you can or cannot hear and understand my thoughts."

"I can read your thoughts, woman and am amused by you," Reilly sniffed.

"You amuse *me* often, although most of the time you annoy me," I said with a smile. "Why don't you go and make yourself useful? You could go and do my shopping for me, for instance."

"You know they don't like me in the shops...I can't understand why."

"They think you'll steal their food, and not only that, you would be considered a health hazard!"

"*Moi?* A health hazard? Oh yeah...maybe they're right...if they tried to shoo me out, I would show dem just *what* a hazard I could be! I would scrag their bags of wheat and sugar and flour; I would knock down dem big displays of canned food; I would dance among their lettuces and cabbages with my claws unsheathed; I would chew on their packets of cat biscuits and also get into their freezers!"

"Hopefully you mean *open* chest freezers," I suggested.

"Of course dat's what I meant!"

"How did you know they would have open freezers?" I asked him suspiciously.

"How do you suppose? I sneaked in one day and had a look! Boy, whatta freezer! A cat such as I could go madly, wonderfully crazy in there. As long as I didn't stay in it too long, of course, otherwise I could get a nasty chill."

I had a sudden vivid picture of the reaction from the owner and his assistant when Reilly entered the corner dairy-cum-restaurant in Carter's Beach a few years ago. It was not a good reaction.

"Did anyone see you?"

"Oh I expect they did," Reilly said airily. "But no one said anything, although I did think I heard a lot of muffled laughter."

"Oh please tell me, what did you do, and what shop was it?"

"I don't know what shop it was...just some smallish place down at the shopping centre. Someone left a nice tasty sausage roll on the table so I hopped up on a chair and snaffled it quickly before it was taken away. Actually...now that I think of it, when I sneaked away I thought I heard someone say 'who stole my sausage roll?'"

I looked at him sceptically.

"Well...okay, I *did* hear someone say that, but of course I had to call out, 'not I, sire' and then I moved in closer behind a table. I heard a man say: 'who said that?' and I answered: 'T'was but a wonderful, glorious cat...fancy that!' And I secretly was amazed that someone else could actually hear what I was saying. I was also very proud of my bit of poetry, and I think the man was too because he then said: 'A blasted cat! Huh, how about that! It's amazing what they let in, these days! Oh well, I s'pose each shop owner has his or her own funny ways!'"

I looked at Reilly in an even more sceptical way. "Are you telling me that everything you said just now is all true?"

His eyes widened in apparent shock and hurt. "I am grievously stricken and torn! Are you telling me I am a liar? Oh...next think you'll be telling me I am not only a liar, but I am also a *thief!*"

"Well, is *that* the truth?"

"Is *what* the truth?"

I could see he was playing for time.

"That you are not only a big liar, but you are also a thief!"

"Ohhh, so now it's a *big* liar, eh? Well, I like that!"

"Well? Are you a liar, or what are you?"

"Me? I am Reilly the Gorgeous, Reilly the Wonderful, Reilly the Caped One, Reilly The Most Glorious...etcetera..."

"Reilly the Big-Headed One," I added cynically.

"Reilly the Fathead," said Chloe, who had entered the room quietly.

"Fathead? If anyone is a fathead, it is *you*, Chloe Arabella! By the way, you never *did* tell me if you got the number of the bus you ran into."

Chloe seemed to smile a secret smile. "Actually, it was Number Seven. A very big red bus with an extremely bold yellow sign that said Number Seven."

Reilly was momentarily disconcerted. "Number Seven? Why Number Seven?"

"Because that's what I read on the bus when it stopped just down the street, silly!" Chloe said gleefully. "And do you know what, Reilly? You didn't know I could read, did you? Also, it so happens that Number Seven is my lucky number..."

"How do you know that?"

"It brought me here in the end, didn't it? That nice young couple had to travel with me on a bus and they kept me covered up until they got here. I am so thankful to be here and even though I don't like being covered up, I knew it wouldn't be for long. And not only that, I have another cat to spar with! Oh, joy to the world!"

"Dat's the sort of thing I should be saying! How *dare* you copy me?"

"Haven't you heard that imitating is the best and sincerest form of flattery?"

"Are you flattering me?"

"I don't know. *Am* I?" Chloe said silkily. "You tell *me.*"

"Do you think you need to flatter me?" Reilly began to preen.

"Not really. Your ego is big enough to cover about two dozen people or more."

"Huh! For that you will feel the edge of my claws!"

"Hisss!"

"Oh you silly cat, go and have a hissy fit...see if I care!"

Chloe hissed at him once more and turned her back on him. Reilly leaped on her and began to box her, but I could see it was more in play than anything else...although it was evident he wished to remind her about who was boss in our house. It was time I intervened.

"Cut that out Reilly! Leave Chloe alone! Anyway, *I* am the boss in this house and it's time I reminded you of that fact."

"Oh come on Chloe, let's go outside and play. The magpies are back. I think it's time to beat up on them again. The woman gets so boring."

"Ungrateful, miserable cat!"

"Foolish, sentimental woman!"

"Wretched, cheeky, rude, egotistical cat!"

"Ah, *now* you is getting somewhere, little widdy woman..."

"I will remind you that I am *not* a widdy woman!"

"You might as well be..."

They pranced outside and raced up the pepper tree to begin terrorising the magpies. The magpies paid lip service to their presence, but decided that it was time to be discreet, and flew off, warbling noisily.

It was just five minutes after they had gone outside that I realised Reilly had not answered my question about whether he was telling the truth about going down to the shopping centre and stealing a sausage roll, and telling me in his own way about how the man could understand what he, Reilly was saying. That cat had proved himself yet again at what a master of deceit and wiliness he could be!

**

Big Mike visited again with his new dog Sarah. She took one look at Reilly and when she started yapping, he stood his ground, then hunkered down ready to spring at her. A very surprised Sarah took several steps backwards, and then ran to the ranchslider door so Mike could let her out.

"It's not a good idea to bring her inside Mike," I reminded him yet again. "You're bringing Sarah onto two cats' territory now. They could easily gang up on her and claw her eyes."

"Sarah would be too quick for them both," Mike said proudly. "She'd probably eat them alive!"

"Not if I have anything to do with it!" I said grimly.

"Where's Chloe, anyway?"

"I don't know. Maybe still outside somewhere, conferring with Reilly on how they can get rid of Sarah! They just chased off the magpies, so now they need something else to do."

"Still think those cats can talk to you, do you?" Mike said with one eyebrow raised in a disbelieving manner.

"Of course they do!" I defended. "We have some wonderful conversations! Some not so wonderful, I might add."

"Too catty for you are they? Their remarks, I mean?" He said with a wide grin, showing his perfect teeth.

"Very funny, Mike," I said sourly.

Mike moved to the dining room window to watch his dog's antics.

"Oh, lookit that! Sarah's rolling over on her back!"

"Asking for trouble, she is. That dog of yours is a hussy, to be sure."

"Ohhh, I think she's rolling in something." Mike peered out the door. "Sarah! What are you rolling in?"

I hope it's only treacle, I thought. *Or maybe it's something much worse.*

"Sarah! Get out of that! Ooo, Amber, I think she's rolled in some poo. She's got brown on her back."

"Well, you needn't think she can come through the lounge like that. Maybe it's only dirt."

"One of your cats must have pooed on the lawn!" Mike snapped.

Personally, I thought he had a cheek, speaking to me like that. Frankly, it was none of his business if my cats *had* used the lawn for their toilet, but I knew they hadn't. Maybe it was a sneaky dog from down the street that had leaped the fence, especially to leave a deposit in my back yard. The local dogs were so good at that. They seemed to think I would appreciate it. Dogs can be so stupid, I thought drolly.

"Probably Sarah did it, then rolled in it thinking she couldn't let that aroma go to waste! What a thrifty dog!"

Mike looked at me in an annoyed fashion. "Probably one of your *pussycats* did it!"

"Well, there's one way to find out isn't there Mike? Actually, I think it looks like a bit of dirt. Go and catch her and give her a sniff!"

Big Mike moved quickly out the ranch slider door and managed to catch the very quick little Sarah, who got away from him and ran around the side of the house to the driveway. She thought Mike was having a wonderful game with her. I opened the front door to see what was happening, just as he caught Sarah for the second time.

"Now that you have caught her, give her a sniff," I suggested, tongue in cheek.

Mike did just that. His face went very red and his eyes rolled in his head.

"Poooooooo! She don't half *stink!*"

"Now Mike, you know that's not a nice thing to say about a lady!" But by then I was doubled up with mirth. In between bursts of mirth I told him that she wasn't coming back inside; that he would have to hose her down or take her straight home.

"I'm gonna take her home," he said morosely. "I only bathed her yesterday, too!"

Which only made me laugh again.

"She doesn't like the smell of the shampoo you use on her," I said with a grin.

"Bleedin' heck. It cost me an arm and a leg, too!"

"Which must make it all the harder for you to handle her," I said sweetly.

"I'm going home," Mike said. "I should be getting me bleedin' groceries but she'd probably put 'er stink all over them!"

"Very flavoursome, I *don't* think!"

Mike took his leave, Sarah grinning at us out the back window. I decided I really did like Sarah, after all.

**

The cats moseyed back inside. They seemed unperturbed that Sarah had paid us a visit. Safety in numbers, I guess.

"Gone again, have they?" Reilly wanted to know.

"Yes they have. Sarah rolled in something nasty and Mike smelled it. You should have seen his face. Red as a beetroot and his eyes rolling."

"Sounds very scary, heh, heh. We coulda told him, but he wouldn't have heard us anyway. We sat up the pepper tree and watched. A dog from down the street came in here yesterday.

The wind musta blown open the gate and in this dog came. What a mutt it was too. I couldn't even be bothered scaring it off, but when I saw what it did on the lawn, you can bet your boots I shooed it off!"

"I didn't hear any dogs running scared and barking," I said.

"No, that's because I gave it such a good scare it didn't have the time to bark! Oh I must say, I enjoyed that! I haven't chased a dog in ages! You should have seen dat dog airborne when I whacked him on his fat rear! I forgot to tell you dat da dog left its deposit on the lawn. Pooed in fright, I guess. Dat's what Sarah rolled in. What a *stupid* dog!"

"I guess she liked the smell of that doggie doo better than the shampoo Mike used on her last night."

"Da shampoo sure must smelled real bad, den," Reilly smirked. "Oh, aren't I glad I was born into this world a wonderful, adorable, *clean* cat!"

"You were born into this world a tiny kitten," I reminded him.

"Semantics, woman! Now, be a good girl and go get us starving cats some food...decent stuff too, I might add. None of that *canned* stuff!"

"What did your last slave die of?"

"What do you think?"

"Overwork?" I suggested.

"Got it in one, woman!"

"If I died of overwork, who would look after you cats? Who would do your shopping for you, cuddle you when you are lonely... take you to the vet...?"

"Dat's *it!* You mentioned that filthy word, *vet!* Get to *work*, woman! We'll make you work so hard you will be too tired to ever take us to da vet again." Reilly stopped in his tracks. "Which reminds me, wasn't dat vet gonna come and have afternoon tea with us?"

"I am not so sure about that," I said warily. "I think he may have branded me as one of those potty women who are soppy about cats."

"Dat vet is a very wise man," Reilly said succinctly.

"If that is the case, and you agree with me, you would also have to agree that I am indeed potty about cats!"

"Well of course you are! You've got us! We *do* appreciate you, yer know!"

"I'd like to think that was true, cat."

"Of course it is! Have I ever lied to you?"

"Probably," I said shortly. "In fact, on numerous occasions."

Reilly went off singing the Eurythmics big hit song of the 80's: "Would I Lie To You?"

I don't know how that cat does it, but he always manages to come out tops in the repartee stakes!

***

CHAPTER SEVENTEEN

"Strange Tastes"

A new day had dawned. We had gone through our new routine of toast and coffee for me while sitting in bed, and Chloe having some of my toast, and then looking pleadingly at me for more.

"If you think I am going to get out of my warm bed at this extremely early hour to make toast for you, my girl, then you have another think coming!"

"Well, it was worth a try."

"At least you're honest!"

"Huh! Aren't I honest too?" Reilly came leaping up my bed to stare into my face. "So where's *my* toast?"

"You told me you didn't like it."

"Yeah well, maybe you're right."

"I *am* right."

Reilly walked down my legs a few paces and stared out the window. He had, by his body actions, changed the subject...well, almost.

"Like I have said in the past, toast and jam is for sissies."

"I don't recall you actually saying those words, Reilly!"

"Calling me a liar now, are you? Like you tried to call me the other day?"

"I'm surprised you brought that subject up, Reilly. After all, it was you who shifted the subject sideways and then went off singing that song Would I Lie To You? Incidentally, I should have called out to you when you were making a getaway - that the answer to that question is...*yes!*"

"You see Reilly, our mother is smarter than you give her credit for."

"Mother? So it's *Mother* now, is it? You didn't call her anything before. Oh, what a crawling cat you have turned out to be, Chloe Arabella!"

"I have noticed you do a fair bit of crawling yourself, Reilly, literally and metaphorically speaking."

"I don't like dem big words, even though I know what they are."

"Why not?"

"Coz I like da language of da Bronx!"

"Shut up, Reilly! You are changing the subject again. I'm already very tired of hearing about that damned Bronx! I said before you have done a fair bit of crawling yourself...especially when it comes to wanting supper."

Hmmm...the little round cat with the saucer eyes could be a spitfire!

Reilly said nothing further, but glared at Chloe and stormed off, taking a swing at her on passing.

"Ow! Mother, did you see that?"

"I most certainly did! Reilly, you come back and apologise!"

"Apologise I will *not!* It should be the other way round," Reilly called from down the hallway.

"Gee, what did I do?" Chloe's eyes looked more enormous than ever, this time with a measure of hurt in them.

"You did nothing Chloe, except put Reilly in his place."

"She should apologise for speaking to me like that, as if I were an infant," Reilly called.

I was so amused. "Infant you are *not,*" I said, imitating his words. "In fact, you are getting to be quite an old cat now, heh, heh."

"Old? Did you say *old?* How dare you say that to me! After all, I am an *ageless* cat!"

"Oh, but didn't I hear you say some years ago that you were fighting on the beaches and in the trenches? That would make you a *very* old cat!"

"It's memories, woman! *Memories!* We cats are so evolved we have super memories, far better than elephants, even!"

"You liken yourself to an elephant? My word cat, as I have said once before, you are a much bigger cat than I first thought."

Reilly shot back into my bedroom. "Yeah, so just let me sit on you for a while, den you will appreciate the weight of me!"

"Fat too," I observed, when he leaped onto me and sat on my legs. His tummy bulged out his sides.

"Huh. Dat's not a nice thing to say about your boy cat. If I were a sumo wrestler, maybe, but I am simply an aristocratic, wonderful, handsome cat."

"An egotistical fat cat from the Bronx, or so he says." Chloe added her money's worth.

"You are an insolent cat! Why, I liked Katie O'Brien much better dan *you!*"

"Only because you were able to bully her far more than you try to bully *me!*"

"Huh! I like that!"

"I'm glad that you do, Reilly. Now, let's have some peace, shall we?" I yawned. "I have to get up soon and Reilly, you sure are heavy."

"Sumo wrestler," Reilly muttered. "Hmmm...I kind like dat idea!"

With a chirrup, he leaped off the bed and ran into the 'smallest room'.

"What are you up to, cat?" I called after hearing him making odd bumps and bangs.

"Nothing much." But his voice was muffled.

I decided to climb out of bed and investigate. Reilly was down the toilet, having a drink of water.

"I haven't seen you do that for ages!" I exclaimed.

Chloe ran out to have a look. "What's he doing?"

"Having a drink from the loo."

"That's disgusting!" Chloe snapped.

"My toilet is clean," I defended, a little bit hurt. Actually, it had pleased me, seeing Reilly do that. It reminded me of being on the West Coast, and enjoying all the cute things he used to do over there. Okay, so maybe some of the things he did were not so cute, but time has a habit of taking the edge off memories that were not so good. But in this instance, it was a cute memory.

"Sorry Mother," Chloe said. "I didn't mean to offend you. But what if you had that fancy blue cleaner stuff in there?"

"Oh my gosh, you're right! I think I *do* have some left! Reilly, get out of there!"

Reilly remained there for a few more seconds. His rear end looked most comical, with his tail hanging over the front of the toilet bowl.

"He is rather fat, isn't he?" Chloe remarked. "And he doesn't have much taste, either! Well, just for...ugh...drinking from toilets."

Reilly emerged and leaped down, taking a swipe at Chloe. It wasn't meant to hit her, I could see that, but she took fast steps backwards anyway.

"I will have you know that I *like* to drink from the toilet."

"What's wrong with drinking from your bowl?"

"Boring, as I have told you many times in the past."

"But I haven't seen you drinking from the toilet for ages and ages."

"Dat's because you ain't around when I have been."

"So why do you? Drink from the toilet, I mean."

"Because, as I said before, I like it! *Yuk*, I do have a bit of an awful taste in my mouth, though."

"You drank up the last traces of that blue cleaner I had in there."

"Yuk! I could have been *poisoned!*"

"You should have checked first, that the water was clear."

"Ugh! It reminds me of that time at Carter's Beach when I had a drink from the neighbour's toilet, and she had real blue stuff in it! I tell you, I wanted to call out the environmentalists! Dat stuff is dangerous to our ecology! And *you* should not have had dat stuff in dis toilet!"

"I only use it occasionally," I defended.

"Well, get off my back, will ya?"

"Did you get out of the wrong side of the bed this morning, Reilly?"

"Yeah, I should be able to have your bed all to myself. I shouldn't have to share it with two females."

"You should be so lucky, Reilly," I said coolly.

"Right, for dat remark, I am off to chase dogs."

"Off you go den...er, then, but do be very careful. You're not so young now, you know."

"Neither are you, and nor is a *baby*, for dat matter. It gets older by the hour! I am gonna start my day by annoying da neighbours!"

"What method will you use this time? Stare through their kitchen window until they feel sorry for you and give you something to eat?"

"Hey now, dat's not a bad idea! After all, I have only had a drink of loo water dis morning."

"You have cat biscuits in your bowl."

"Boring, *boring!* Give me filet steak any day."

"It used to be rump steak you would demand, but I see your tastes have become far more exalted now." I returned to my bedroom and began to get dressed.

"Of course! Dat's because I have come to the full realisation of what a perfect specimen of a cat dat I am."

"I know one thing that I would give you full marks for," Chloe said.

"Oh yeah? Da liddle round pussycat actually would give me full marks for something?"

"Yes Reilly, your ego. It is well and truly intact, but its inflation could cause it to burst if you're not careful."

"I'm sure there are plenty of beautiful girl cats around to catch me should I fall."

"Well, you needn't think I would be one of them."

"Who says you're a beautiful cat? Did I say you're beautiful?"

"No, I don't recall that you did."

"Well then...looks like you would definitely *not* be one of the beautiful girl cats who would catch me should I fall."

"Mother, Reilly is not being nice to me."

"Well Chloe, I think you're a very beautiful cat!"

"Thank you. I'm glad you appreciate me."

"Of course I do! Reilly, it's about time you went outside, since you're not going to eat your biscuits. They're nice and tasty, you know."

"How do *you* know that? Been eating them when my back was turned, eh?"

"Don't be silly, Reilly. I read it on the packet, and read about all the things in it that are so good for you."

"Give me red meat any day. Or give me fresh fish straight from the sea...or give me whipped cream. Or some fresh oysters, maybe!"

"You give me the money to pay for all that, and so I shall," I retorted. "Now, off outside you go."

"Huh, spoilsport!"

Then off he went, chirruping and scampering. A few moments later I heard "shoo! Get off there! Stop staring, you horrible cat!"

I realised Reilly must have climbed up onto the neighbour's trellis that had clematis weaving through out and made a lovely sight. It was also a nice spot for Reilly to sun himself on. His next move would have been to leap onto the fence, run along the railing and sit in front of the neighbour's kitchen window. Well, he had completed his first promise. In due course I expected to hear the sound of yapping dogs.

"BOYS, PLEASE! NOTHING PERSONAL ...

...BUT YOUR MUMS REALLY ARE...!!"

It didn't take long. Barely ten minutes later I heard the people from two houses away come outside to see what the commotion was all about. I climbed onto the big drum by the first neighbour's fence and stood up to have a look. Reilly was, by that stage, sitting on *their* neighbour's tall fence and reaching down, swiping at the two big dogs with his paw, knowing he was well out of reach of both of them. He was smart enough to know that these were dogs *not* to chase! They were big and fast; one was a Rottweiler, the other a Doberman and they were guard dogs. Their owner ran a paint and panel shop and also did mechanical repairs and the dogs were necessary security measures.

But all the same, Reilly could not resist the lure of baiting the dogs, any dogs for that matter, or the neighbours. When opportunity knocked, and all that...

**

Walt Disney, that great man of imagination and the ability to look into the minds of adults and see the children still there had this to say: 'Somehow I can't believe that there are any heights that can't be scaled by a man who knows the secret of making dreams come true. This special secret, it seems to me, can be summarised in Four C's. They are curiosity, confidence, courage and constancy, and the greatest of these is confidence. When you believe in a thing, believe in it all the way, implicitly and unquestionably.'

I absolutely agree with that great man. But I would like to add a personal rider to his statements: I can't believe there are any heights that can't be scaled by a cat who knows the secret of making dreams come true, *definitely* has curiosity, courage, confidence and constancy, and *does* believe in himself implicitly!

Reilly has the curiosity of ten cats, the confidence and courage of a lion and his constancy in his self-praise and in his demands for expensive food! Could I add more to that? Well of course I can. The subliminal messages he is so good at, and he also regularly slipped in hints of moving from this place at Parklands to returning to Carter's Beach. While thinking about that right now, I am tempted to say something to him, but thought better of it. Two sets of huge golden cat eyes looking at me in a mixture of outrage and hurt was more than any normal person could bear for long. Although why Chloe should look outraged was beyond me, unless Reilly had been quietly working his subtle, or sometimes not-so-subtle brain-washing on her!

Having said that, I have often been told I am 'not like other people', so perhaps that explains my long-term patience with a cat who, while embracing all the good things about cats, also embraced the full meaning of bad things about cats! Such as staring at me in his outraged way.

But I must count my blessings again, and think about these facts that: Reilly had not leaped onto the drapes since we had moved to this house; he had not come home with someone's very dead pet budgie in his mouth, or returned home with a kingfisher bird, complete with small branch in his mouth, and nor had he stolen anyone's thawing beef olives off their kitchen bench. And nor had he stolen someone's lovely piece of fresh fruit cake and fresh rump steak – as had one other cat I had once upon a time...

"How do *you* know that I haven't done all those things?"

I spun around in fright.

"Crikey, cat, where did you spring from? I thought you were still baiting the neighbour's dogs!"

"Naw...I got bored with that. Anyway, as I said before, how do you know I haven't done all that? You know, those things you were thinking of before."

If I have said it once, I shall say it again, even though I had long known that Reilly could hear my thoughts, there were times when I was still disconcerted by it. This time was one of them.

"Well, have you done all those things? Stolen someone's nice fruit cake, or steak, or beef olives...or eaten their pet budgie, or killed and eaten a rare and protected bird?"

Reilly sniggered. "That's for me to know, and you to find out, woman!"

Then off he scampered, returning outside. I hadn't discovered why he and Chloe had been staring at me in such an outraged and hurt way. Soon I heard him baiting the magpies.

Perhaps I could have added an 'F' to those Four Cs mentioned earlier: 'foolishness'. On the other hand, Walt Disney himself may have argued with me if he had still been around, perhaps saying: 'But in some people's eyes, hadn't they viewed bravery and courage simply as recklessness or foolishness? Until they realised when time passed that the seemingly foolish person was one of great fortitude and strength and implicitly believed in what he or she was about to do?'

Okay, I get the point, I thought, my mind still 'twixt and tween' Walt Disney's quote and my imagined quote of his. But I still mulled over Disney's actual words when I heard the warbling and shrieking of the magpies.

I needn't have worried however. Reilly came scampering back inside, with some magpie feathers in his mouth. Several steps up from the budgie of years ago, I guess, even though it hadn't been him who'd caught the neighbour's budgie. Okay, I got the point again. Reilly had all the courage and fortitude imaginable of a cat, and many times more and I have to admit it, I was truly very proud of him.

Until my arms smarted in the shower from the fresh scratches on them, that is.

***

CHAPTER EIGHTEEN

"Safely, Safely Go The Cats"

A week or so later Mike called around. It was nearing the dinner hour and as I had not started preparing my evening meal, Mike suggested we should buy some takeaways. I agreed and so off we went, Reilly's calls of 'bring us some fresh, battered oysters, woman!' ringing in my ears. My usual reply was "oh, if only!" Oysters were very expensive, and much as I loved the taste of them, unless I was a lot better off financially, oysters were definitely *not* on the menu!

Off Mike and I went, to have a quick look at the shops before they closed for the day and then carried on up the street to the nearest takeaway shop. While waiting for our order to be cooked, I noticed a free promotion where I could win a four-wheel drive vehicle.

"Gee Mike, that would be nice!"

"Yeah, and fifty thousand other people are probably all thinking the same thing!" Mike said cynically. I knew he was right, but I am of the belief that you have to be in to win, and so I filled out my details as per requirements.

"What's the catch?" I asked the takeaway owner.

"None, as far as I know," he said.

**

Reilly complained that we didn't buy him any oysters.

"Out of season," I said briefly, glad that it was true and that I didn't have to fob off my big cat, who really did have a penchant for the delicacy.

"Harumph!" Reilly snorted. "Well, I suppose I have to make do with ordinary old fish again."

"This is not ordinary fish, Reilly," I said. "This is succulent, juicy, absolutely fresh fish, and you can't have it all. Chloe wants some too, don't you Chloe?"

"I don't mind if I do, but just make sure the pieces aren't too hot and nor too big, and nor too cold."

"Did you hear that, woman? Madam doesn't want her food too hot, and nor too cold! Icky, spoilt, *dilly* little round cat!"

"Don't speak that way to Chloe, Reilly," I said gently, although I do have to admit to thinking Chloe was getting just a wee bit too fussy.

"You and them damn cats! Still think you can talk to them, eh?" Mike said with a wicked glint in his eyes. "You'd better watch it girl, or them men with the long white coats will be coming to take you away!"

"He heeee!" I added, musically, making Mike look sideways at me. "Hey now, I was only adding that extra bit about it. You know, ha ha, ha *heee!*"

"Bloody bonkers, if you ask me!" said Mike.

"I didn't ask you," I said with an edge to my voice.

"If *I* went around saying the things you do, I'm sure they would lock me up!"

"I'm sure they would too, Mike!" I said sweetly.

"Get on with it, woman! Can't you see we cats are starving?"

"All right, all right, don't get yourself in a dither over it!" I eyed Reilly's fat sides and decided a few minutes more before he got his portions of fresh fish would not hurt him in the least.

I spread out the feast of fish and potato chips and plump sausages in its wrapping, onto the coffee table, and fetched tomato sauce and two saucers so I could break small pieces of fish into each of them.

One of life's treats, I thought, sitting in front of the telly in a warm house, eating delicious takeaways straight from the paper wrapping and sharing the meal with a friend and my cats.

Chloe sniffed suspiciously at her small pieces of food. "Too cold, Chloe? Too hot? Should I test your food with a thermometer first?"

"Sarcasm doesn't suit always you Mother," she replied.

Huh, I thought. *I think I prefer Reilly's ways, evil as they can be at times!* Chloe's sometimes air of suffering and outrage, mostly unaccountable, was most annoying. Add that to her habit of yowling in the middle of the night and I often thought that Mike's involvement in helping get her for me was a mixed blessing. I felt permanently tired.

"Mumsy-wumsy might find you somewhere else to live, if you ever speak to her like that again," Reilly commented when he had gobbled up his fish.

Chloe swung her enormous eyes onto me and looked at me in such a reproachful manner I felt terrible about having any cross thoughts with her at all. It was a similar look to what I had experienced from both of them about ten days before.

"You are such a sucker, woman!" Reilly said, correctly interpreting my look of remorse. "It doesn't take much to upset you. Why...I only have to tell Chloe that you don't want to go back to the beach and there you are..."

So that's why they sometimes looked at me that way – with such reproach. "I know I am a sucker," I agreed. "Especially when it comes to pussycats. But Reilly, you should not make up stories to tell Chloe about me."

Mike rolled his eyes at me. "You and them cats! You get more weird every day!"

"Not everyone thinks so," I said mildly.

"Lucky for you!" he snorted.

"Yes, isn't it?" I said with a smile. "And aren't *you* the lucky one, having me for a friend!"

"Sometimes I wonder," Mike returned.

"You don't have to come around here, you know, if you think I am *that* weird!" I said sharply.

Mike grinned. "I quite like coming here, actually, and anyway, you're my best friend!"

"So there, woman! Now aren't *you* the lucky one, having da giant corncob for your best friend! I wonder what a whole field full of giant corncobs like dis one here would look like?"

Reilly had chosen to ignore my earlier comment – the one about making up stories about me to tell Chloe.

"Very large, I would imagine," I said with a smile. "And all speaking with a sort-of Liverpudlian accent!"

"Bleedin' heck! Call out th' bleedin guards! We've got a blimmin' mutiny on 'our 'ands! Bleedin' giant corncobs are takin' over th' bleedin' country!" Reilly said in a very good imitation of a Cockney accent.

All that bleeding everywhere, I thought wildly.

"I'm buggered if I know what the hell yer talkin' about, but I think it involves me!" Mike said suspiciously. I fought the urge to laugh. He had a piece of fish hanging down from his beard, giving him a very rakish look.

"We were talking about giant corncobs," I said easily.

"Yum! I love big juicy corncobs, hot and running with butter!" Mike said with glee.

Reilly gave a big snigger. I felt like a big snigger of my own coming on. "Perish da thought," Reilly said. "Now *dat* is far too scary a thought for even da likes of me."

I laughed out loud.

"Blimey, I didn't think what I'd said was *that* funny!" Mike said in puzzlement.

"Oh, you are a naturally humorous guy," I said, my stomach knotting with suppressed mirth.

The rest of the evening went very well and Mike left, taking Sarah with him. She'd stayed out in the car while we ate, and when Mike was due to leave for home, he let her have a run around my back lawn.

"I have to take her home and cook tea for her," he said.

It seemed an anomaly: we ate takeaways and the dog had her meal cooked especially for her a little later on. *Maybe that's what Liverpudlian people do*, I thought; *live off sausages and liver while their dogs get the steak. Maybe dat's...er, that's where the 'liver' part of Liverpudlian comes into the picture!*

**

About two weeks later I received a telephone call from a woman who told me I was a winner in a promotion I had entered recently. I was thrilled.

"Oh, what have I won?" I said happily, hoping it was the four-wheel drive vehicle. Alas, it was not.

The woman told me I had won a personal alarm, plus a small book about home security and there were one or two other small things I had won as well, those being pamphlets about keeping oneself safe. My heart sank a little. But, as I consoled myself, it was better than nothing.

"One of our representatives will deliver it for you," the woman said. "You just name a day when you will be home this week and we will have him deliver it to you personally."

"Oh, why can't you just send it to me by mail?" I asked warily.

"No, we don't work that way. We like our winners to have their prizes delivered to them personally," she said in warm tones.

"How nice," I said warily. "What's the catch?"

"There is no catch at all," she said, her voice light and charming. "Well, congratulations again and enjoy your prize."

She rang off and I was left wondering, why such a fuss about such a small prize?

"Da person who comes around here to give you your prize will try to sell you something, woman. You mark my words," Reilly said.

I had the sinking feeling he was right.

**

A large, smiling, ultra-charming man complete with identity badge swinging from his suit lapel came to visit me the next day.

"Hello! My name is Trevor and I'm here to deliver your prize to you!"

"I will sink my claws into his leg, if he gets too close," Reilly said warningly.

"I don't think you need worry," I said.

"Pardon?" said Trevor.

"I was just talking to my cat."

"Oh, ha ha! Many of my lady clients do that very thing too!" he said in a too-cheerful voice.

"Dat's coz they find your conversation so boring they would rather talk to their cats!" Reilly snarled.

"What's the matter with your cat? He seems very aggressive, I must say. Is that wise to have such an aggressive cat?"

"What do you mean, aggressive? Reilly is my watch cat. He does an excellent job of it too!" I defended. "Now, can I make you a cup of coffee or tea?"

"I wouldn't give dat man anything, woman! He's trying to sell you something you don't need and can't afford anyway!"

I smiled at Reilly, and swung my gaze back to the security man. He was still smiling and eyeing me in a way I did not care for.

"A cup of coffee would be most pleasant and then we can get down to business!"

"Business? I thought you were here to deliver my prize to me?" I said as I went about making coffee and putting biscuits on a plate.

"Don't give him any chocolate ones, woman! Dat man is too fat as it is!"

I compromised by putting some gingernut biscuits as well as chocolate ones on a plate.

"Dat man will take da chocolate ones, you mark my words!"

"Your cat does seem to yowl a lot," Trevor remarked, still smiling, although I noticed his smile was not as wide as when he first arrived on my doorstep.

"Actually, he's talking to me," I said gently, doing my best not to let a grin escape.

"Oh yes? And what does he say?" said Trevor, taking two chocolate biscuits off the plate.

"Cat talk," I said, my stomach beginning to knot with mirth as I watched him stuff the chocolate biscuits in his mouth, two at once. "Anyway, what's this business you are talking about?"

"Well now, if you would just sit down like a good girl, we can get started," he said smoothly, while licking biscuit crumbs from his fingers. I figured he had that down pat, after all the biscuits and cakes he ate at ladies' houses. I eyed his protruding stomach with disgust. My hackles rose at his statement and I longed to knock the smoothness from his voice. A good whack across the kisser would have done the trick, I thought. I looked at the prize I had supposedly won, as Trevor showed each part of it, handling the small items as if they were made of gold and rubies.

I agreed privately that the personal alarm worked very well.

Reilly and Chloe both shot out of the house at top speed when Trevor demonstrated how well the alarm worked. I felt like smacking my ears to get them working again. The ringing was still in my head several minutes later. Then he showed me a tiny booklet on how to keep one's house safe and a couple of small pamphlets along the same lines. These latter three things were part of a *prize?* Sheesh! Prior to giving me these items, he'd asked me about a dozen questions on personal safety; what did I do to ensure my safety in the house, did I live alone, etcetera. I told him I did not go around telling people I lived on my own...in any case, that would technically be a lie, as I had my two cats with me.

The fact that I answered all his questions correctly appeared to annoy him. Here was one blonde who knew how to take care of herself, seemed to be the unspoken statement. Oh *drat*, could have been his next thought, if his face was anything to go by.

"So now I will take you through this book I have with me..."

"Alice in Wonderland?" I asked, tongue in cheek. "Through the looking glass into the book?"

"Oh, ha hahahaha...no, not quite!"

His laugh was grating on my nerves, but fortunately, there were other amusing things about the whole scenario to keep my humour in good order.

"What, then?"

"This good book we use for our prospective clients."

"I was not under the impression I was a client, prospective or otherwise," I said suspiciously.

By this time Reilly had re-entered the dining room where we were seated at the table, Trevor next to me with his fancy flip catalogue, oozing the scent of cologne...Trevor that is, not the catalogue, although I would not have been surprised if that was part of his sales pitch. You know - have the scent of lovely men's cologne waft to a lady's nostrils each time he flipped a page over. Hmmm...now that I am thinking about that, I *do* believe a waft of cologne wafted to me each time Trevor flipped a page over. I had been slightly puzzled about the amount of wafting that was going on. It was then obvious that it was a set-up for all prospective clients; wafting cologne, not only from the sales agent, but also from the book in question...giving subliminal messages. The perfume is gorgeous, and therefore the product will be too.

But I hadn't come down in the last shower.

"He's gonna try and sting you for thousands of dollars," Reilly said as he came to sit near me. I was willing Trevor not to get smart with me, because Reilly would have bitten his leg, for sure. "He's using that fancy smell to get you under his spell! Oh my goodness me, I am a *poet* again!"

I fought the urge to laugh.

"So, here we go now..." Trevor began.

"Are you trying to *sell* me a security system?" I said a few moments later. As if I didn't already know what he was driving at! "Is this some kind of false advertising?"

Trevor looked alarmed, so to speak. "Oh, I'm not pushing you into *any*thing, Amber Jo. My main interest is in making sure you and your house are *safe*, Amber Jo!"

Another lie, I thought. Reilly echoed my thoughts.

"Sure an' dat man is a big liar an' all!"

I gave a chuckle, but of course Trevor didn't know that I was chuckling at Reilly. He took it as my assent for him to continue. And so he did, with me interrupting him every so often to tell him that he was wasting his time; that I could not afford a security system, and would not be able to in the foreseeable future, either.

"What about cats? Is the system affected by cats coming in and out?"

"Well Amber Jo, you have to realise that this system is recognised as a world leader and that it is very sensitive..."

"I have known of many world leaders who were *any*thing but sensitive!" I said, with a little more heat in my words than I had intended.

Reilly chuckled gleefully, over and over.

"What's the matter with your cat, Amber Jo? Is he having a fit or something?"

"No, he's laughing."

Trevor's eyes went very cool, although he tried to keep warmth instilled in his voice. It didn't work.

"Oh yes, ha ha, I must say. Rather amusing, Amber Jo."

I knew that the frequent use of a prospective client's first name was a marketing ploy, but he didn't know that *I* knew that. I was surprised that the ploy hadn't been dropped from marketing seminars long ago, as I found it most annoying. And if I found the very frequent use of my first name annoying, then I knew I could reasonably assume that many other people did too.

"How much does this system cost?"

"Have a guess."

"Guessing games, eh? Why don't you tell me outright?"

"Bearing in mind, my dear Amber Jo, that this is a very sensitive system..."

"You didn't tell me before whether it was affected by cats or not," I interrupted, already of the belief that this man was an out and out *prat*.

"Well, actually, yes, it is *that* sensitive. If a cat walks in front of the beam, the alarm would go off. We do allow up to five callouts over a short period of time, but if there are more then we have to charge for it."

I saw dollar signs flashing before my eyes...oh yes, alarms were definitely ringing!

"Then there is absolutely no point in my having an alarm, is there? You have seen that I've got two cats. The alarm would be going off all the time!"

"Well...there is an alternative..."

"Oh yes, and what's that?"

"You could find new homes for your cats."

Too late to stop him, Reilly sunk his teeth into the man's leg.

"Ow! Get this cat off me!"

"You shouldn't have said what you did," I said with a grin.

"*Lady*, (oh, so I was *lady* now, and not '*my dear Amber Jo*') I can see with half an eye that you already have a security problem *inside* your house!" Trevor rubbed at his leg after Reilly reluctantly let go.

"Well, I did tell you that Reilly is my watch cat, and you suggested I get rid of him and Chloe. He heard what you said and didn't like it. And frankly, neither did I."

Trevor looked abashed. "Only trying to do my job," he mumbled.

"Well, of course you are!" I said, feeling just a tad sorry for him. His face still looked pained. Perhaps I should tell Reilly not to bite quite so hard in future, depending on the circumstances, that is. "Now, about the price, and don't make me guess, although I would imagine a system such as this would cost at least two thousand dollars."

"Perhaps I should show you."

Gee, he still *couldn't tell me*, I thought.

Trevor flipped over to the last page (another few wafts of expensive male cologne...*commissions on security systems must be pretty good*, I thought) which gave a blatant message about how much do you value your safety, the safety of your family and that of your home and pets? Would you even *dare* to put a price on the safety of your family, home and pets, blah blah...

"Three thousand, four hundred dollars?" I exclaimed when I saw the price written boldly in red. "Is this for real? But there's hardly anything to it!"

"You can pay it off, if you want," Trevor said quickly, aware that he was fast losing a possible sale.

Correction, he never stood a chance of a sale in the first place, and as soon as he suggested that I find new homes for my cats, well...there was even *less* than *nothing* of a deal!

"What did I tell you, woman? Dat man wanted thousands of dollars outa ya!"

"Yes I know, cat," I said, and Trevor looked at me oddly.

"Could you manage to pay it off in monthly instalments?"

"Look, all throughout your visit, I have been busy telling you that I cannot afford your security system, whether outright, by time payment over the next ten years, or ever. But you have been busy ignoring me all the time. And, quite frankly, what is the good of having a system that's going to send out an ear-piercing sound every time one of my cats walks through the beam? Would you people pay for my cats to have therapy afterwards?"

"We don't do cat therapy," he said crisply. For a wee small moment I thought he was going to turn out to be a genuinely nice, kooky guy with that statement, but when I looked at him, he wasn't even smiling.

"A pity," I said with a grin. "There are not enough cat therapists around. Have you considered a change in career?"

Trevor got swiftly to his feet, not amused at me at all.

"Do you offer to pay for tests for the hearing impaired... namely me...*now?*"

"We don't do hearing tests," he said, looking grimmer than ever.

"A pity," I repeated. I'm sure my grin must have been even wider than before, despite the persistent ringing in my head resulting from the shrill alarm. "I'm sure I have just been deafened."

"I have to make a phone call!" he announced, ignoring my last comment.

I had a sudden feeling it was going to be to the lady who had phoned me about my 'prize'.

"Are you going to phone Kath?"

Trevor looked at me warily. "Yes, as a matter of fact, I am. How did you know?"

"Just a feeling I had," I said smoothly. "I'm a bit like that you know. Some people have even called me 'spooky'. By the way, everyone who entered that promotion received the same things, didn't they?"

"Er...yes..." Trevor said hesitantly.

"So it wasn't really a nice little prize at all, was it? That's false advertising! It's just a lure to get into people's houses and try to sell them your security systems for inflated prices that would way more than cover any giveaways as well as your commission and the security system itself."

"Well, I suppose so. So...are you interested?"

"I have to give you full marks for one thing, Trevor."

"Oh yes? What's that?"

"Persistence, even after I have said *no* to you at least a dozen or so times during this visit."

"I should bite him again, I should!"

"No, don't bite him, Reilly. Let his make his phone call and we'll say goodbye to him."

Trevor glared at us both even though he was smiling again, but his eyes gave him away. He made the call from my foyer and we could hear every word.

"No...she's not interested. She's got a cat that would scare off any burglar. She's...the woman that is, is small and blonde with a lot of long hair...you'd think she would have been a pushover, but she's not to be trifled with!"

"He got dat bit right! *I* know you can be soft, but you can be tough with blokes like dat!"

Trevor took his leave a few minutes later, not realising we'd heard what he told the lady Kath.

I watched Trevor walking down my driveway. "Hey!" I called to him. He spun around. "You mean I don't get the four-wheel drive vehicle?"

"Not a chance!" He snapped.

"Maybe there wasn't one at all...maybe that was just another ruse to get people interested! Most people love a free promotion or a raffle."

"You've got it wrong, lady!" Trevor snapped, beginning to turn on his heel again. For such a big man, he was surprisingly nimble on his feet.

"Oh no, I've got it right! I've just saved three thousand, four hundred dollars today! Yippee!"

Trevor spun back on his heels. Any minute now and he'd start leaping like a ballerina. I hoped he would. I badly needed some entertainment, although to give him his due, Trevor had already provided entertainment of a sort for the past couple of hours.

"Isn't it a lovely day!" I called to Trevor as he got into his car.

"Is it?" he said shortly.

"Oh yes indeed! To reiterate, I've just saved a lot of money today, namely - three thousand, four hundred dollars! It's been a really lovely day for me!"

Trevor drove off with a squeal of his tyres. I had a final glimpse of his face, looking grimly forward.

"You are becoming a curmudgeon woman," said Reilly, who was sitting at my feet, on the driveway. He appeared to be smirking.

"Curmudgeons are miserly, ill-tempered people," I told Reilly as we went inside.

"Dat's what I mean! Fancy depriving dat man of a sale. You didn't give me a chance to bite him again!"

"Journalism and life has taught me a thing or two," I said crisply.

"Yeah, dat you are only a pushover when it comes to *animals!*"

"Not always, Reilly," I smiled. "But I do thank you for biting that man! I felt a bit like doing that myself, but I did not want to be grovelling at his feet."

Chloe came wandering back inside.

"Has that awful man gone?"

"Yes, Chloe, he's gone."

"Thank goodness! My ears are still ringing after that demonstration he did. I will probably have tinnitus permanently after this!

"You can put a ring around dat one, woman!" Reilly snickered, and ran off, giving Chloe a playful bopping on his way.

I thought I heard him singing Abba's big hit 'Ring, Ring', but maybe I'd got that wrong. Maybe it was the ringing still in *my* own head!

***

CHAPTER NINETEEN

"Call Me Gypsy"

I had been feeling a bit unsettled for a while, and realised that it truly was time to seriously consider moving on again. It was already October, and although we still had the rest of spring and summer to go through, I knew I could not bear another winter in the house. I'd talked to the cats about another move months before, but the days had drifted by while I considered my options. The truth is that I didn't have many.

Pamphlets began appearing in the mail, promoting Halloween. Although so many people believe it's a fun time, the origins of Halloween put me right off. Besides, I did not like the more-than-a-hint of extortion, when people came to my house and demanded sweets or anything else I could give them, or else they would give me a nasty fright.

"I *told* you that you're a curmudgeon, woman," Reilly said one day when I had voiced my opinions to him.

"Then that makes two of us!" I retorted. "What about people who have a nervous disposition? What if one of them answered the door and an ugly witch or warlock, or someone with one of those horrible rubber masks let out a big BOO! That person could die of a heart attack!"

"What if! What *if!*"

"I'm stating just *one* possibility!" I reminded him. "I don't think it's nice going around frightening people!"

"*You* would have no trouble doing it! You would only have to stand there and knock! One look from those steely blue eyes of yours and that'd be *it!*" Reilly said, and then ran off before he could hear my wrathful words.

**

On the evening of Halloween, some people 'dressed to kill' came to my door. I watched them from my lounge window, where I knew they could not see me. There were small witches and a couple of big warlocks, as well as a big man in ordinary casual clothing.

"Trick or treat, trick or treat!" they called. And when I did not go to the door, one of them added: "If you don't come to the door, we'll come in and *find* you!"

And I'll have you charged with breaking and entering, I thought wrathfully, wishing I had a megaphone and one of those ugly rubber masks complete with warts, gaping wounds, big crooked nose and ugly, bulging eyes. Why, if I had, I would have gone to the door, opened it with a flourish and yelled: "BOO!" through the megaphone. That would have set them rocking on their feet!

My friend Bob phoned. I told him how I felt and what I would have liked to do.

"No need to go to all that trouble," he said drolly.

"Why not?" I asked. "I think it would be a good idea! They'd think twice about coming to my house again!"

"No, just show them your cat. That would be enough to frighten the life out of anyone!"

"What? You mean Reilly? Ohhh, that's *awful!*"

"No, I meant the other one. Whatshername...Chloe. Ugliest cat I have ever seen. It gave me a hell of a fright I can tell you, when I saw her face!"

Bob can be such a kidder. But he'd said something of that nature one other time. All the same, I was glad Chloe could not hear what Bob said. She would have been very hurt.

"Did I hear my name?" Reilly asked, striding inside as if he had been for a wonderful, leisurely walk, which I have no doubt is what he had just been doing.

"Yes you did. I'm talking to Bob on the phone."

"Who've you got there? A boyfriend?" Bob wanted to know.

"No, my cat Reilly," I said.

"Talk to your cats like humans, do you?"

"Of course I do!"

"I suppose they understand you too, do they?"

"Oh yes indeed! We have great conversations at times!"

"Bloody bonkers, if you ask me!" Bob said snappily. "I can't stand cats."

"Then you must have a very deprived life," I said coolly, thinking of the time recently when Big Mike had also said I was bonkers.

"They're always scratching up my nice garden and tearing out my new plants," Bob complained. "And leaving their calling cards dug into my garden!"

"That's one way to get your attention!" I retorted.

Not surprisingly, soon after we rang off. Bob said he wanted to get to bed. I knew he went to bed early, so that was reason enough, but had we not had the small exchange about cats, I'm sure he would have wanted to chat longer.

I went looking for Chloe to give her an extra cuddle, simply because I felt bad about Bob's remarks about her and cats in general, even though the remarks, some of them anyway, *were* quite funny. Chloe was sitting on my bedroom windowsill, sound asleep, but when I entered, she fell off, half asleep still. She shook her head and blinked a couple of times as if to say: 'who pushed me?'

**

Christmas came and went, with plenty of church activities to go with it. One morning after returning from a service, I had the desire to go to the shopping centre and see if there were any free realtor books left. There was, just one, and one was all I needed. I took it home and lay on my bed, thinking about our future. I had a talk to God about it.

"And what did He say?" Reilly asked, landing on my bed with a thud. I was now sleeping in the small spare bedroom that I normally kept for guests. It was too noisy for me to stay in the main bedroom any longer and despite being in Parklands for just over two years at that stage, I still had not become used to the sound of traffic.

"I have the conviction that I should go ahead and see if we can buy a place of our own."

"Back on the West Coast?"

"No, but certainly near the beach, so we can go back down there again."

"It's far too cold on this side of the island. Those easterly winds fair cut a body in half!"

"It's not that way in summer," I said.

"No, it's far too *hot!* I want a milder climate! I want to go where I can hear the birds properly...somewhere I can go stalking and wandering without fear of a car running me down."

"You hear the magpies here," I reminded him.

"I'm fed up with magpies!"

"You don't want much, Reilly. Perhaps you should go and look for a house for us to buy! Perhaps *you* could make the negotiations."

"You are a silly little woman! How would I do that?"

"You told me you could write, and that you are Reilly the Wonderful, etcetera...I thought you could do *anything!*"

"Oh I can," Reilly said airily. "But I don't see why I should have to, when there is a perfectly good little woman here who can do the work."

"You called me silly a moment or so ago."

"And so you can be too. All that feminine mush and gush. But I do agree you can be useful at times."

"Big of you!" I said waspishly. "Anyway, I have told God that if He means us to stay in Christchurch, He has to give us the means

187

to buy our own place, otherwise we're moving right out of the district. I can't bear the thought of ever having to rent again."

"I think I like that idea of having our own house. What about you, Chloe?"

Chloe had just walked sleepily into the room.

"What about me?"

"Wanna move house – into our own? The woman's finally made up her mind to shift again."

"I don't mind if I do. As long as there's enough room for us all."

"Good, then that's what we shall do. I am going to put things into action today."

"You've got no money, woman."

"No, but I do have a lot of faith!"

"I think you'll be needing it."

**

Those were the same words the real estate agent said to me when I looked at one place. It was a three-bedroomed unit, one of two, with a gorgeous kitchen. Brand new whiteware went with the property and I was delighted. I thought I could sell off some of my own whiteware, put the money towards lawyer's fees and perhaps there would be some left over to go towards the agent's fees.

But it was not to be. A person came along offering cash for the property and that was that. I was disappointed and told Reilly and Chloe about it.

"You've often told me that there is always a reason for things turning out the way they do," Reilly informed me. Chloe just sat there looking at me with her huge eyes blinking owlishly.

"Yes, and I still believe that. Maybe there was something wrong with the drainage or something."

"I'm sure you'll find out, woman."

I did find out, just a month or so later. The neighbourhood had deteriorated, according to a friend who knew the area well, with hoons causing disturbances late at night, driving at high speeds up and down the road, and houses had been broken into.

When the agent had phoned to tell me that the unit had been sold, he told me about another place, which I had a look at. It was even nicer than the first, and still near the beach. It didn't have whiteware to go with it, but I decided that whatever the situation, it was part of God's Plan. It was a rent-to-purchase situation and I knew I could manage it.

"You still don't have any money, woman!" Reilly snapped when I told him I'd had a look at the unit.

"All the money in the world is God's, and if He chooses to have me stay in Christchurch, then He will choose a way for us to have that place."

"If you say so, woman."

"Oh ye of little faith. I have been told many times that I am a very determined person, and this is just another time when I am going to live up to my reputation!"

"Steely, would be the word."

"Whatever. I don't care. I refuse to rent in Christchurch again."

"That's telling him, Mother," said Chloe.

"Oh, so the cat can speak, can it? I was wondering."

"Well Reilly, you can wonder no more. Of course I can speak, as I have done so before, but you do most of the talking around this place anyway. I can hardly get a word in. Why, I was almost forgetting how to speak!"

"The fat little round girl cat is also sarcastic."

"I have to make the most of the time when I *do* get the opportunity to speak."

I was amused at their exchange. It always made me feel better when Chloe had her say. It was good to see Reilly put in his place for a change, even though I knew it wouldn't last for long.

**

If ever I thought I was a determined person, then I had to pull out all stops this time. The fact was, mortgage brokers tended to put me in the 'too hard' basket.

"But I don't drink, nor do I smoke. I don't have magazine subscriptions, I don't go to movies or nightclubs or the pub. I live very simply and frugally. Surely that's got to count for something?"

"Perhaps. But what do you do for entertainment?" asked one mortgage broker, whom I am sure smiled so rarely that it was a surprise to him when he actually *did* smile, because of the different facial muscles he had to use.

"I go to the library, or go for walks. I watch television and I write. And I have my cats for company. They can be most amusing."

"I bet," the man said doubtfully, eyeing Reilly who was eyeing *him* with a jaundiced eye. Reilly began to growl. "I'd say that having a cat like this would be a hazard."

"He hasn't bitten you yet, has he?" I said, trying not to laugh.

"No, but is he likely to?"

"Oh yes, he *could* be! Perhaps if you say yes to a mortgage for me, he won't bite you!"

"I do not succumb to bribes like that!" he snapped.

Sheesh, the man had no sense of humour whatsoever.

"Dat man has no sense of humour," Reilly said, echoing my thoughts.

"I know he doesn't," I replied, looking down fondly at him.

"You talk to your cats too?"

"Of course I do," I said sweetly. "Doesn't everyone?"

"No, they do not," the mortgage broker said firmly.

"More's the pity," I said. "They must lead very deprived lives. Having a cat or two in the house is good for the soul."

"Well now, let's get down to some more business," the mortgage broker said briskly. "What size deposit do you have?"

"I don't have one at all!" I said airily.

"Then what makes you think you can get a mortgage?" He said tersely.

"I saw in the realtor magazine that one company would lend up to 100% of the value of the property."

"Yes, but that depends on the circumstances."

"And what are those?"

"Mainly that there are two people in the household, both with good jobs."

"Then they should have stated that criterion, rather than give people like me false hope." I sat back with a smile. "But I *do* have something else to offer!"

"What might *that* be?"

"I have *faith!*" I announced.

"Then you'll be needing a great deal of that!"

"I've heard those words before, but you know, I am not the sort of person to give up easily!"

The mortgage broker packed up his briefcase. He gave a very small smile that did not reach his eyes. "I wish you well. Faith or not, it's money you need. If you had a deposit, now *that* would make all the difference." As he was about to go out the door, he added: "put it this way, it's highly unlikely, but not *improbable* that you would get a mortgage, given your circumstances."

"I do not give up easily!" I said with a wide smile. "We shall see what we shall see."

"I wish you well then." It was obvious he had no intention of getting back to me with other options I might consider in my endeavours to buy a property. I didn't care. He never did get back to me, not that I was expecting him to do so, but I had often read that success was in the follow-up. So...I would do following up of my own. There were other brokers around, even though the first one, a young woman, had already given up on me.

The real estate agent phoned me to ask how I was getting on with finance. I told him 'not so good', but I wasn't going to give up. He was more helpful than either of the brokers had been. He put me in touch with another one, a woman, and from there, things were set in action.

It took months of work and determination, with even the lawyers' receptionists getting short-tempered and beginning to argue with each other, but I thought of the line from a stage show, 'Always look on the bright side...' and so I did. I even laughed when my lawyer's receptionist told me bluntly: "Amber Jo, you have to be one of the most tenacious people I have ever known!" My response to that was to tell her that the sky would not fall in if the transaction was not completed by a certain day, and anyway, God knew all about it! She'd given a small snort that I interpreted to mean that she thought God must have taken a few weeks off, then. I smiled anyway, knowing that it was all part of God's Plan. Besides, as I'd also told the receptionist, I couldn't see any people beating a path to the door in the hopes of purchasing the apartment I was in, so I felt I was safe. The receptionist gave another snort. Maybe she was working herself up into a possible scenario with the other woman, in which she, the first woman, would win hands down, of course.

But despite all the scenarios, real and imagined, finally my cats and I moved into our new home, just before winter set in. I was warm and happy and the cats settled in right away, even though there was a smaller back yard, albeit a very pretty one.

God had answered my prayers again. And the receptionist would have to revise her thoughts about God taking time off!

***

CHAPTER TWENTY

"The Early Bird Catches The Worm"

It took a few weeks for me to recover financially from the big move, but the thought of less work to do around the house was bliss. It was a light and airy place and the ladies who had owned it were so sweet and patient while the lengthy process of purchase-by-instalment was going through. I had everything I could have wished for, even though I knew it would be two years maximum that we would live there.

How did I know that? Because God had told me so. The first time I walked around the house while it was still empty; the morning I took over ownership and had brought over my first carload of gear, I walked around the house and it was then I was told I would have the house for a maximum of two years.

"Okay God, if it's two years, then I am grateful for that." And I meant it. A lot could happen in two years.

One of the first major things to happen was when I told my cats soon after moving into the new house that they would need worm tablets. I was sitting at the dining table, enjoying the late afternoon sun streaming through the big kitchen window and casting a glow off Reilly's fur.

"I absolutely *refuse* to take that stuff!"

"I refuse too, actually," Chloe said mildly, while washing her paws.

"Then you both shall have worm paste."

"I shall *not* have worm paste! Have you any idea what that stuff tastes like, woman?"

"Of course I haven't! I am not a cat. But our mother made my sisters and I take some medicine many years ago, because she thought we were eating too much. She thought we had worms, but we were simply growing girls and there wasn't much to eat anyway. Times were very tough then!"

"Eccentric, was she?" Reilly smirked.

"Oh yes she was."

"It shows!"

"It does?"

"Oh yes," Reilly mimicked. "It shows in *you!*"

"I have to be eccentric, to put up with *you!*" I retorted. "By the way, that medicine we had to take - looked like syrupy blood."

"Yuk! Maybe that's what it *was!*" Reilly leaped onto the table and loomed in close to my face. "Hmmm, are you really a vampire in disguise?"

"Certainly not!"

"But you just told us dat you and your sisters were given syrupy blood to drink as a medicine."

"I did *not* say that! I said the medicine Mum gave us *looked* like syrupy blood! We didn't need it anyway. We were young teenagers and growing fast. Gee Reilly, you sure can twist things around!"

"Gee I love it when you get angry! Do you realise, woman - that as long as your hair is, it still seems to stand on end? A *miracle!*"

"That should be an interesting sight," I said, cooling down.

"Believe me, it *is!*"

Reilly leaped off the table and ran away chuckling. He returned a moment later to add: "spray some starch on it when it's on end like that and you could be used for a chimney sweep – a very *wide* chimney, dat is!"

"Luckily, we don't have a chimney here," I said mildly.

"Yes, lucky for you, isn't it?"

"Ah bien, c'est la vie," I replied.

"Er, I think that's French, woman. I thought you were supposed to be learning Spanish?"

"I still am, but not the same now. Singing has almost taken its place completely."

"Yes, I hear you singing like a little bird...correction, *big* bird, every day. Why do you think we clear off outside?"

"You don't like my singing?" I was immediately on the defensive. Hmmm...now that I think about it, I was often on the defensive, when it came to my cats' remarks.

"It's not that. We cats have very sensitive hearing."

"So you *don't* like my singing then?"

"I told you it wasn't that. You're just very *loud*."

"Huh, I'm loud, I'm eccentric and silly...what other compliments do you have for me?"

"Do you really want to know?"

"No, I don't think I do. Now, I'm off to do my singing...like the bird you think I am. Hey...which reminds me...you *very* cleverly got off the subject of being wormed!"

"Darn it all! Another strategy bites the dust! Chloe, head for da hills!"

"Oh no you don't!" I quickly closed the latches on the cat door so they couldn't escape and fetched the worm tablets. With a flourish born of years of practice, I sat Reilly down in such a way he did not have an escape route and popped a worm tablet down his throat, then massaged his neck to ensure he didn't spit it out.

"Arrrgh! I *hate* you, woman"! He glared at me and stalked off under the table to smoulder in silence.

"And now Chloe, it's your turn. Come here sweetie," I coaxed.

I took hold of her and tried all sorts of tricks to get a tablet down her throat, but she too, had had years of practice in *avoiding* worm tablets being pushed down her throat.

"Nah nah, nah, na nah nah!" Reilly taunted, sing-song. "Mumsy-wumsy can't get a little pill down Chloe's throat! You *should* be able to. Chloe's got a fat enough head!"

"You are a nasty horrible cat, Reilly! Arghh! Get away from me!" The last part was said when I made another attempt to worm her.

I gave up in the end. She was stressed enough as it was. I hadn't given up completely though. I fetched the worm paste, which I remembered I'd had to use on her in the past – and within a few seconds it was all over.

"Huh, I didn't like you doing that much, but at least the flavour was nice!" Chloe said, licking her lips.

"What did it taste like?"

"Chicken liver, actually. One of my favourites."

"Why didn't you give *me* paste?" Reilly complained.

"I thought you would rather get it over and done with quickly. Do you *like* the idea of having internal parasites?"

"Don't be silly. Of course I don't. But if humans are supposed to be so clever, why haven't they discovered a nice way to get rid of parasites? Why haven't they..."

"They have," Chloe butted in. "I've just eaten some of it. Yum yum!"

"Gimme, gimme!" Reilly snarled at me from under the table.

"You are a greedy cat. You have had your dose and you are not getting any more for three months."

"In that case, I demand porterhouse steak for my dinner."

"*I* don't even get that! Now cats, let me get on with my singing."

"Uh oh, time to bail out, Chloe."

I unlatched the cat door and off they went, Reilly pausing to growl at the neighbour's tabby cat who had come to see what was going on in our house.

**

Soon after, the cats returned, prompted I am sure, by the scent of meat cooking. The cats were in a good mood and it was almost as if they had not gone through the business of being wormed. It appeared I had been forgiven again. Smiling to myself,

I went to the mailbox and to my delight, a letter was waiting there for me, from my friend Joe, who is American-born, extremely funny, and who lives in the far south of the South Island. I could hardly wait to open his letter.

The cats clamoured around me when I sat on the sofa, chuckling.

"What's happened down south *now?*" Reilly wanted to know. He's often heard me talking over the phone with Joe, and laughing fit to burst from time to time.

"Shall I read it to you?"

"What are you waiting for?"

"Okay. Here goes. Joe is telling me about the mugging of his dog Tip."

"His dog got mugged? Now what sort of a dog allows himself to get *mugged?*"

"A very stupid one," Chloe chipped in.

"A dog named Tip," I said.

"Well, I rest my case. Any dog named after a rubbish dump *surely* must be the kind of dog that allows itself to get mugged! Mind you, I have always considered dogs...oh must I puke again... to be rather stupid!"

"Why do you say 'must I puke' when you're talking about dogs?" Chloe asked, blinking her huge eyes at him.

"What, are *you* stupid too? It's because I feel a bit sick each time I mention the word dog. Ohhh...suddenly I don't feel well again!"

"Stop being such a drama queen...er, king, Reilly. Now, do you want me to read this, or don't you?"

"Get on with it, woman!"

I glared at him, and then I forgot my slight annoyance when I scanned through Joe's letter before reading aloud.

"'I think I may have told you about the recent mugging of my dog (actually, he hadn't). Well, no sooner did that occur - then here is my word picture of Ernie and two of his six pig dogs. Ironically, these were the two that gave him the trouble. It was

Patch that sniffed him under the rib cage, then blew out like it was a bad smell...'"

"The dog named Patch was sniffing under *Ernie's* armpit?" Reilly interrupted. "How *gross!*"

"No, Patch was sniffing under Tip's ribcage..."

"If the dog was doing that to another dog, named Tip, then I am not surprised Patch huffed out like he did. Tip probably smelled like his name...Tip, and a particularly stinky tip at that!"

"Stop interrupting, cat! Now, where was I?"

"Patch was busy sniffing under armpits," Reilly said with a smirk. "Not that I would ever do such a thing."

"Stop it Reilly! That wasn't what I said! Anyway, I remember you doing that to a guy once! You clawed him as well!"

"I most likely thought he smelled terrible!" Reilly smirked. "Oh yes, I remember dat man now, and he *did* smell terrible! Okay, get on with da story then, woman! Crumbs, do we have to wait around all day to hear the punchline?"

"If it wasn't for you interrupting me all the time Reilly, I would have already told you the story!" I snapped.

"Gee, and spoiled half the fun, too!" Reilly chirruped, and sat on his haunches in front of me, like a child being read to by his teacher. It was rather sweet, and even more so when Chloe came to sit next to him. Reilly glanced around as much to say: *who put this thing here? Oh well, it can stay for a while. It so happens I am in a good mood, and feeling particularly tolerant.*

"Back to the story, then. 'Mistake number one was to allow the dogs to sniff him. And then with five other dogs sniffing him all at the same time, he flinched. That was mistake number two. It was a dog named Jake that growled, another snarled and then it was all on for about fifteen seconds. Once Ernie snarled at *them*, they all scattered. But old Tip had quickly worked out which one of Ernie's dogs had snarled and then he took to Jake. Poor Jake wasn't even looking at his attacker, but for support from his mates. Of course they had already been snarled at by their master, so they just lost interest. Tip was doing a good job on Jake but I could see Ernie was getting apprehensive so with reluctance I called Tip off before Ernie stuck his pack of dogs back onto Tip. I had to laugh because Tip really had his hackles up, with a look on his face that said: "Treat me like that would you, you bastard!'"

Joe had added in his letter that not many people liked Ernie, although he, Joe did. It *had* to be that way because Ernie was a dangerous fellow – likely to shoot you if you squealed on him, glared at him in dislike or argued with him. Joe referred to him as 'Ernie, Ernie, and he drives the fastest drug cart in the West!' Well, in this case it was away down south, not to the west. Talk about having a different set of laws away down south! It was a similar situation on the West Coast too.

I gazed into space for a while until Reilly cleared his throat.

"Another story coming on?"

"Yes," I said as I put Joe's letter back into its envelope.

I remember one time when interviewing a really tough looking man named Lex. He told me he used to be with a biker gang, and I believed him. All the signs were there! And yet this man grew beautiful, healthy nursery plants, but the only ones I ever saw were the legal kind. Naturally he was too smart for a snoopy journalist and would have had any illegal plants well hidden from view - especially with knowing that he had an interview coming up with a journalist, namely, me. He asked me if I would like to see where his tame eels were and of course I said yes. I did wonder briefly if this was a new slant on 'wanna come up and see my etchings?' But Lex had been on his best behaviour so far and I had no reason to suspect that it would change. We tramped for several minutes through scrubland known as *pakihi*, due to its relative infertility. And indeed, soon we came to the small stream where Lex's tame eels were. While we were watching the fascinating big eels in the small, water-cress lined stream slither up to us, Lex told me about the time, not long before, when he was standing in almost the same spot when to his fright, an enormous man leaped out of the scrub, brandishing a wicked-looking meat cleaver. He asked Lex if he had seen anyone pass that way, and gave the description, explaining that the person he was looking for had been rustling his cattle. Lex said he hadn't seen him, and just as his heart was settling down to a reasonable rate, a second man came leaping out of the scrub – a more frightening looking person than the first one, although smaller. This man was waving a slasher, and there was no doubt in Lex's mind that if the man in question had been caught up with, he would have met an untimely death.

As Lex continued with his story, I asked him to describe a little more, the huge man brandishing the meat cleaver because I had a feeling I might have interviewed him. When we swapped more notes, he indeed was a man whom I had interviewed, and he truly is the largest man I have ever met. In fact, an absolute giant of a man – somewhere near seven feet in height, very strongly built and sporting a massive scar on his forehead. When I first met the man, on glancing at the huge scar I reasoned that either the man had been involved in a serious accident, or someone with a personal death wish had taken him on in a fight.

Perhaps the cattle rustler, years later, is still on the move!

I finished telling the cats this story and their response was simple: they yawned widely.

"I didn't think I was that boring!" I said with aspersion.

"You're not! We yawned because we wanna go back to the Coast."

"You're already on the Coast," I reminded him.

"I'm talking about the West Coast, as well you know."

"To my knowledge, Chloe has never been on the Coast!"

"Well who cares? I just like hearing about the West Coast, but it makes me homesick."

"But can't you hear the sea at night?"

"Of course I can, but it ain't the same!"

"So I keep hearing from you, cat," I said drily.

"Ya gonna hear it again and again, woman."

"So what's new?" I said, also yawning.

"A story! Give us a new story from Joe!"

"All right, I will, but just wait, will you, while I look for his other letter."

"There's no hurry, but make it snappy, would you?" Reilly said with a snigger.

I glared and walked into my bedroom, hearing Chloe say: "Actually Reilly, you can be rather an amusing cat. A pity you're so egotistical."

"If I don't love me, who will?"

"Mother, I would think. I can see she's a soft touch when it comes to animals."

"Lucky for us, eh?"

"I have to agree, lucky for us!"

Naturally, I never let on that I had heard them!

***

CHAPTER TWENTY-ONE

"Larry Feeling Sheepish"

I returned to the lounge and planted myself comfortably back onto the sofa, smiling as I withdrew Joe's next letter from its envelope. The man was so funny and didn't even know it. Perhaps that's the best kind of humorist, I thought.

"Hurry up, woman! We haven't got all day!" Reilly complained.

"And neither have I," I said shortly. "You cats should be grateful that I am prepared to sit here and read to you!"

"Don't hand us that one! You *know* you love to sit and read to us. You've been like that in all the years I have known you."

"A lot of years," I said with a small grin. "You is getting ter be an ol' puddy tat."

Reilly promptly sat up and looked large and very, very young.

"Sometimes you come out with ridiculous things. Now, are you going to read to us, or shall Chloe and I leave home?"

I smiled wider. "Leave home if you must, but I must inform you that I have some nice whipped cream in the fridge!"

"Gimme, gimme!" Reilly leaped onto my lap with a thud, reminding me that yes indeed, he was still very agile and also very big! Chloe too, rose up and tried to look big, but all she achieved by this was to make her look rounder than ever. Even her paws looked very round. As for her eyes, they were like saucers.

"Afterwards, cats, I shall give you a small treat of some whipped cream."

"Make it a big treat and I am your man."

"Don't you mean, cat?"

"Cat, schmat...whatever...and now for the story!"

"Okay, here goes...this is more about Tip the dog. 'Well, talking about Dog, did I tell you he has taken legal advice and is thinking of suing me for slander? It is really true! The days of "Man's best friend" are well and truly over, Amber Jo. That point was driven home to me today when I went out to get some firewood, and left the door open to the kitchen. Coming back, who did I meet on the way out but Dog. He had a pottle of butter in his mouth and when he saw me he almost dropped it. Almost, I say, as he quickly regained it and hoped that I had not noticed the pottle hanging off the end of his nose. I suppose I should have had a guilty conscience as I reluctantly removed it from his jaws. I have already told the government that I want him muzzled and a microchip inserted. I think they heard me and are following legislation along those lines.'"

"If I had a pottle of butter hanging from my mouth, I am sure you would notice," Reilly said.

"I am sure I would too," I replied with a smile. "I wonder if Joe actually did get a microchip inserted into Tip?"

"I think if he told the government officials the reason why, they would have him dismissed as an eccentric."

"You can be such a clever cat, Reilly."

"I know. All the time, actually." He yawned, as if to underline the fact that clever as he is, it was all very ho-hum, really. Chloe blinked at him several times. I knew she had his number. She just chose her times carefully, when she wanted him to know what she thought of him. Today was one of those times.

"How terribly dull for you, Reilly, being so smart, and the rest of us so inferior."

Reilly smirked. "If you say so, Chloe! Who am I to contradict your words of absolute truth?"

Chloe chattered at him in an annoyed fashion and turned back to me. "Please read us some more Mother. I can only take so much of Reilly's waffle."

"Clever waffle though," Reilly added.

"Stop it, you two. Now, where was I?"

"You were telling us about Joe's dog named Tip; the dog he sometimes refers to as...Dog. Suddenly I do not feel well."

"Go outside if you are going to be sick, Reilly. What a weak stomach you must have!"

"Only on occasion, when the subject of...ugh...dogs, is mentioned."

"Here's some more of Joe's letter, cats. He's telling me about Larry the Lamb."

"Flamin heck...lambs now eh? I well remember the lambie dog called Mickey. Ugh...I do not feel well again."

"Shut up Reilly, and let Mother read to us again. The longer you interrupt, the longer it will take before we get our cream!"

"Who do you think you are, Chloe? Speaking to a cat such as I, like that?"

"In case you have forgotten, my full name is Chloe Arabella and I am a purebred Blue Cream Shorthair Persian cat."

"*Short* being the operative word. Now woman, get on with the story!"

I sighed. "Are you sure you have finished?"

"Naturally!"

"Then I shall continue. 'Did I ever tell you the story about Larry the Lamb...?'"

"No you didn't but are about to," Reilly interrupted.

"That's what Joe is saying in his letter, Reilly! Stop interrupting me!"

"Yes Reilly, stop interrupting!" Chloe parroted.

"Stop it Reilly, stop interrupting, Reilly!" The big cat sniggered even while he mocked.

I continued with Joe's story. "'Well, Larry is no longer a lamb, or a ram, but a three year old whether, or wether, or is it weather? Anyway, he was born with a broken pelvis. At that time Michael's girlfriend from the U.K. was staying with him and she took pity on him...'"

"Took pity on whom? The lamb or the man?" Reilly interrupted yet again.

"The lamb, of course. I will continue, hopefully this time without interruption. 'So he (Michael) took Larry the Lamb to the vet and they placed him on medication, as well as set his hip. When it came time to go to his family's crib (small holiday home) at Lake Hayes, Larry had to have his medicine. So Michael loaded him into the Land Rover crate and took him on holiday. Later on, whenever they went on tour to Arrowtown or Queenstown (or is it Queerstown?), they would load Larry into the crate and show him the sights. Maybe it was this that made him so wacky, but he has never been a well-adjusted lamb and appeared to lack the usual graces associated with such creatures.

'But when the vet bill arrived, it cost Michael over four hundred dollars. Maybe that's why I was asked if I would take him onto my place. I thought it might be better if he recouped some of his losses, but Michael thought otherwise, so that is how Larry ended up here.'"

My cats both leaped up to sit beside me, one either side like little children eager to hear more of a favourite nursery story. It gave me such a wonderful feeling of well-being. I gazed at each in turn, smiling at them and stroking their silky heads. Sighing happily, I continued with the story.

"'Perhaps it was the fact that I don't take him on holidays, that he had such a dour attitude. Anyway, when he first landed at my place, he went and head-butted each and every ewe on my property. For weeks he would sit in one corner and they would sit in the opposite. In time they came to tolerate each other. The ewes came from Michael's place too, and I can thank him for those as well. They are great huge things that have never reared a lamb. No good as mothers, but great grass to crap converters. Well anyway, cutting a long story short, one of these "fat ass" things went down where I usually have my fires for burning rubbish. But it was first thing in the morning in the middle of a drought. This poor thing had been cast all night. She was trying to get up when Larry came along and saw this great huge rear end flapping around. Well, he just saw "red", and you could almost see his eyes bulging out. As she rolled around immobilised, Larry pawed the ground, took one step back and charged! He hit her straight in the rear and she plopped up on all four feet. She stood there, half-dazed for a minute, as if to say: 'Oh, I'm up.' Next thing was annoyance: 'Who dared do that?' When she looked behind her substantial rear she saw Larry standing there, still pawing the ground like a bull. She took off after him and they exchanged half a dozen head butts amidst the clouds of ash dust. What a sight! Meanwhile, I dropped to the ground in hysterics. Oh Amber Jo, what have I done to get all these eccentric animals?'"

"The man is a real eccentric, and attracts creatures of the same," Reilly said. "Just like *you* do, woman!"

"Think about what you just said, cat."

Reilly gazed at me for a moment. "I've thought about it."

"And?"

"And...nothing. My mind is a complete blank!"

"What, again?"

"There is no need to be sarcastic."

"It makes a change!"

"Harumph. I can see it's time for another story. We can't have the little woman getting bored and resorting to sarcasm, can we?"

"Indeed we cannot," I said with a grin, not put out this time, by the fact that he too was being sarcastic, and so ensuring the shift away from any further suggestion of his mind being blank. "What about a spooky story?"

"How spooky?"

"Not very, although the small flat I was living in *was* haunted."

"I don't want to hear the story if it's too spooky."

"What, my big strong cat...afraid of a ghost story?"

"It's not that at all! It's just that supernatural things make our fur stand on end...it gets very uncomfortable, y'know! Isn't that right, Chloe?"

Chloe turned and looked at him from across my lap. "I have a plush coat, in case you hadn't noticed. It does not stand up on end! It is not only very soft, but also very thick..."

"Like the rest of you!" Reilly butted in gleefully.

"I'm not speaking to you, Reilly..."

"Gasp! I am distraught! I am aggrieved!"

Reilly rolled over onto his back and gave a false mournful look. Neither Chloe nor I were fooled. Chloe yawned and gave him a disdainful look.

"Now, on with my story...I was living in this tiny haunted flat in Westport. All sorts of things would happen, such as the television blaring loudly on my return from a walk, even though I knew I had not turned it on in the first place, and also all the lights were switched on, when it was daylight when I went for my walk, and I am careful with power anyway, and would not have been likely to have all the lights turned on..."

"Frugal, isn't that the word?"

"Call it what you will. I was in no position to be extravagant with power, or with anything, come to that. There were other things that happened; framed photographs being turned around the other way, soft toys and other items found in places where I had not put them; feelings of great chill when I would be about to go to my bedroom. Ohhh, and so many other things that would make your hair stand on end. My friend Keith could only visit me for a short while. He'd sprawl out on the sofa and I'd be sitting in the armchair opposite, and then he would get a certain look in his eyes and I would say to him: 'ready to leave so soon, Keith?' and he would reply: 'I don't know how the hell you can stand living here!' I would reply to the effect that it was as good a place as I was likely to get, at least for the time being, and that I would move in due course. A ghost or two didn't frighten me.

"One of the main problems with the flat was the fact that it was right next to a railway line, so for the first five months or so I had broken sleep every night. By that time I was feeling rather ragged. Then one night I was actually beginning to have a lovely sleep, then a slight sound woke me suddenly..."

"A spook?"

"No, it wasn't a spook. I heard something just outside my window...it was just a faint sound that was like heavy breathing..."

"You should be so *lucky!*"

"Pipe down, Reilly, or I won't tell you the rest of the story!"

"Yes, do pipe down Reilly, there's a good chap...er, cat," Chloe said.

"I thought you weren't speaking to me?"

"I have been known to make concessions, depending on the circumstances."

"You surprise me, Chloe," Reilly said with a sly look on his face.

"In what way?

"I am surprised because there are times in which you actually sound quite bright."

"Here's another surprise, Bighead!"

Chloe leaped across my lap, hissing as she went and gave Reilly several boppings with her little round paw.

"Ugh! I *like that!*" Reilly said in surprise. "Well, I really like *that!* Huh!"

"Good! Because there is more of where this came from if you're not careful! Now shut up, because I want to hear the rest of the story!"

Chloe resumed her comfortable position next to me.

Reilly shut up, but every so often I would hear a muttered 'I'm gonna getcha' ...or at least, that's what it sounded like. I continued with my story, a part of me amused at Chloe's retaliation. She reminded me a little of myself...able to be pushed just so far... then look out!

"Anyway, as I was saying, there was this heavy breathing sound, then a kind of rustling sound. I lay there in the darkness, trying to work out what the noise could be. Was it a hedgehog? No, their sounds were very distinctive. Was it a night bird...?"

"Is it a bird? Is it a plane? No, it's Superman...er, superwoman!" Reilly interrupted yet again.

"I think that's a compliment! No, it didn't seem to be either, and suddenly I felt angry, because I suspected it was a person outside my window. I sat up in bed and tried to reach the light cord...one of those old-fashioned things. I couldn't find it, so scrambled out of bed and went into the tiny lounge and switched that light on. 'Right!' I said aloud. 'For the first time in months and months I was having a good sleep...and now it's been *ruined!* I'll fix whoever it is! YOU are *for* it, whoever you are!'

"I was still in my white night shirt. I rocketed around the back of the flat and saw the tail end of someone running away around the corner of the adjoining flat."

"Dat person is probably even now, years later still running, and recalling the most scariest night of his life! I thought you said dis wasn't a spooky story? Heh, heh, heh! By the way, did dat person ever come back? I just bet he didn't! As I said before, dat's probably coz he's still running!"

"No, never," I said, remembering the event as if it had happened only a few weeks before, instead of a few years ago. "That was before you came on the scene, Reilly. I mentioned the incident to an acquaintance of mine. He told me I should never have gone outside by myself. I told him in no uncertain terms that I had waited until I was sure there was just one person there and then I rocketed outside. Besides, as I had said to my acquaintance, named Jim, whoever it was got such a fright at seeing this woman in a white nightshirt with long hair flying that he probably thought *he* had seen a ghost!"

"Spooky, spooky!" Reilly sniggered.

"'What would you have done if you had been confronted by this person?' Jim had asked. 'Given him a jolly good punch in the nose!' I'd retorted."

"Ghosts seem to be getting scarier all the time! Now they don't just fly around corners, they also punch people! Chloe, be on the alert! Make sure you never go sniffing and breathing heavily under the woman's bedroom window."

Chloe gazed at him disdainfully from her position on the other side of my lap.

"I, Reilly, am not a heavy breather."

"Thank the gods for dat, then! Now, isn't there something you were meaning to give us, woman?"

"Yes," I sighed. "Some whipped cream."

I went to the fridge and retrieved the can of whipped cream.

"Gimme, gimme!" Reilly said, as he has done so over the years, whenever a can of cream has been in my hands.

I squirted cream into their bowls and watched them contentedly licking it up, while sitting side by side as though they were the best of buddies. Maybe one day they *would* be, I hoped.

***

CHAPTER TWENTY-TWO

"On My Knees Again"

I loved my new little apartment. It was pretty and there was no doubt that the two ladies who had lived there for the past nine years had also loved it. The many roses and other plants, and pretty drapes and clean carpet told me that.

Whenever I felt restless again, I reminded myself about the fact that I was there for a maximum of two years, and that I should make the most of it. It was noisy, but most of the neighbours were friendly and I thanked God for the blessing of good neighbours.

I also had a small garage with internal access. That was great, until the day when, in a hurry to go across the city to my friend Hubie's house, I tripped while going down the steps into the garage. I tried to save myself but didn't manage to. I hit my arm hard against the big internal sliding garage door and when that gave way, down I went, my right foot twisted awkwardly. I gave a yelp of pain.

The cats came to investigate.

"Why are you sitting on the floor?"

"I've hurt myself. I think I have twisted my ankle."

"That'll teach you for trying to do too much for too many people!" Reilly said with a gleam in his eyes.

"Well, thanks very much for your sympathy, I don't think!"

"Dis'll mean you have to stay home and pay attention to Chloe and me!"

"I already pay you two cats far more attention than most people would for their cats! Now, what about helping me up?"

"Think we're Amazons, or something?"

"Reilly, I swear you get ruder as you get older!"

"Dat's the privilege of getting older ...and smarter. Now, while you sit there and have a rest while you think about the best way of getting up, I am going to have a drink of water."

Off he went into the bathroom, and down into the toilet.

"Hey, I must admit the Christchurch City Council produces great water. Far better dan the West Coast stuff! Dis is even better than at Parklands, even though the water there was great."

Reilly's voice sounded muffled. Normally I would have been rather amused, but my ankle was hurting badly. I had promised Hubie I would help him with his gardening, and not being the kind of person to break promises, I managed to get to my feet. I phoned Hubie and said I would be running late as I had hurt myself.

Reilly emerged from the bathroom just as I was hanging up the phone. "Don't tell me you're still going across town when you look like dat?"

"Like what?"

"Washed out. Anyone would think you were in pain!"

"As if I wasn't used to it! Now cats, move out of my way, please. I have to get a few things ready."

"I tell you, Chloe, dat woman gets more stubborn as she gets older! If I were a bit bigger I would stop her from going."

"There is no fathoming the human mind," Chloe said as she scampered past me.

**

When I arrived at Hubie's lovely Housing Corporation unit some twelve kilometres away, I told him that I would be doing very little in the way of gardening, as I had fallen down my steps and was pretty sore.

"Did you say one for me while you were on your knees?" Hubie said humorously.

"I was too busy asking God to help me get up. You should be grateful that I am here!"

"Oh I am, I am!" Hubie said with a grin. "Let it be known to all and sundry that I am *very* grateful!"

Cheeky sod, I thought, and hobbled outside to start on some gardening. I didn't know which part of me hurt the most – my hip, ankle, elbow, neck or knee.

"You missed a bit there," Hubie remarked, while standing to one side and watching me with an eagle eye.

"Really?" I retorted. "Just be glad I am here at all!"

"By the way, say one for me while you're down there, as I mentioned before. I don't recall that you did that."

I'm sure I must have had smoke coming out of my ears by then.

"I'll say one for you all right, and it might not be a *prayer!*" I said testily, as I pulled out some oxalis.

"That's not very nice Nellie Kelly," He said mildly. "And here's me with me arthritic knees, sore back, pains in me joints and whatnot."

I did not ask what the 'whatnot' was. I might not have liked the answer! And he always called me Nellie Kelly when he knew my 'dander was up'. Well, it sure was up right now! My ankle throbbed mercilessly and so did my elbow and my knee, and I struggled to get up from my gardening and general weeding work. Without Hubie's help, I might add. My neck and hip had settled down to a steady throb of pain, but when I turned my head to one side my neck gave a loud click and immediately felt a bit better.

When I thought about it, I was amazed that I had driven across the city in heavy traffic, for over 12 kilometres. I did only a minimal amount of work for Hubie and went home. By now it seemed that every part of me ached unbearably.

"Look at you! Just *look* at you! You have to be the most stubborn woman I have ever known!" Reilly snarled when I returned, white faced and exhausted.

"Known many women?" I said sarcastically.

"A few," Reilly replied succinctly. He gave me a smug look. "Do you mean in the cat realm or human realm?"

"Either way, I don't care."

"Like I said, a few. Now woman, you look like you need a doctor!"

This was one of the few times I agreed with my big cat. Fortunately I was home in time to call up the doctor and explain what had happened. When I visited him the next day, he dismissed most of my pain, doing what so many busy doctors seem to do now, prescribe pain relievers and tell their patients to 'take it easy'. And that I should make another appointment with him if I didn't improve. I felt my visit was a waste of time and money.

Over the next few days the pain worsened. I called up a Swiss chiropractor, by the name of Steffan, who had been recommended to me and he was most sympathetic when I saw him.

"You poor little lady. You have a sprained ankle," he said after examining me. He checked out other sore spots. "Oh dear, you have a badly sprained left knee as well. Ohhh, look at your elbow! It is very large!" My right elbow was very inflamed and painful to touch. Steffan checked out my foot again. "You have some slightly dislocated bones here too," he added. "You must have fallen down a lot of steps!"

I felt embarrassed when I had to tell him that it was only a few, but that I had tried to save myself and in doing so, had caused further injury, some of it to my hip and neck. So, I needed an enforced rest, which was not easy for a person like me to take.

"Mother, isn't it about time you were kinder to yourself?" This time it was Chloe to have the say. She was right.

"I have too much to do," I said. "But I know you're right."

"But if you're using those injured limbs Mother, you won't be much good to us, will you? Who would look after us?"

There! I knew there was a motive behind her apparent sympathy!

"I would struggle along as usual!" I retorted.

"The last of the big martyrs!" Reilly sniggered.

"Go away you cats and leave me alone. I need some time to myself!"

"We want food, and we want it *now!*"

There was only one thing for it. If I was to have some peace, then food for the cats it had to be. I fetched some from the fridge.

"Room temperature would be nice," Reilly said loftily.

"A velvet cushion to sit upon perhaps? Some caviar and cream?"

"Gee thanks! *Now* you're talking!" Reilly sniggered again.

I tried to stalk out of the room in high dudgeon, but all I could manage was a painful hobble.

Somehow it didn't have the same effect.

**

Later that evening when I felt a bit better I remembered a situation a few years before when I'd fallen out of my friends' four-wheel-drive. Am I a clumsy person? No, I don't believe so, but arthritis and its aftermath can result in changes in walking habits. Muscle atrophy in my lower back meant that sometimes I did not raise my feet quite enough when walking, and hence the occasional accident.

I was in Balclutha, a small town in the far south of the South Island, visiting with my friends Kevin and Shelley Jenkins, who had moved to Balclutha to take up new positions, Kevin in management and Shelley in administration.

"Want to hear a story, cats?" I asked, my good humour restored, despite the throb in my knee, elbow and foot. And the persistent ache in my left hip.

"Is it a good one?"

"Do I ever tell bad stories?"

"No, but there's always a first time."

"Tell us, Mother!" Chloe added with her sweet little chatter.

"Okay. I was with Kevin and Shelley. We were getting out of their four-wheel-drive Lada when I tripped over the high sill. I was wearing a long skirt and didn't notice that the sill was as high as it was. I landed straight onto the concrete footpath outside the church. Shelley asked me if I was okay and I said yes, as I got to my feet and dusted myself down. My right hand stung from the impact and so did my right elbow..."

"Flinging yourself about the place again, woman? Haven't you learned yet that human flesh and concrete aren't a good combination?"

"Stop interrupting me! I am well aware that concrete does not have any 'give' to it, believe me! Anyway, off we went into church and after about ten minutes I felt this trickling feeling. I lifted my long skirt up..."

"You lifted your skirt in *church!* Well, I mean to say, what sort of a Christian woman *are* you?"

"A Christian woman in pain, I would think!" Chloe said. "Now Reilly do shut up and let Mother get on with the story."

"Sisters in arms, eh? Oh, how *cosy!*"

"Shut up Reilly!"

"Shut up Reilly, shut up Reilly!" he mimicked annoyingly.

"You are just the most *annoying* cat, Reilly! Anyway, I nudged Shelley and let her see the blood trickling down my leg. She nudged Kevin on the other side of her, and gestured to my leg. He calmly pulled out a handkerchief, handed it to Shelley who handed it to me and I calmly wrapped it around my knee. Soon it was time to go up to the altar to take communion. I couldn't kneel, so had to stand, mostly on one foot. Luckily I didn't fall over."

"You would have stolen the show!" Reilly said with glee. "Just imagine! Your skirt and petticoats up around your waist, bloodied bandage around your knee and blood still dripping, ta *dah!* All eyes would be on you."

"That's not what I wanted! I just wanted to go up for communion, say a prayer and quietly go back to our pew. Which is what I did. But when I sat down, I wondered why my sleeve hung the odd way that it did and then I discovered that it hung that way because the knit fabric had laddered when I fell onto the footpath. The lady vicar told me at morning tea afterwards that she had noticed it when I went up for communion, but didn't say anything as she thought it was the latest fashion!"

"Good heavens woman! See what an impact you made...pun intended or unintended! You even started a fashion trend. I *told* you all eyes would be on you."

"Well, they weren't. Not that I had noticed, anyway. So later on that day we decided to go for a walk up on the cliff top and visit an old lighthouse..."

"I told you earlier you are a martyr. A masochist as well."

I ignored his remark.

"On the way down the track, Kevin and Shelley followed. I had an idea they were keeping an eye on me. I tried not to limp."

'Are you limping, Amber?' Kevin had called.

"I wouldn't say that," I'd replied.

'What *would* you say, then? Have you got a sore leg, Amber?' Shelley called, the stiff sea breeze muffling her words.

"No," I'd replied, quite truthfully. My leg didn't hurt at all, but my knee was beginning to hurt.

'If I know you Amber, you'd have a broken leg and still say it was okay!' Shelley called.

"Oh, you could be right!" I called back cheerfully, the sea breeze trying to whip my words away.

**

Shelley's words were prophetic. That evening as I knelt on the lounge floor to study a large map, intense pain rocketed from my knee down my leg. I flew up in the air with the pain.

"I felt that!" Shelley said.

"Possibly not as much as me!" I returned, breathing heavily. I felt faint and nauseous, but glossed over it as best I could, not wanting to make a fuss.

I was supposed to return to Christchurch the next day but stayed another day, on their advice. It was good advice too, as the thought of driving for around six hours or so with a very sore knee did not enthuse me. Besides, snow was setting in and driving was too risky.

I drove back the day after and almost *fell* inside, exhausted.

"Oh yeah, I remember that incident! You told me about it then...gee I had almost forgotten it." Reilly was contemplative. "Dat was one time when you got the giant corncob to look after us! It would have been all right, except for dat stupid lambie dog… puke puke, er, God rest his soul. He was so *annoying!*"

"Yes, just like *you* can be, Reilly," little Chloe chattered in amusement. "Now, please let Mother get on with her story. She might give us some cream afterwards."

Chloe looked at me winningly.

"Of course I will," I said with a smile. Oh, what a pushover I could be, when it came to my cats!

"Anyway, the pain did not go away, and so after two weeks I visited a chiropractor who was also a specialist in other medical fields. He examined my knee. 'Oh my, no wonder you've been having trouble with this. You have a slight dislocation here.' With a firm tweak there was a 'clunk' sound and instant relief. I asked him if he would check out my shin as I had odd bruising down near my ankle. He did as I asked. 'Yes, you have a small hairline fracture here.' I told him what my friend Shelley had said. 'Well, she was more or less right, wasn't she?' he said good-humouredly.

"I went home amused and telephoned Shelley that evening. 'You remember when you said to me on the cliff top that I would probably still say I was fine even if I'd had a broken leg?' Shelley remembered well, she said. 'Er, it was fractured, just a hairline fracture though. And I had a slight dislocation to my knee.'

"You've been walking around on that?" Shelley asked. I replied that I had been. "That figures, you mad Irish washerwoman!"

"Why does she refer to you as a mad Irish washerwoman?" Chloe wanted to know.

"Hmmm…I think because we have Irish ancestry and perhaps when they have visited I have had washing on the clothes line or have been about to do some washing…"

"And the 'mad' bit?" Reilly interrupted, his big eyes gleaming with amusement.

"Perhaps they find me amusing in some way," I ventured.

Reilly gave a snort, which said a lot…just in that one short blast.

**

Later on in the day I telephoned my sister Sandy, who told me that she'd just come home from work to an awful burnt smell in the house. 'Don't worry,' said her husband John. 'It's only Jerry.' Jerry is their large black and white cat – a wonderful cat of great looks and character. He was feeling cold during the day so while his people were out and the Woodsman fuel burner was going, Jerry snuggled up close. The only problem was that his fur was up against the heavy glass door. John returned home soon afterwards to the smell of burning fur; fortunately Jerry was unharmed apart from singed fur on his side.

"It *would* be on the white patch too," Sandy said, adding that she would have to explain to their neighbours that it was Jerry himself at fault, not through any wrongdoing on their part. Jerry was apparently quite miffed about the brown patch over his lovely white patch of fur on his side.

I told my cats about the incident.

"So they had a hot cat in their house, instead of a hot dog?" Reilly commented, yawning.

"You could say that," I said.

"I just did!"

"Which reminds me..."

"Oh my, Chloe, Mumsy-wumsy is going to launch into another story."

"I won't tell you, then!" I said sourly.

"Tell me, tell me!" Reilly pleaded.

"Tell me too!" Chloe added her sweetly sultry voice.

"In that case," I smiled. "I shall resume. I was living with my son and three cats in my first house in Carter's Beach..."

"*Three* cats! Ye gods! What happened to them? Did they all move out together?"

"No. Reilly, stop interrupting! I told you years ago about my cats – Butch Cassidy, Rafferty O'Reilly and Muffy – my colour-co-ordinated cats, I used to say."

"Oh yeah, I remember now. They went to nice new homes and you went to live in Australia."

"That's right. Well anyway, Butch Cassidy did a similar thing as Jerry did. The day was cold; my heater was going and Butch got too close. I was busy at the kitchen sink and suddenly smelt this awful smell of burning. At the same time I turned around to see my son laughing as the heat suddenly hit big Butch and he leaped away, his fur singed."

"Lucky you were in the house at the time."

"Well naturally, if I had been out and about I would not have left the heater going!"

"Maybe, maybe not," Reilly said. "But didn't Shelley refer to you as the mad Irish washerwoman?"

"Yes, she did and still does."

"Isn't it likely then that you might have gone out and left the heater on, for your poor abandoned cats to get burned from?"

"Don't be ridiculous, Reilly! For one thing, they were *not* abandoned, but three very well cared for cats and for another thing, no, I would *not* have gone out and left the heater on!"

"Has anyone ever told you you're beautiful when you're angry?"

"Yes!" I snapped. "Several times...namely *you.*"

"I thought you wouldn't be averse to a little bit of flattery, woman! Most women are."

"Mother is not 'most women,'" Chloe observed.

"No, indeed not," Reilly smirked. "She's *most* unusual! I've heard tell dat she is a mad Irish washerwoman!"

"*Reilly!*" I shouted, and hobbled after him.

"Not only a mad Irish washerwoman, but one dat has got a bung knee, a bung hip, bung foot and goodness knows what else is bung!"

My head, I thought waspishly, in tolerating Reilly's jibes for all these years.

He ran away sniggering, and after a while I had to have a little snigger too. Exasperating as he was, he was and is, still the most amusing cat I have ever known.

***

CHAPTER TWENTY-THREE

"On The Move Yet Again"

I was very much aware of the swift passing of time and the need to be out of the apartment by the time the two years were up, and also importantly, to be out of there before winter. I had contracted a particularly nasty virus the previous winter and having two bad bouts of laryngitis two weeks apart – on top of the virus, I had felt extremely miserable. My cats were affected too, mainly because they had grown to enjoy my stories and looked forward to being read to each day. For several weeks I was barely able to whisper, and I was despairing as I thought I might never be able to sing again.

"Bleedin' heck!" my friend Big Mike said with a laugh. "I phone up the girl and she can't even talk ter me. That makes a change! Normally I can't get a word in edgeways."

That of course, was an exaggeration, but I was not in the position to give him cheek in return.

But each day I would try a little bit...even a line or two and I gradually was able to build up my strength again. In all, it took a complete year to get my voice back to the strength it was at before I became ill.

I believe the problem lay in the fact that the apartment where I lived was built over an ancient swamp, and despite paying to have thick polythene ground sheeting placed under the apartment, the damp still rose up. Sometimes it would drip off the walls. It wasn't like that when I purchased the apartment, but the situation evolved when the expressway was being developed to the rear of my rear neighbours' properties. Much draining of a swampy area was done and I guess the damp had to go somewhere. It seemed like it was all congregating in my apartment. I pulled back the lowboy from the wall. The lowboy had fungus growing on the back of it. I was shocked at how fast that had happened and promptly removed the fungus and aired the lowboy and took out the clothes from the drawers and re-washed them.

I talked to my cats about the situation. "When I first came here cats, I knew we had this place for a maximum of two years."

"It can't be two years already!" Reilly snorted.

"No, it isn't – it's not yet eighteen months, but it will take a few months to sell it."

"On the flamin' move again! What is it with you, woman? Are you some kind of gypsy?"

"Each time I have moved, it has been necessary," I said primly. "Besides, God told me I would have this place for a maximum of two years."

"That's right - blame it on God! Doesn't everyone?"

"No, we do not. I'm willing to go where God wants me to go."

Reilly heaved a sigh. "As long it's near the beach, I suppose we don't mind, do we Chloe?"

"Oh no, I'd like that very much," she said sweetly.

I smiled. "Who knows? This time we may be able to manage it." I was aware that Reilly hadn't mentioned a beach on the West Coast, namely Carter's Beach. Much as I would have loved to be there again, it was in too remote a spot, and returning to Christchurch for medical tests would involve a lot of travel.

So, I would leave it at that and in the meantime, do my best to start looking at houses near the beach. Real estate was becoming a major investment market and I knew I should get a good price for my property. By the same token, I knew my timing must be right, so that I could still afford to buy again.

The real estate man who had worked so hard to get me into this lovely apartment came to visit one day, bringing a calendar. As I was about to leave to go to my singing lesson, I couldn't stay and chat, much as I would have liked to. I was so tempted then to say to the real estate man that I was thinking about putting my apartment on the market, but thought I would keep quiet about it for the time being. I felt the time wasn't quite right yet. Besides, my cats kept grumbling.

"Listen here woman, you hardly get the old dust out of a house and your...correction, *our* furniture set down than you're thinking about moving again! What is it with you?"

"Now *you* listen here Reilly," I said sternly. "God told me when we first came here that it would be for a maximum of two years. So blame God, if you want to blame someone!"

"Oh yes dat's right, like I said before! Blame God; blame Him for everything dat happens!"

"Well, don't *you?*" I countered. "Besides, I am not blaming God at all. If He says we are here for a maximum of two years, then that's what it is. I figure God knows His own business best."

Reilly gave a cat-sized sniff. "Huh. Anyway, I don't blame God for *everything*...why, I blame fat Chloe here!"

He pounced on her, giving her a swift *whop* and she screamed at him. And struck him in return, with her little round paw.

"If youse thinks dat's gonna hurt me, then youse gotta nother fink coming!"

"I really don't understand why your speech sinks to that level when you're being nasty, Reilly. Leave Chloe alone. She wasn't doing you any harm."

"No, but she might have, mightn't she? I'm just bopping her in advance!"

And he promptly leaped onto her again. Chloe fought back and gave as much as she could against the much bigger and stronger Reilly. I managed to part them. Chloe stalked away in high dudgeon and Reilly sat back on his haunches, a look of absolute smugness on his face.

"Sometimes I feel so *ashamed* of you, Reilly!"

"Oh goodie, den you can have da shame for both of us, heh, heh. I wouldn't want yez ter think I was without *some* modicum of compassion!"

He bounded off around the corner into the kitchen and just before I heard the cat door open, I heard that distinctive snigger of his.

"I shall get my revenge on him, Mother," Chloe announced, returning as soon as she heard the cat door bang back into place.

I sighed. "You know Chloe, in many ways I have been trying to do that very thing for years, but somehow he always gets the upper hand."

"Don't you get fed up with him?"

"I do, but he's still my cat and I love him very much..."

"More than me?" Chloe's gold eyes were huge and plaintive, in much the same way that Katie O'Brien's used to be.

"I love you so much Chloe, and in a different way, but by no means less," I said.

At that Chloe seemed content. She sat down and tucked her front paws under her in that absolutely charming way cats have, and her huge eyes look on a faraway look.

"What are you thinking about?"

"I'm thinking about when we go to live near the beach...about how nice it will be."

"It will be too," I replied. "But first I have to get this house sold and buy another one."

"It'll happen," Chloe said philosophically and began to gently purr. "And sooner than you think, Mother."

"That's nice Chloe," I said, somewhat abstractedly as my mind was already racing forward with the knowledge that I would have to put things into action if I wanted to be out of this apartment by the time two years was up.

"You'll see, Mother," Chloe said, looking a bit mysterious but still purring.

It was obvious she saw things that I did not. I left the lounge room without further comment and began preparations for my evening meal.

**

The next day I put the wheels into motion of selling the apartment.

"Here we go again," I thought as I looked through real estate weekly magazines, listing so many houses with colourful descriptions to make them sound so much better than they were. "Huh...listen to this," I said as Reilly came leaping with a flourish through the cat door. "'Warm and cosy'. Interpret that as small and out of date. Here's another... 'character home in need of that tender, expert touch from a loving hand'. Interpret that as an old house that's about to fall down, yet is saved by its interesting old age. How about this one? 'All the charm of yesteryear, just waiting for that genuine buyer...' Interpret that as very old, with no renovations done, hoping for a buyer who doesn't care whether or not a place is renovated, and is happy to buy as-is."

"Found any nice places by the sea? I sincerely hope you have, otherwise I shall not budge from here," Reilly informed me.

"You can hardly expect any prospective buyer of this house to take *you* on, cat," I said.

"I would expect them to consider it a privilege to have me here!" Reilly loftily retorted.

"Big head!"

"But a gorgeous big head, wouldn't you say?"

I grinned. "If you say so, cat."

"Big, yes I agree, but I am not so sure about the gorgeous part of it. Egotistical I would have said - if you had asked me," Chloe put in.

"Oh, but I don't recall *asking* you, fat cat."

"I am not fat; I am healthy and well-rounded, curvaceous, even."

"Fat, with eyes too big for your head!"

"You are rude and unappreciative of my good looks."

Reilly snorted. "Well, to coin the woman's phrase, if you say so, cat!"

Chloe turned away in disgust. "I really cannot be bothered talking to you, Reilly."

"Den what is da little fatty cat doing, if not talking ter *me?*"

"Ignoring you," Chloe said sweetly, and smiled a cute pussycat smile.

Reilly snorted again and turned *his* back on Chloe. "Harumph. Woman, show me some of dem pictures. I wanna see where we're gonna live!"

"It ain't...er, isn't that simple, Reilly."

"Why not?"

"There are things like mortgages, loan applications and the like to consider. Not to mention the lawyers' fees."

"Well, don't mention them, den."

I took a deep breath. I could see that this forthcoming move was going to be no easier than the many others I'd had.

"I won't mention anything about moving at all, if you're not careful. We could stay here, of course!" I said testily.

"Ah, but aren't you the little woman who said that God told her we would stay here for a maximum of two years? You know you can't go back on what God says and pretend He didn't say it!"

"Sometimes I wonder why I tell you anything at all, Reilly!"

"Dat's because you love me and like to share things with me! What's more, I'm your loveable boy cat!"

Chloe gave a funny little sound. It was almost like suppressed laughter.

"What are you thinking, fatty cat?"

Chloe turned back to face Reilly. "Oh, were you speaking to *me?*"

"Of course I was, fathead."

Chloe promptly turned her back on him again and didn't say another word.

"In other words Reilly, foolish talk is sometimes better to be completely ignored!" I said with relish.

"And dat is why I am now gonna ignore *you!*"

He promptly leaped back out through the cat door. I thought it banged even louder than normal, but that could have been my imagination. Hmmm...

"He has to be the rudest cat I have ever met," Chloe said.

"He *is* the rudest cat I have ever met!" I replied.

"But he does have a certain...panache..."

"Yes, darn it all, he does indeed!"

"But we can't let him know about that, can we?"

"Too late Chloe. He already knows about that!"

I heard sniggering again...this time from underneath the dining table. Oh when had he sneaked back inside without us being aware of his return?

**

I was beginning my singing practise one morning when, as usual Chloe wanted to go outside. Okay, I know I can be loud, but Chloe emphasised that each time she yowled to go out. I comforted myself with the thought that it wasn't my singing that upset her inasmuch as the volume and cats have very sensitive ears.

"You *are* loud, woman!" Reilly said, as he too, wanted to go outside.

It never ceases to amaze me that cats know our very thoughts.

I carried on singing, lightly amused at the fact that both cats wanted me to go to the trouble of opening the sliding door onto the patio while singing, rather than go in the other direction and go out via the cat door. Reilly headed off over the back fence and Chloe sat on the patio. Then she dragged her bottom over the concrete and had such a silly look on her face that it was all I could do not to laugh. My voice wavered as I sang. But then Chloe sat in a ray of sunshine; the light shone through her cinnamon-coloured eyebrows as she sat there like an old, old man; her little grin still adorning her flat face. I imagined her thinking: 'oh my, my, that sure felt great!' I burst into laughter and Chloe spun around, sudden annoyance at being caught out in her every movement.

It took me several minutes before I could resume singing.

**

The months rolled on and during that time quite a few people came to look at my apartment. But not one person came to buy.

In a way I didn't care as I still had quite a lot of time left before the allotted two years was up. Reilly had other ideas though.

"I'm fed up with all these people traipsing through the house, woman! For all we know, they could be trying to *case* the joint!"

"I'm sure you would know, Reilly," I said with a grin, mindful of the time he acted like the good watch cat he still is, while we lived in Pine Avenue in South Brighton and a young man of obvious ill intent came looking for a previous tenant. Reilly had in no uncertain terms let me know that the man was full of evil. His yowling, loud growling and tail swishing had given me a clear warning. Perhaps that's the *real* reason why the man did not stand directly in front of the door when I opened it, and not the fact that he was a shady character and expecting someone to shoot at him. I'm sure Reilly's growling and yowling were audible from several houses away!

One day about a month later I received a phone call from the nice real estate agent, Alan, who, by this stage had placed a 'for sale' sign out front. He had some people wanting to look through. The lady who had arrived with her sister informed me later on that she loved the apartment as soon as she walked up the driveway.

Six weeks later my apartment was sold, a near-new house bought and I was heading out to the beach, my car loaded with final bits and pieces plus of course, my cats. When God puts His plans into action, things happen very quickly! It was just a month short of the allotted two years God had told me was the maximum time we would be living there.

Chloe didn't like the trip but Reilly loved it as he always did.

"Can't you go a bit faster, woman?"

"Certainly not," I replied. "We could get pulled up for speeding!"

"I'd soon sort out dat police officer! I'd show him what road rage *really* meant!"

"Oh sure. And what would *you* do?"

"Bite him, of course! And tell him to stop picking on poor little women and their pussycats!"

I grinned, picturing the situation. And the astonishment of the officer who was not only newly bitten by an aggressive cat, but told off by that same cat!

"Fair enough," I said, still grinning. "But even if we didn't get pulled up for speeding, the trip would be over too quickly and you wouldn't get another long car ride for a while."

"True," Reilly agreed and lapsed into silence, all the while watching other cars and trucks on the motorway. I was aware of the strange looks and fingers being pointed at us. Some people were laughing outright at Reilly, who stood on the small space left on the passenger seat and had his front paws placed firmly on the dashboard.

"Let them laugh and point and stare, I say! It's about time people took notice of me again!"

"But I take notice of you, and so does Chloe," I said as we rounded a corner and passed a couple of cars in the slower lane.

"Yeah, but now I want people to take notice of me *en masse!*"

"You can be sure they will when we've got over the big move and go for a walk down to the beach."

"I can hardly wait."

"I want to get out of here!" Chloe wailed.

"Sooky, fat round baby cat! We'll be there sooner that you can say Jack Robinson!"

"Jack Robinson. There – I said it. Are we there yet?"

"Near enough," said Reilly and sniggered.

***

"FASTER, WOMAN!.....

...OR I'LL SHOW YOU ROAD-RAGE.!!"

CHAPTER TWENTY FOUR

"Coming Full Circle"

We arrived about ten minutes or so before the removal truck. I had enough time to let the cats out to explore their new home and to do some exploring of my own when the truck arrived.

By that evening I was so weary I could hardly stand.

"But we're here now Mother, and didn't I tell you it would all happen sooner that you thought?"

"You did, Chloe, that you did." I stretched my aching back.

"Feed us woman, and then you should feed yourself and go to bed. Tomorrow is another day, and all that," Reilly announced.

I knew he was right, but as is my habit, the more tired I am, the more I try to potter around and get little chores done. When I got to the stage where I was picking things up and putting them down again and forgetting where I had put them, I finally decided to heed Reilly's words. I had a cool shower as the water hadn't fully heated and then I went to bed.

The next day dawned a beauty; blue skies with a soft ocean breeze whispering through the cabbage trees that stood in line, as sentinels guarding the gravel driveway. A matter of metres away I could hear the same breeze rustling through the willows, creating a sound not unlike gentle rain. The air was so exquisite I breathed it in deeply. Then I promptly felt a bit dizzy with the increased oxygen.

The scene from the deck was of layer upon layer of fresh greenery in different hues. It was so pretty I could not seem to get enough of it. Although there were few flowers in the garden, that fact was more than made up for by the massive amount of foliage. To the rear of the house and self-contained sleepout that I had earlier earmarked for my office was a back yard that reminded me of a grotto, so filled with shrubs that it was. There was also a shade-house with late flowering clematis hanging picturesquely from it, and several varieties of passion-flower, complete with their alien-like flowers adding to the clematis' small display. Apart from these, there were few other flowers. But the colourful foliage, not only from the cabbage trees to the side of the property, but also to the rear created their own garden. It seemed like a Garden of Eden. And the cats thought so too. They raced around and around as if they had been confined for months on end.

The novelty of the large section with plenty of shrubs wore off only long enough for the two cats to be 'refuelled', and off they went again. To see them so happy together was manna to my spirit. I could feel the heaviness of past months lifting as I watched their obvious joy. I took another deep breath of the sea-scented air and thanked God for the blessing of this new property.

**

The days rolled by and as they did so, I could feel my strength returning. I lay in bed early one morning in my room in the chalet-like house with its warm, wood panelled walls and gazed out the window at the cabbage trees, tall and straight with their spiky leaves and some with their clumps of musky sweet flower heads dispelling extra perfume into the air. I could hear a tui warbling exquisitely in a treetop.

So much beauty; it was almost too much to bear.

Reilly bounded in through the cat door in the back door.

"Get up, woman! This is too good a day to waste!"

"Oh, but I'm not wasting it at all. I'm savouring it before I get up," I said dreamily.

"Huh, you have a goofy look on your face. Are you in love, or something?" Reilly placed his front paws on the edge of the bed and peered into my face.

"Yes, you could say that, cat."

"I just did. Who is he? Not some deadbeat, I sincerely hope?"

"This goes to show that you shouldn't jump to conclusions!"

"I see what I see, and what I see is a goofy woman!"

"Don't you recognise contentment when you see it?" I retorted.

"Oh, is *dat* what it is? Maybe it's been so long since I've seen you happy! That's apart from the expected happiness of having we cats live with you, of course."

"I just knew there had to be a rider to the first part of your dialogue."

"Talk properly, woman. Don't cha know I'm from da Bronx?"

"Rubbish, cat! You're from Nelson...or near to it."

"But my *spirit* is from a long way off," Reilly persisted.

"Maybe so, cat, but I know for a fact that your mind is in a place not far from this very room, in fact. The fridge, for instance!"

"Did I say so?"

"No, you didn't have to. I can see it in your face. Besides, you just dribbled on me!"

"I wouldn't have done if yez had got out of bed early and had fed us poor, starving cats."

"Starving and poor you are *not*," I said firmly. "Now, move out of my way so I can get out of bed!"

Reilly sat back on his haunches and observed me changing out of my long nightshirt. He seemed to be grinning.

"What's that look on your face, for?"

"You've lost weight, woman, but you still look like you need an operation!"

"Good heavens! Whatever for?" I blinked in surprise.

"To get rid of dem lumps yez have!"

"Shoo! Scat!" I said and clapped my hands at him. Reilly ran off, sniggering.

A few minutes later when Chloe entered the house via the cat door, I heard him telling her that I needed an operation. She gave a meow of protest.

"Who will look after us while she's away having this operation?"

"You'll see," Reilly said.

I stood just inside my bedroom door and waited to see what nonsense he would come up with this time.

"Oh dear, what's wrong with Mother?"

"She's got big lumps."

"Lumps? Oh dear, that *does* sound ominous! Where are they?"

"On her chest!"

"Oh really Reilly, you are so *rude!*"

"Really Reilly, oh *really* Reilly! You are so *rude!*" he mimicked.

"Amen to that," I said, emerging from my bedroom. "Perhaps you could go without breakfast for your rudeness?" I suggested.

He assumed a nonchalant look and yawned. "So, what's for breakfast?"

"Cat food. Fresh out of a can and its hearty beef with lamb."

Reilly rushed down the hallway saying "gimme, gimme."

I followed him. "Do you think you deserve breakfast after being so rude about me?"

He stopped short of the entrance into the main living area and turned to face me. "Let's put it this way, woman. If I wasn't rude to you and uncouth sometimes, wouldn't you worry about me? Wouldn't you worry that there was something seriously wrong with me?"

I grinned. "You have a point, cat. Okay, breakfast time."

I retrieved a new can of cat food from the pantry and opened it. It smelt savoury and delicious. I could see how many elderly people on tiny incomes were tempted to eat cat food as a cheap substitute for ordinary cuts of meat. I was *not,* however, going to venture down that path, delicious as the cat food smelt!

Scooping several spoons full into each of the cats' dishes, I was amused at how Chloe's good manners temporarily deserted her. She gulped her food down, purring all the while. Reilly was much the same, except that he looked up every so often to check the food level in Chloe's bowl. I knew that he had plans to wolf his fast enough so he could ease Chloe away from her bowl and finish off her serving. I stood between them so Reilly didn't get the chance.

A few minutes later they were both replete and I took pleasure in hearing them both purring as they waddled back down the hallway and exited the house.

**

I knew that I would be able to begin to write again here. The peace was tangible, broken only by the sounds of the exquisite little iridescent bellbirds. Their song is the most beautiful I have ever heard, and here they were, in the treetops on my property, singing their hearts out on this lovely day. I wanted to enjoy them for a while longer before Reilly broke the spell.

Two minutes later the birds flew off. Reilly had been making an attempt to climb the fast-growing Lucerne tree. The bellbirds were not going to stay around for idle chit-chat.

"Huh! Spoilsports!" Reilly called. I smiled in amusement.

Chloe didn't say anything, but much in the way that Katie had, she blinked her huge eyes a few times, then carried on with washing herself while sitting and purring in the sun. The mark of a very contented cat.

Reilly was restless. "Why don't we explore around the river?"

"That's a good idea," I agreed. "And then we could go on down to the sea." The writing could wait for a bit longer, I decided, as it was too good a day to waste indoors.

"Oh, joy of joys!" Reilly leaped about.

"I'll just have to lock up first." The cats came in with me. Chloe suddenly sat down in front of the open spare bedroom door. She dragged her bottom on the carpet, not looking where she was going and hit her face on the door.

"Now I see how you got such a flat face, Chloe! It wasn't a bus at all! It was a door, correction, *doors*, over time – you running into them!"

"Don't be so horrible, Reilly," I said, giving myself a quiet reminder to buy some more worm paste, in case that was the problem.

"*Horrible?* You call *me* horrible! What she was doing was disgusting!"

"You should mind your business, Reilly," Chloe said sweetly. "I bet *you* get an itchy bottom from time to time! You just wouldn't want anyone to see you."

She blinked at him and walked slowly off to the ranch slider door.

Reilly grumbled and chattered to no one in particular. "I do not let *anyone* see me having an itchy bottom!" he declared loudly.

"I rest my case!" Chloe called back.

Off we went, through the big gate at the entrance to the driveway, down the sealed road to the small council reserve, and then up the river stop bank and onto the gravel road atop the bank. The road went for several kilometres and is a daily walkway for many of the locals. A few of them passed me and smiled at my cats following me.

"Do they always do that?" asked one very stout lady in a bright pink tracksuit.

"Reilly does, but Chloe not so often. She may come with us more often though, since we've moved out here to the country."

"Ohhh, aren't they just gorrrgeous!" the stout lady trilled, her enormous bosom jiggling.

Chloe moved to the side of the walkway and blinked owlishly at her while Reilly preened.

"Well, if you insist," he said.

"Reilly, you have such a big ego!" I said in amusement.

"Eh?" the stout lady blinked at me. "Did he say something?"

"Oh yes, he always does! He usually has *too* much to say!"

The lady gave a little laugh. "It does seem that way doesn't it, that they can talk to you!"

"Stupid woman," Reilly growled.

"Oh dear, why is he growling?"

"Coz of your horrible tight pink tracksuit! It offends my eyes!"

"He wants to get going," I said easily, stifling the mirth that threatened to rise. I agreed with Reilly. The pink tracksuit, just a tad too bright and too small on a very large woman *did* offend the eyes!

"Oh I say, well, I mustn't keep you then, must I?"

"No, you must *not*, you stupid fat pink woman!"

I gave a sudden laugh and the stout lady looked hard at me, sure that what she had said wasn't *that* funny.

"Nice to meet you!" I said gaily as we moved on, leaving the stout lady staring after us before she too, turned and walked on in the opposite direction. In fact, the short exchange had been very funny, even though the pink-clad lady might have thought otherwise, especially if she had known what Reilly was saying. I felt a bit sorry for Reilly having been so rude about her, but at least she was saved from knowing what he had said. Anyway, I'm sure that Reilly was not the only one to comment on her too-tight, bright pink tracksuit!

We ambled on down through the roads that meander among the ancient willow trees that border the riverbed. It is a beautiful spot; the sun dappled the leaves and created a fairytale place that reminded me somewhat of the picturesque wooded area in Switzerland that my friend Fritz had taken me for a beautiful walk through some years before.

Soon after, the cats and I retraced some of our steps and headed back up to the riverbank walkway, to continue on down to the lagoon and then the beach.

The bird life was wonderful; pied oystercatchers, stilts, godwits and gulls, plus numerous other species that were too far away for me to recognise, apart from the occasional heron that rose majestically upwards from the side of the river mouth. Somewhere fairly close by came the deep booming sound of a bittern, cleverly camouflaged amongst the reeds.

With the sound and scent of the sea filling our heads and minds, we skirted the lagoon as it was too deep to wade through and went onto the beach. Reilly was ecstatic. He whooped, gambolled and skittered in the sand.

It had been far too long since he could freely do this. In a way I felt responsible for his deprivation, but had no other choices at the time. The right time to return was now, and Reilly for one, was making the most of it. Chloe was enjoying it too, but in a more subdued way.

I think she was happy to be entertained by Reilly, rather than be an active participant.

I thought of Carter's Beach and suddenly had a fierce longing for it. I knew that I would go back there, but not just now. For the time being, this new beach was more than just a substitute.

It has as many, if not more things of interest than Carter's Beach.

Full Circle

Lest I forget the times
Of joy – of a multitude of things
That my Reilly did;
Lest I forget the rhymes

I composed while we walked
The beaches and hedgerows
And explored mossy creeks
And Reilly casually stalked

A fluttering butterfly –
Lazy in the warm coastal breeze
And content in his element,
And I would sit on a rock and sigh

At Nature's perfection and bounty.
Small birds would skylark –
Chattering in the old blue sky,
Flittering and dancing so musically.

I sit awhile and dream
Of days, some years before;
Days nostalgically the same
...or so it seems

In my blissful reverie.
I watch Reilly dart here and there
And marvel at his silver colours,
His great gold eyes and his energy...

And I think of Carter's Beach.
Sometimes it seems
So many dimensions ago
And so out of my reach

And yet here we are this day,
In a place so like it,
But even better than before.
Again we will come this way.

I smell the sweet damp undergrowth
And feel the slight chill of the dying day.
A crying seagull soars overhead:
The nostalgia affects us both.

Reilly sits contentedly with me,
His purr a precious sound
Mingling with the forest's rustles
And drones of fat honeybees.

Lest I forget, this is a new and better place;
We have come full circle.
Reilly runs and prances with glee,
Even now at his usual pace –

On some small thing that moved,
Or might not have moved at all –
But to Reilly, was simply there
And was strange, exciting and new.

O yes, as I sit and gaze
At my cat, with a backdrop of cabbage trees,
Forest, moss, stream and sky
I think of our endless days...

So lest I forget,
I will remember Carter's Beach
And all its sand and wonders
And remember the glorious sunsets

And I sit awhile to watch the sunset here
And I marvel at the glow on Reilly's fur.
He comes running to me again:
I realise afresh we have come full circle...
How wonderful have been our days -
How precious and how dear.

**

Chloe remained sitting by me while Reilly continued his prancing and dancing in the sand. Gulls circled overhead and added to the glitter of the sun glinting off the calm sea that was broken only where the river chuckled its way down to merge with it. The air was so exquisite that I felt intoxicated by it.

Reilly galloped closer to where Chloe and I were sitting, by now side by side on a dry drift log that was also glinting – silver from the years of sun and sea.

My big cat began to dig a trench in the wet sand.

"We fought on the beaches...we fought in the trenches...and now I'm gonna dig for some shellfish!"

We had come full circle.

THE END

GLOSSARY

Bittern......................Swamp-dwelling bird, allied to herons

Crib...........................Small holiday home; also known as a bach

Hangi ....Food cooked in an earth oven

Pakihi.......................Infertile wasteland

Tui............................Sometimes known as parson-bird. Native to New Zealand

Skerrick....................Small amount, orig. British dialect word; survived as Australian and NZ colloquial English